Daisy McIntosh

Roger H. Panton

To Maureen

Hope you find this story interesting.

11/9/15

Copyright © 2014 by Roger H. Panton

ISBN: 1497592690
ISBN 13: 9781497592698
Library of Congress Control Number: 2014906806
CreateSpace Independent Publishing Platform
North Charleston, South Carolina

ISBN: Softcover
        E-Book

All rights reserved. No part of this book may be reproduced or transmitted in any form or by any means, electronic or mechanical, including photocopying, recording, or by any information storage and retrieval system, without permission in writing from the copyright owner.

This is a work of fiction. Names, characters, places, and incidents are either the product of the author's imagination or are used fictitiously; and any resemblance to any actual persons, living or dead, events, or locations is entirely coincidental.

ACKNOWLEDGMENTS

I would like to thank Grace Smith Henry for her suggestions and overall support and Donna Panton for her valuable editorial assistance and comments throughout.

ONE

"Twenty-one, twenty-two, twenty-three," Daisy counted breathlessly as she skipped beneath the mango tree in her neighbour's yard.

Miss Martha, a barely five feet tall, slim, bespectacled lady, thought it was unusually hot, so she stood in the doorway of her house, shaded by the mango tree, instead of down by her petite flower garden that was bathed in the intermittent Jamaican sunlight that darted through the leaves of the pimento tree. She was glad for the daytime company as she fanned her dark face and counted in silent union with the youngster. Daisy's score was always well short of her own averages as a thirteen-year-old schoolgirl. The child really should have been more proficient at a simple thing like skipping, but Martha thought it wouldn't do to make comparisons. What Daisy needed now was a bucket-load of encouragement, and that was exactly what Miss Martha, a very kind Miss Martha, intended to give her.

"Come now, Daisy," she said, smiling broadly, not waiting for Daisy's feet to tangle with the rope. Daisy knew she had done well for Martha to interrupt her. "You did very well this time, my dear," she continued. But instead of talking about the number, she said, "You know something—I need to have a chat with your mother. You are getting a big girl now. Come, come. Let me make you a drink. Sit down. Use mi fan."

This was a real treat for Daisy, using Martha's fan. She sat on the nearby stool, her polka-dot dress sticking to her sweaty body. She swept her long tresses back and let them drop behind her before pulling at the neckline of her dress, and just as she'd seen the women doing in church, she held the fan lightly, flicked her wrist rapidly, and aimed the rush of air down the top of her dress. Daisy was sure she knew what Martha had in mind about a chat with her mother, as she had heard her mumble the same thing a few days earlier.

Watching Daisy fan herself, Martha, with her flowery skirt brushing the floor, continued to fan herself with her little white hat that seemed too small for the purpose. She thought, *I must create the atmosphere for this chat.* She was fully aware of how sensitive May had become of late to any discussion concerning her daughter because of the rumours. Before mixing the drink as she had intended, Martha searched through the cuttings of material on the floor by her sewing machine for a suitable piece of cloth. She was going to get Daisy to do a nice piece of hand sewing to show her mother just how clever she was with needle and thread.

Unlike many of the girls her age, Daisy had few friends. Although she never used the term, she would have described Thelma, who lived two doors away on the other side of Martha, as her *best friend.* In reality, Thelma was her only true friend. But, if asked, Daisy probably would have admitted to liking her classmate Gladys more than she did Thelma. Gladys walked with her to school and shared her crayons and pencils with her, and Daisy shared her abundance of fruits with the girl. However, once they were in the vicinity of home, the two would part company. They remained friends whilst in Plummers only through exchanging smiles and pleasantries.

Daisy secretly wished Gladys went to the shops, ran errands, fetched water, or even stayed behind a few minutes after Sunday school so they could share more friendly moments. She knew, however, that that would not happen: Gladys's mother was the church organist, and such open familiarity would not have been acceptable to her.

Thelma, small for her age in both height and build, was a year older than Daisy and was the only other girl being taught to sew by Martha, mostly at holiday time. Though the two girls were rarely there at the same time, Thelma provided Daisy with so-called grown-up stories. She told Daisy of her first sexual encounter, which had been with one of the monitors at school. She spoke of it triumphantly. The girls from OutaBridge had their own stories about Jeffrey, and she just had to experience him for herself. She said she had done it three or four times with him, but she stopped after a good talking-to from Martha. She still did not know how Martha knew about it.

Thelma also told Daisy about a couple of the men in the district who tried to get her to do it with them. She mentioned the names of some who had exposed themselves to her and invited her to touch them, one even going so far as to grab her hand and press it on his erect penis. She also told her of a man who she would not name, saying he held her down on Martha's bed and forced his fingers into her. Daisy was not too surprised by the last story because of her own experience with Martha's husband, Mr. Mills. She was, however, shocked when she heard some of the other names Thelma mentioned, as they included some of the most respected men in the district. Daisy thought that if she and Thelma had fathers around, the men would have been more respectful. As young as she was, Daisy was astute enough to work such things out.

The bigger girls also taught Daisy a lot, not directly, but by their careless chatter, which she overheard. She didn't know then that many of their stories were exaggerated; some were in fact blatant lies to show off their imagined sexual prowess. She didn't realize that other girls could have told her stories of just how choosy these girls were, how little experience they had, how pure they were. For Daisy, the dangers of early sexual experience were for people like Martha to tell.

The walk along the road was brisk, with the head held straight and with the shadow of a smile. It was difficult to maintain such a change for long periods. Still, it had to be done. She had to behave differently as a matter of self-preservation. To her, the journey was a test. Perhaps Martha had her people checking on her along the way, and so she had to do exactly as she said. She couldn't let her down.

On approaching the shop, Daisy was aware of the usual noise of the domino players—laughter, curse words, the dominoes being slammed into the little table. Then, when she was just a few feet away from the steps, there was a sudden silence. Her first real test had begun. Obeying the briefing, she did not look at any of the men as she climbed the three steps into the shop. The chatter and banging of the dominoes resumed. She was satisfied she had passed that test. Had she glanced over her shoulders as she passed by, she would have seen the exaggerated licking of lips, winks, and smiles of the men who were old enough to be her father and, a couple of them, even her grandfather. Had she listened intently, she would have heard the comments about how lucky Soldier was. How they envied him his nice young thing.

The rumour that Daisy was having dealings with Soldier with her mother's blessing persisted despite the denials. It was uncomfortable for her because of her playfulness with a couple of the boys, which was common knowledge. She feared she might be told that she had brought it on herself through her behaviour with the boys. Daisy did not share with her mother or Martha the fact that some of the men had told her to her face that now that she had turned thirteen, she was on their list for "action." She knew what they meant. She also kept from them that they had also said they wanted a piece of what Soldier enjoyed so much. She didn't tell anyone that some had groped her as they passed her on the way to or from the river when she was fetching water or on late evenings when she went to the shop. She didn't think she would be believed.

As she stood patiently in the shop, she watched as a man tipped a little rum from a flat-sided bottle onto the counter and set fire to it with a match. After a few moments, he put the flame out, satisfied that the rum had not been watered down. He paid, smiled at Daisy—a different, polite smile—and left, forcing the bottle into his back pocket as he left the shop.

"So what you want now, Daisy?"

"Half a pound of flour and half a pound of salt beef." She waited patiently whilst the young man weighed and wrapped the goods. Every now and then, she stole a glance behind her but found no one watching her. The domino game was reaching its climax. That was more important then. After paying and collecting her purchase, she pulled at her sleeves and checked that her dress was hanging properly. She turned and left the shop, remembering what Martha had told her. She headed up the slope towards home, walking on the side where there was more shade.

The wind had picked up a little in the short time she had been in the shop, and each step she took was accompanied by a little puff of dust as her bare feet spread out in quick, short steps. What the men were noticing, however, was the little wiggle as she leaned forward into the gradient, making her backside more pronounced as she walked away from them.

Top Ground only existed as an area separate from Plummers to those who lived there and wanted to differentiate themselves from the rest of the electoral district. They saw themselves as the elite—the bastion of the church and the power seat of the area.

The little houses in the rest of Plummers were scattered on land where the boundaries were not noticeably identified. In Top Ground, however, there were hedges with colourful leaves appropriately named Joseph's coat and evergreen plants called never dead. Most folks, if challenged, would not have been able to produce the legal papers to prove ownership of the land they claimed was theirs. That did not bother them, however, because land in Plummers was handed down through the generations. Very rarely was any sold.

Many of the families were related, and children learned their family links at an early age, some of them being told that a particular man living with his family in some other household was their father. That was just the way things were. The children also learned pretty quickly who to have more respect for, who would have the right to chastise them or even give them a whipping whilst out, and whose complaint against them their parents would accept without even trying to get their version of the incident.

The implication was that grown-ups don't lie. The children soon learned, however, that that was not so. The older girls were told who they should not be seen with at night or bear children with because they were closely related, something they mostly obeyed, even when they weren't told how the relationship came about. It usually fell to the grandmothers or even the great-grandmothers to pull the girls aside and tell them these things. These women felt that the young men could not be trusted to put a stop to the relationships, as they were generally considered as beings that had no self-control.

Problems occurred in other areas, especially with girls not being sure who the father of their children was. Again, the old women had a way of dealing with that. They would inspect fingers or look for specific marks on the baby and then reach a decision based on characteristics known to them, sometimes those of a deceased family member. There was rarely any argument as to the accuracy of the decision. The important thing for the folks was that the children were accepted and looked after as kin.

Forty-four-year-old Soldier from OutaBridge was a slim six-footer. He took pride in his appearance and felt it gave him an edge if ever he needed to impose his authority as ranger of the Dalbeattie plantation. He loved the power the job gave him, and he was sure he could have been a successful soldier had he passed the test. He had thought of trying out for the police force, but he learned that the police test was harder than that for the army. He at first thought it a cruel joke to be nicknamed Soldier, but he grew to like it and so began to ensure he looked the part of a soldier, those he had seen in the movies and those who visited Dalbeattie. He presented himself likewise and was content that he had succeeded.

Being ranger was a job Soldier took very seriously, and he enjoyed catching the odd person who stole produce or allowed his livestock to destroy saplings on the property. He delighted in sitting atop his horse proudly and having the culprits walk ahead of him, the stolen goods on their heads or hanging by a rope from their shoulders or errant livestock being pulled along behind them. Prosecutions were rare. Soldier, however, delighted in humiliating some people, especially the younger men who made their dislike of him very clear. He would march them to Mr. Carlisle's shop and let them go after taking the stolen produce from them, or he'd give the animal owners a telling-off and force them to publicly apologize for destroying the saplings.

Everybody knew that the foodstuff were distributed in the dead of night to his favourite people like Mr Carlisle, the most influential shop owner, with only a portion of the money finding its way back to the Sandersons. The Sandersons knew it, too, but they were not concerned because, in general, Soldier was doing a very good job for them.

Kenny Sanderson, born in Scotland in 1881, was the youngest of three sons to Robert and Eileen Sanderson. His mother died when he was an infant, and he, like his siblings, was brought up by family members. By 1921, he was running the family hotel in Singapore whilst one of his brothers was serving in the Indian army. His other brother and his father had died during the First World War. A new acquaintance would invariably ask Kenny when he'd arrived in Singapore expecting the answer to be no more than a few weeks prior. Such was the paleness of his skin because of his dislike for the sun and the opportunities he had to keep out of it. It came as a shock to him when he was ordered—not asked, but literally ordered, military-style—by an older cousin to travel to Jamaica to take over the running of the Dalbeattie plantation.

He was not at all eager to make the move to the other side of the world, but he knew that as a Sanderson male who had been brought up by relatives, he had to take on any responsibility put before him. He took comfort in the fact that at least he would still be in the tropics. Others did not understand that he loved the heat; he just did not like being in the sun.

Hoping for a gradual introduction and mentoring from his uncle Gordon before taking control of the plantation, Kenny felt cheated when he found that his uncle had passed away and been buried a couple of days before his ship docked in Kingston. Although his family members denied it, Kenny felt that the family had known of his uncle's rapid decline and had intentionally kept it from him.

He decided that since he was running the plantation for the benefit of the wider family, he would take it easy and let the staff run things whilst he enjoyed the beauty of the place and relaxed after the hustle and bustle of Singapore. As it turned out, this was a good decision. The staff at Dalbeattie, accustomed to the mature, older Sandersons, took some time to accept Kenny's authority, especially as he knew so little about farming.

Reluctant at first to join her husband in Jamaica, Jean Sanderson spent her early years at the Dalbeattie plantation making watercolour paintings, discovering the names of the local fauna and flowers, and learning how to make sweet potato pudding and other local specialties. This was vastly different from the way she'd spent her time in Singapore, where she had been immersed in the British society of tea parties with so-called proper ladies and gentlemen. She was surprised to find that she missed those parties, and after a while, she began to invite overseas visitors to afternoon tea at Dalbeattie. Weekend stays followed when she became disenchanted with the brief stays of the tea party guests, which did not allow her enough time to interact deeply with her visitors. Her untimely death after twelve years at Dalbeattie was a blow to her staff and the local people who adored her.

The present Mrs. Sanderson was born Morag MacDonald in Scotland in 1905, the only child of Alistair, the local vet, and Ana, the midwife. As a young nurse, Morag had been selected from many applicants to be the resident nurse in the household of Sir Iain Kirkpatrick, who made his fortune shipping goods between the United Kingdom, India, and the Far East.

Red-haired Morag, tall and with a pointed chin, wore the hint of a permanent smile. She was an astute young lady and was well known for enlightening the staff about political and social events. Lady Kirkpatrick, who found Morag too knowledgeable for her liking, vowed to get rid of her. Sensing that his wife's dislike for Morag might also be because of her good looks, Sir Iain decided to dispense with her services. He arranged for one of his friends, a fellow member of his club in Piccadilly, to take Morag into his household. Morag knew the reason for her leaving, and she vowed that she would not keep quiet. She saw no reason to stifle her knowledge; she knew she was smart beyond her profession and would one day prove it. When the teenage daughters of the new household also felt threatened by her good looks and what they saw as her pushiness, Morag ended up working in a hospital.

Through the contacts she'd made in the private households, Morag got a job as a private nurse with a Harley Street consultant, a highly prestigious position. It was whilst she was there that she came into contact with the Sandersons, marrying Kenny a year later.

On arrival at Dalbeattie in 1934, Morag, at twenty-nine, was not popular with the Plummers residents who were used to dealing with the more mature, gentle, and kind Jean Sanderson. To them, Morag was just a pretty young nurse who'd managed to snare a grieving—and wealthy—man into marrying her. She also had an unusual hostility towards the servants, which led to stories that Kenny had to coach her on the proper way to behave towards them, bearing in mind that they prepared their meals. The older ladies delighted in speaking in glowing terms of Jean, who they saw as a proper lady, whilst others defended Morag, saying her actions could not be described as hostile and that people should learn to respect other people's property. As there were no children by Kenny's first marriage, they hoped there might be at least one child with his new wife.

Problems between Daisy and her stepfather, Soldier, had begun two months earlier, when she turned thirteen. She never knew when it was coming, so she had no way of escaping. Usually it was a single blow. Other times it was a series of slaps as he walked by.

Daisy grew accustomed to hearing her mother being called worthless and wicked for letting Soldier loose on her own daughter. She wanted to defend her mother by telling whoever would listen that things were not like that. But she had to keep quiet. She would not risk the beatings for being rude to an adult, whatever the circumstance. She had no choice but to listen as the women spoke of the situation in deliberate tones, loud enough for her to hear, almost daring her to respond or even repeat what they said, especially to her mother.

Feeling sorry for her mother, who she knew wanted to protect her from Soldier, Daisy longed for the day when she would have the courage to let her mother know just how wise she was about what was going on, that she knew how much her mother loved her and that she was just trying to make life easier for all of them.

The area where Daisy slept was close to the partition, which had large gaps between the boards, and she spent hours awake at times, just listening. She knew the difference between the sounds of the goings-on between Soldier and her mother and that of the wood contracting in the coolness of the night. She also knew from the discussion she overheard between her mother and Soldier why she had to move from the partition to sleep on the far side of the room.

Martha felt that Daisy might get some comfort from talking with Thelma. She was confident that Thelma was a good girl who was taking up the various sewing techniques and had taken her advice and stopped fooling around with the boys. If it were not so, Martha would have heard. She had been tempted to ask Thelma what Daisy told her about what was going on, but she never had the courage. She was not sure that she wanted to hear the details.

Thelma became involved in the Girls' League and was even teaching some of the other girls to do basic hand sewing. Independently from Martha's encouragement, she was the one who talked to Daisy about pregnancy and how easily it could happen. She was also helping Daisy to improve her reading and shared a book about the female body that Martha had let her read in secret. Thelma was also the one who put the fear of childbirth into Daisy by relating the details of the obscenities she'd overheard when her aunt was in labour.

Things were different with Martha, though. Whenever Martha and Sister Geraldine wanted to talk about what was going on around them, especially about specific church sisters, they would usher Daisy out of the house. If they were outside, they would send her inside. There was an understanding about these things between Daisy and Martha so that even when the girl was tempted to stand near a door and try to eavesdrop, her fear of losing Martha's trust prevented her from doing so.

TWO

According to the story passed down through the years, due to a falling-out between the two Sanderson brothers after the death of their father in the 1860s, one brother sold and gave away a portion of the land that forms the greater part of what is now the district of Plummers. Nobody knows where that brother and his family went afterwards, though most believe they returned to England. The other brother stayed on, and the property remained in the hands of his descendants.

Plummers, like the neighbouring districts, lay by the coast, encircled by the Dalbeattie property, whilst the Dalbeattie house sat atop a hill, linked to the coastline-hugging districts by the gently sloping landscape that led to the sea.

The Green and Red Rivers were on either side of Plummers. The Green River was a wide-mouthed river that often had stagnant water caused by the sand building a barrier to the sea, only to be opened up in times of heavy rain. The children swam in the sea away from the mouth, and despite the warnings from parents about the dirty water, when it was time to leave the beach, they would go to the area where the fresh water seeped like a sieve through the sand into the sea so that their skin would be free from the salt that would otherwise glisten on their dark skin as they dried in the sun.

The Red River, on the other hand, flowed down the neighbouring valley just under two miles or so away. This was a smaller river that flowed constantly, even if at little more than a trickle at times. It had a narrow, deep riverbed and got its name from the colour of the water when it rained, as the water stripped the land upriver of its red topsoil.

The rivers played an important part in the lives of the Plummers residents. You were said to be from OutaBridge to denote that you were not a native of Plummers but from Jenners, the district on the other side of Green River, or Clover Hill, on the other side of Red River. If you were from farther away, you were referred to by the name of your district. OutaBridge denoted a form of neighbourliness that was unique to Plummers.

The use of the name OutaBridge could easily give the impression that the people from Plummers were not very welcoming, but that was not so. Because Plummers sided with the brother who had left, the other brother took his revenge and hardly hired any of the residents to work on his plantation. The people were thus forced to concentrate on their own personal farming and became tradesmen—carpenters, blacksmiths, stone masons, boat builders, and the like.

Although it was first to be considered the location for the Methodist church for ministers who came from England, Plummers later lost out to Clover Hill. The latter was chosen because of the intervention of the resident Sanderson brother, who persuaded the church authorities to give the honour to Clover Hill.

Nobody can point to how it started, but the story is that the people of Plummers were so upset at losing the church to Clover Hill that they set about deciding on a suitable revenge, and they chose education. Whether the story is true or not, it is a fact that Plummers began to draw attention to itself through its interest in education, so much so that when the public works department set up a base in the area, the Plummers folks got the vast majority of the jobs. Whether by coincidence or not, the church authorities went back to their earlier choice and set up in Plummers.

The shift in the location of the mission house from Clover Hill to Plummers created rivalry between the two districts, which extended to cricket tournaments. In later years it became more pronounced in the political arena, with the districts supporting opposing candidates.

The house where Daisy, her mother, her baby brother, and Soldier lived was among the first of a group of houses as you entered the lane. It was close to the junction with the main road and backed on to the Dalbeattie property. Next was Martha. Her house was a little farther back from the path, and a row of guava trees marked the boundary between the two properties. Sister Doris, Gladys's mother, was next. The front of her house was almost in line with May's house, with a pretty hedge running across the front and continuing by the side towards the back. It was so high that you could only see the houses beyond it if you were almost past Doris's house. Also in the lane were two couples from OutaBridge who did not feel that welcome. The menfolk were two friends, also from OutaBridge. They were farm labourers at Dalbeattie and the best cricketers on the Plummers team.

Martha was a teenager when she arrived in Top Ground in the early 1920s, her mother being housekeeper to the Sandersons. Her mother, Miss Sarah, was not liked by the locals, as they felt she was not as kind as the previous housekeeper, who used to give them little presents of sweets and cakes for the children. They knew Jean Sanderson was not happy with what she regarded as an overly generous level of kindness by the previous housekeeper, but some of the older folks also felt Jean was just being spiteful, getting back at them because of the generosity of the Sanderson brother who gave part of the Dalbeattie property to their forefathers.

Within days of starting work at Dalbeattie, Sarah insisted her daughter learn a skill. She had no idea what the skill would be, but she did not want her to follow her into service. It so happened that the prominent dressmaker in the district was looking for a little girl to help her out by first learning to baste and sew buttonholes. If she showed promise, there would be an opportunity to learn the more intricate skill of stitching and, finally, learning to cut and make a dress herself. That was how Martha got started in dressmaking.

Due to ill health, Sarah stopped working for the Sandersons when she was in her early fifties. As if she knew she did not have long to live, she encouraged Martha to get married. She wanted to see a ring on her daughter's finger before long. Unknown to Sarah, Martha already had a suitor who wanted her to live with him, and she was planning to do just that when her mother suddenly stopped working. She died from typhoid fever before her dream was fulfilled.

At Dalbeattie, May did the bed making, washing, and ironing and any other work she was called upon to do, except the cooking. That was the domain of Miss Agnes, a tiny lady with a deep voice, and with wrinkles that seemed to change her facial expressions without effort, giving her little cause to express her feelings in words. She was not one to be challenged. She lived in and was the real boss. Whilst the Sandersons called their staff, including Geoffrey Marshall, the bookkeeper, by their surnames, they always referred to her as Miss Agnes. She always dressed in light blue, a sort of uniform with white cuffs, more like a nurse. She commanded respect and attention from all at Dalbeattie.

Working in the Sanderson household was a prized position in itself, and May knew she was envied. It was something she was aware of but did not glorify in. She simply devoted herself to the task of doing whatever she could so that her little girl would be able to avoid that sort of working life. All that changed, however, when she took up with Soldier.

Unlike his fellow villagers (except for the churchgoers), Soldier did not drink alcohol. But that did not stop him from hanging around with the heavy drinkers, chatting about boxing, politics, cricket, or women or listening to war stories from the old soldiers. He was also very proud of his treasured scrap book, an old exercise book the Sandersons had thrown out. He mixed paste from flour and water, adding a little lime juice to deter the cockroaches from eating the paper. He then cut out and pasted his many pictures from magazines, which were plentiful over at Dalbeattie. Many were of the royal family, and he delighted in being able to name the kings and queens of the previous centuries. He also cut out and pasted pictures from the newspapers of cricketers and boxers. Soldier was active in local politics, being among the first to want to organize a political meeting. Once that had been accomplished, he melted into the background so he could have the freedom to be mischievous with any of the parties or individuals he chose to have issues with.

Strangers who did not know Soldier and heard him talk about politics, the history of the royal family, and other subjects would think he was a learned man with a formal education. They, like the people of Plummers, did not know that he had a fantastic memory for facts, especially from the radio broadcasts he listened to over at Dalbeattie. He also learned a great deal from eavesdropping on conversations there.

Soldier was always well turned out, with his shirt well ironed and trousers well seamed. Unusual among the men, he ironed his trousers himself. He took pride in doing it when he was living alone, much to the disgust of many of the men, who saw it as him just being mean, when he could pay a woman to do it. They felt he would get himself a better deal than what he got from paying some of the so-called slack women for sex before May teamed up with him. He used to iron his shirts, too, but as Daisy got older, he stopped doing it, saying it was something she should do. He was very forceful about it, even when May offered to do it instead.

Soldier was also the local cricket umpire and was well known for not favouring giving someone out through the lbw rules. "You have three wickets to aim for. Lick down one o' dem," he'd often say.

Martha was correct about how long Soldier had been living with May—just over four years. The only other woman they knew he'd lived with since coming to Plummers had lasted just a few weeks. Rumour had it that she could not cope with his sexual demands. The story was that his idea of good sex involved inflicting a great degree of hurt or discomfort on the woman and that he delighted in women pleading with him to "take you time" or "no go down so far" or whatever else came to them that they felt would get him to be gentle. There were many stories about him in that respect, some told by some of the women, who always said they heard that so-and-so had had a taste of Soldier and how "him batter 'er up."

Agnes admired Soldier. She saw him as a dedicated, kind person who was just a bit power mad. She was always pleased to see him when he took a break from his horseback patrols and popped in for a chat.

He kept her in touch with what was happening in the district, as the ladies did not trust her to keep their stories from the ears of the white people. They took the same attitude when dealing with the parson's wife because they said that soon after she arrived, she knew everybody's business, including who was sleeping with who and who was the father of this or that child that was a regular in church. Those who did not attend church laughed at this, as the parson's wife seemed interested only in the stories of the regular churchgoers.

It was quite normal for young girls to live with families other than their own and do a few chores in return for a better life than they would have had with their own parents. This arrangement was more common with relatives. In the case of Daisy, the nearness of her house to Martha's made the prospect easier for her mother to contemplate. Martha thought she could do with a little help, and who better to help her and learn a little dressmaking than little Daisy?

Martha was aware that Daisy did not go to school as regularly as the other girls. She was also aware that neither her stepfather nor her mother did much in their little house. It was as if they'd decided that because they served the Sandersons, little Daisy had to serve them. May was aware that many of the women talked about how she seemed to be punishing Daisy for the fact that the girl's father had gone away, never to return, blighting her prospects of getting a decent man, one who would respect her the way many of the church people seemed to be respected by their men.

Martha suffered silent pains as she watched little Daisy clean non-stop in the mornings and late into the evenings. She often commented, "Surely there can't be that much cleaning to do in that little house." She also noted that the floor was spotless and shiny from Daisy's efforts. The girl was always on her knees, pushing the coconut brush back and forth in front of her in a steady rhythm until the floor glistened from the sunlight that broke in through the gaps in the boards.

Shading her eyes from the early morning sun, Daisy wondered what Martha was fussing herself about. She pulled both knees up to her chest, her bare feet flat on the grass wet from the overnight dew. She pushed herself up with both hands into a sitting position and winced from the pain that ran through her body. Martha noticed that her flimsy sleeping garment was wet. She hoped it was from the dew. Then she saw her face.

"Oh my God! Him do it again—and you face swelling up fast, fast, fast."

Daisy touched her face and winced as the pain shot through her again. She closed her eyes and tried to recall how she came to be on the wet grass at the break of day, why her face was aching, and why Martha was fussing herself so much. Then she remembered the look in Soldier's eyes and the half smile that had pushed up the left side of his top lip. She knew it wasn't a real smile, but an expression that said she was not going to enjoy what followed. She remembered walking slowly towards him as she had so many times before. Then her mind went blank. However much she tried, she could remember nothing else.

Martha grabbed her by the hand and helped her up as she had done a couple of times before at the break of dawn. On previous occasions, Martha had kept Daisy until her body returned to a relaxed state. She would then send her back over to her own house to wash and change. Today, however, would be different. Daisy would stay with her all day. It didn't matter that Soldier would come home during the day and would, as usual, want Daisy to pull off his boots or pour him a mug of water. Martha decided that today, Soldier would have to do everything for himself. Making that decision gave her a sense of satisfaction, a sense of power, a feeling of doing something special for little Daisy.

"You eat yet?" Martha asked, and before Daisy could answer, she added, "What a stupid thing to ask. Girl, just sit yourself down on the bench. No…no…come, come…I really don't know what I am doing, you know. Tell you what—sit on the stool. I'm going to get your clothes." Then, walking towards her own house, she mumbled quietly to herself: "Lawd…mi head no good today at all. This man affecting me as well. Not good. Not good. Have to put a stop to it." As she was about to climb the steps to her house, she turned and made her way over to Daisy's house, which was just a few yards from her own, and no fence between them. After a couple of minutes, she returned with clean clothes and a basin for Daisy to wash herself before having breakfast with her. She sent her inside. Daisy knew where to go. After a few minutes, she came out with the basin of water and poured it in her little flower garden, taking care to ensure the water went directly onto the earth and not on the leaves.

Near one corner of her house, Martha had a little bench that could seat two people comfortably, though she was the only one who normally sat on it. It had been made specifically for her to relax on after meals, a ritual she'd started after a quarrel with her husband and one she never regretted. It was not that Mr. Mills could not sit on the bench, but if ever he did, he would make sure he got up as soon as his wife was nearing the end of a meal. He would anticipate the sun's movement across the sky every hour or so and place the bench in such a way that Martha would be properly shaded by the overhanging mango and breadfruit trees without having to move the seat herself. It was a gesture she treasured and delighted in relating to her church sisters over and over again. She always ended with, "Him love me so till…"

After breakfast, Martha put some old clothes on the bench and, with Mr. Mills being away from home, carried out the sun-positioning routine. She then beckoned Daisy to lie on the bench. Daisy did as she was told, lying back with her feet hanging over one end. Martha gently held the child's head steady and laid a crushed leaf on the bruise on her cheek. She then returned to the house to fetch her sewing basket, sat herself down on a stool facing the girl, reached into the basket, and began her hand sewing. Daisy slowly drifted into sleep, and Martha watched as her chest heaved with each breath. She wondered how May, a sometimes churchgoing mother, could live with herself, knowing what her daughter was going through.

Martha's concern was not new. Aware that Daisy did not get a good night's sleep most nights, Martha had made a large cushion filled with scraps of leftover material from her sewing for Daisy to lie on. It provided welcome relief for the girl, as at home she was made to sleep on special matting on a narrow wooden bed. Martha knew that May was none too pleased with this gift, but she had allowed Daisy to keep it nevertheless.

Daisy's situation was playing on Martha's mind. She considered different options and decided the time had come for a big decision to be made. Enough was enough. She would tell May that she had to put a stop to Soldier. She would approach the Sandersons. After all, she thought, they were, in the main, decent white people, and she was sure that if Morag knew what was happening, she would speak with May. Having forgiven the Sandersons for their wayward ways when their soldier friends came to visit and behaved a bit strangely after they'd downed some white rum, Martha had a secret admiration for Morag because she knew that if she was in her position, she would not have waited hand and foot on her husband the way Morag did.

Another strategy Martha considered was to join forces with Miss Agatha, who had the ear of the parson. She felt together they could do something to protect the girl from Soldier. She thought of involving the police, but she knew that once the police paid a visit to the district, they would return from time to time, sometimes to cast an eye over the young girls, who saw it as a feather in their hats to be associated with a policeman. It was also known that the police had ways of "seeing off" their rivals by harassing or even arresting them for gambling, a vice the police themselves took part in from time to time. She finally decided that walking for over an hour in the hot sun to the police station would not be worth the hassle. She was furious with her hopeless position, confused and agitated that she could not settle on one clear idea of how to resolve what for her was a big problem.

Hemming a dress was something she could do blindfolded—such were her dressmaking skills—yet here she was, making silly mistakes because she could not concentrate. After a while, she realized she had not checked on Daisy, so she stopped sewing and glanced over at the girl lying on the bench. She stared at Daisy's chest, becoming alarmed when she did not discern any movement. She rose from the stool and moved closer, and as she bent over the girl, she relaxed as she noticed the gentle heaving with each ever so gentle intake of breath. As she returned to her seat and continued with her sewing, she imagined Daisy being her own little girl. It didn't matter that such a thing could never have been because of the operation she'd had some years earlier. From the day Daisy was born, she had treated her just as she would have treated her own child. She was angry now. She was ready to do battle.

Martha looked up to the sky, judging whether she and Daisy would have to shift their positions in order to remain in the shade. Not yet, she decided. She noticed that the birds had gone quiet, although a gentle breeze had sprung up. It was as if nature was preparing itself for a disaster, the calm before the breeze-blow.

Grabbing her straw fan, the one with the embroidered butterflies on both sides, Martha began to fan the sleeping Daisy, as if the gentle breeze was not enough. After a little while, she got up and went indoors and brought out another stool. She went back again and returned with a pretty piece of material, obviously left over from the dress she was hemming. She folded the cloth and laid it over the stool, creating a small table. She went into the house yet again and brought out a tray laden with a pitcher of water, a small bag of sugar, two limes, a tin mug, and a large wooden spoon. Daisy stirred as Martha began mixing the ingredients to make lemonade.

"Daisy," she called. No answer. "Daisy, time you get up and have a drink." Still no response. Becoming concerned, she shook Daisy gently and watched her come slowly to life. She smiled as the child rubbed her eyes with the back of a hand as she came to grips with where she was and what time of day it was.

Martha went into the house to fetch a glass and a cup. She had decided just as she was about to pour the lemonade that Daisy would drink from one of her best glasses; she herself would use the cup. On her way back, she stopped in the doorway and cried out, "Lord, I can't concentrate. Help me. Help me, oh Lord." Daisy was accustomed to hearing Martha talk to herself, so she just smiled back at her.

After they had finished drinking their lemonade, Martha took a break from her sewing and began singing her favourite hymns, clapping her hands to the beat from time to time. It was well known in the district that these song breaks, as they were called, calmed her and helped her get through the day. Daisy drifted off to sleep, almost falling off the bench now and then.

In between songs, Martha lifted the leaf from Daisy's cheekbone, checking to see if the swelling had gone down. It was not until midafternoon that she saw the first signs of the reduced swelling and satisfied herself that Daisy would be all right.

She decided that she would not let Daisy go back into the hellhole the child called home. Seeing the child lying there with that bruised cheek made Martha feel even more protective than usual. She knew that Soldier and May were the contacts who provided young ladies for the soldiers from the British army camp in Kingston who came up to Dalbeattie several weekends each year. As far as she knew, most of the girls were from OutaBridge; only one or two of the local girls from Plummers appeared to be involved. It was a nasty situation, about which May refused to answer questions, saying that what happened in Mrs. Sanderson's house was Mrs. Sanderson's business. Given what she had already heard, Martha had been none too pleased with May's response, and that had made her even more concerned.

She knew that Daisy was an outgoing, industrious child, whose spirit Soldier eventually would break, thereby bringing her childhood to an abrupt end. And worst of all, she thought, the mother, whilst not appearing to encourage Soldier's behaviour, didn't seem to be doing anything to stop it. A good solution, she thought would be for Daisy to live with her. She thought, "*Yes. That's it. Why not? Live with me; be under my roof, under my care. Go to school regularly, be hugged, be smiled at and with, hear jokes that I used to hear as a child, be frightened by tales that make her want me to sit up with her till she falls asleep, live the life that a child should live. Yes, that's what Daisy needs.*" She convinced herself that that was what God, through her, would do for Daisy. That was what Daisy was going to experience, come hell or high water.

All she needed now was a plan. There would be no backing down, no asking or pleading. She was going to rescue little Daisy. She was going to give her a life worth living. She was going to make her glad to be alive and able to enjoy the life God gave her. She was going to start with the fact that it was time the girl was wearing a brassiere. Yes. She would say it at last.

She turned her thoughts next to how May might react to her ideas and how she would counter them. "If May puts up a resistance," she thought, "I could accuse her of using her daughter to satisfy Soldier." It was a dangerous strategy but one that seemed to be worth the risk. On the other hand, if May was agreeable but Soldier was not, she could try to use the same strategy, although Soldier was unpredictable and, presumably, a violent man. She was in a quandary. The fact that they lived in separate houses meant a boundary was drawn, irrespective of there not being any discernible border. She thought that under her roof, Daisy would be safe from Soldier. She wondered whether to tell May what led her to think of having Daisy. Then she scolded herself, noting that May would simply shrug her shoulders, take her daughter by the hand, and lead her back to her house, as she had done many times before.

THREE

As if she knew her daughter would have had a problem with Soldier that morning, when May came in from Dalbeattie, she walked right past her house and went directly over to where she knew Miss Martha would be sitting, in the shade of the mango tree.

"Evening, Miss Martha," said May, maintaining her respect for the older woman and avoiding eye contact with her daughter.

"Evening, mi dear."

Without looking at or even acknowledging her daughter's presence, she replied, "I don't know what to do."

"So you know? And you don't know what to do? Well, I think I know what to do."

"And what is that?"

Daisy listened without moving a muscle as the ladies talked about her and her welfare as if she were not there.

Martha continued, "If you don't put a stop to it, you sure know what going to happen. Is that what you want?"

"No. No. No. What you say you going to do?"

"Didn't say I was going to do anything. Said I *know* what to do. That is different."

Daisy watched as her mother folded and unfolded her arms nervously, looking up and down, left and right, without focusing on anything in particular.

Miss Martha continued, "Perhaps you should let her stay with me. I can teach her to sew good, good, good. She can do a good buttonhole already. She can baste well, too. Look! Somebody want me to rent out Jennifer's room to one of the new teachers. I prefer to have Daisy with me. Let her come and live with me. I have a nice bed for her." Martha suddenly became aware of her use of the word *bed*. She took a deep breath and continued, "Lawd, no vex with me. You know what I mean. Let her come live with me. You know I like her. Such a nice little girl."

May noticed that her daughter was shaking.

"What's the matter, child?" she asked. There was no response. Daisy just stared straight ahead. Then she turned and saw her mother smiling at her. She remembered how charming her mother could be when she wanted to be. She had not seen that smile for quite some time.

"Let her come and live with me," Martha reiterated. Daisy's body jerked, and she began to shake uncontrollably.

"She having a fit?" asked May. Martha moved towards Daisy, but May was faster. She dashed over to her daughter, sat on the bench next to her, and hugged her, realizing she should have made the first move to comfort the child. Martha stepped back and watched mother and daughter in an embrace she had not witnessed before.

"Mama, I want to stay with you. I want to stay with you," said Daisy, tears streaming down her face. The plea was heartrending, and both women soon had tears in their eyes. Martha reached out to touch the child but pulled her arms back and folded them as May tried to calm her daughter down.

Martha had a nice, sturdy house with varnished furniture and a huge wooden four-poster bed. Daisy liked Martha and enjoyed being over at the house from time to time. Martha was teaching Daisy how to sew, and the girl returned the trust by always securing Martha's permission before practicing on her precious Singer sewing machine. Daisy wished her house was like that. She envied Jennifer, a girl a few years older who Martha had taken in when her parents immigrated to the United States. Jennifer had always been kind to Daisy, but she had recently left to join her parents in New York. Martha had treated Jennifer like her own. She did not force her to get down on her knees to wax and shine the wood floor; she hired someone to come in and do that on Saturdays. That in itself was a plus. But the thought of being alone in the house with Martha's husband terrified Daisy.

"Let her come and live with me," said Martha again. Daisy shivered, as if hit by a sudden cold breeze. May removed her arms and stepped back. It appeared that something strange and dangerous was about to happen, and she was not sure how to handle the situation.

"Girl, what's the matter?" stammered May, her eyes wide with fear. Daisy continued to sob as spasms racked her body. The women flanked her, gently massaging her upper arms. They did not know that Daisy was in a quandary, wondering how she would cope with Mr. Mills if she accepted Miss Martha's invitation. They did not know that when Martha was away selling her pretty little dresses, Daisy would be at the mercy of Mr. Mills in a way she did not relish. She enjoyed the attentions of Sammy, her fourteen-year-old friend, who regularly rubbed his hands over her breasts and pressed his body against hers, an exciting encounter for both of them. That, however, was very different from what Mr. Mills had done on her twelfth birthday. Martha had left them alone for just a short while, and Mr. Mills had pinched her nipples, winked at her, and invited her to feel the erect penis bulging in his trousers. When she did not react, he had grabbed her hand and forcibly wrapped it around the bulge. She knew she kept it there longer and held it more firmly than she wanted to, but she had been transfixed with horror at such acts perpetrated by a man with whom she had always felt safe.

Over a year had passed without further incident until a few weeks earlier, when Mr. Mills had put his hands down her pants, stroked her private parts, and remarked, "Nice. You a feather already. Nice…nice. No wonder Soldier so happy." Although she had been terrified by the man's actions, she had been afraid to react in a way that might have offended him. After all, he owned one of the two radios in the district, and Soldier often listened to cricket there, under the mango tree, instead of at Mr. Carlisle's shop, where the other men congregated at cricket Test match time.

Mr. Carlisle's was known simply as the shop. It was the largest shop in the district and the only place to buy things like sewing thread, buttons, flashlight batteries, lamp wicks, bay rum, shoelaces, floor wax, and soap. The smaller shops sold rum (some of it watered down and sold at a lower price) and food items that had a quick turnaround, like bread, bun, cheese, soft drinks, flour, salt fish, and sugar.

Daisy was also afraid of Mr. Mills because he was not gentle with his touches like Sammy. He did not smile pleasantly when he groped her. It was as if he wanted her to be afraid of him. She preferred to live under the same roof with Soldier and have her mother close by rather than be alone with Mr. Mills. But how was she going to get the message across?

May was worried that if Soldier found out that he was suspected of having sex with Daisy, he might well do it out of sheer spite instead of shouting his innocence from the rooftops. She appreciated Martha's offer. Martha even proposed that Daisy need not sleep at her house on weekends, if that would help. Still, May refused. What May did not know was that Martha had suffered abuse as a little girl. She was reliving her own agonies and desperately wanted to protect Daisy from a similar fate.

Ruth Green, well dressed as usual and with her trademark scarf around her neck, was sitting on her veranda, watching the world go by. Folks knew not to say good morning to her first, for fear of not getting a response. However, once she greeted them, they felt obliged to return her greeting.

Folks did not mind because those in need felt it was in their interest to be in her good books, as it meant they could get one or two of the handouts she brought with her from New York. Some of the women felt she was a brazen woman—a woman without shame, a woman who thought memories had died. They were suspicious of her. They were not sure whether her gifts were acts of kindness, if she enjoyed the power of giving, or whether she was seeking to curry favour with the people of Plummers, living on the legacy of the good name of her parents. Still, most of the people in the district could not afford to put pride ahead of need, so they played the game, paying respect in exchange for the odd dress, church hat, handbag, or a gently worn nice pair of shoes.

Nobody in Plummers knew Mr. Green or what he and Ruth did for a living in New York. All they knew was that she had met and married someone from "down the country," as those in the east referred to those who were from west of Kingston. They didn't know whether they'd met whilst in Jamaica or in New York, and the lack of such detail bothered some of them. They also heard that the couple had had children and that the husband and children had died. There were many different stories as to what, if any, part Ruth might have played in their deaths. Again, they needed to know. Such was the nature of the people of Plummers. They were trusting but felt the need to feel comfortable with everyone. It was as if there was no such thing as privacy, despite the efforts of some individuals to keep their business private. They felt they should know how Ruth accumulated her wealth, especially as it seemed to be linked to the deaths of her husband and children. Not knowing led to a variety of stories as to how her riches came about.

"Come here, little girl," Ruth called out as Daisy walked by. Daisy approached gingerly, trying to fix her clothes to appear a bit tidier. "What's your name?"

"Daisy, ma'am."

"And who is your mother?"

Daisy spent the next minute answering questions about who she was, where her house was situated, and her age. She did not know that Ruth already knew the answers. But Ruth did not know that Daisy had been briefed via titbits that they were related, her brother being Daisy's father.

Then Ruth asked, "Why aren't you wearing a brassiere?"

Daisy did not want to say she had never worn one. She was waiting for Martha to push for one with her mother. She then noticed Ruth's eyes fixed on her bare feet.

"Come, take a seat. Over there," Ruth said, pointing to a stool on the far side of the veranda.

Daisy climbed the steps slowly and did as she was told. Her eyes locked with Ruth's, something children were not supposed to do with adults. She was not being rude, just a little afraid, or, at best, curious. After a moment of uneasy silence, Ruth Green went inside and came back with three pairs of shoes. After inviting Daisy to try each of them on, she decided on the pair Daisy should have.

Instead of handing them to Daisy, she said, "Tell your mother I want to see her. In fact, tell her to come and see me tomorrow—no, the following day, after church." And without waiting for a response, she went back inside with all the shoes. When Daisy was halfway between the house and the road, Ruth shouted, "Tell your mother I said you should not be out so late on your own."

"Yes ma'am," replied Daisy, continuing on her journey.

Though she'd been born Ruth Golding, the older folks still referred to her as Miss Golding. She never corrected them, seeming to have the same measure of respect for the older people that she expected from the younger ones.

Ruth was the only daughter of teachers Moses and Edith Golding from OutaBridge. Her brother, Oliver, had skipped his work contract, changed his name, and was working clandestinely in the United States. Ruth was still at school when he left Jamaica on a work ticket, a strong, fit twenty-three-year-old.

The Goldings were leading members of the church community, with Mrs. Golding being the founder of the Girls' League. She was determined to teach the girls self-respect, to encourage them to see education as important and not think of relying on a man to provide for them. "You must see yourselves as working in a partnership," she told them. This was radical thinking at that time, and the men felt threatened. They also felt Mr. Golding was a weak man who could not control his wife. They were even more put out when their bastion, the cricket ground, was out of bounds to them on moonlit nights when the Girls' League met. A few trusted older men, who had the job of keeping the younger men at bay on those nights, simply sat around listening to and watching the girls as they recited poetry, told stories, and played games. It was on one of those nights that Ruth's actions first brought shame on her family.

It was just before they broke up to leave, and Ruth simply walked away from the group and headed towards the church graveyard. Waiting for her there was James, the barber's son. Neither knew that Ruth was being followed by two boys who had spent all night watching from among the banana trees as the girls carried out their routines. The boys watched as Ruth, bathed in the moonlight, stepped out of her panties as she approached James, who sat on a tomb. She dropped her panties a few steps short of where James was, and without a greeting of any kind between them, she lay down on the tomb, pulled up her dress, and said, "Quick—quick." The next day, the panties were delivered to the Goldings with a note saying, "Ruth lef dem 'pon Miss Birdie tomb last night."

At the age of fourteen, Ruth changed from a tall, skinny child to a curvy, beautiful young lady. The other girls who were jealous of her good looks and family pedigree were unkind to her, both to her face and behind her back. She was openly called "the dunce" by her classmates and the older girls. There was no doubt that she attracted the attention of the nicer young men, and she was also the target of some of the older ones.

Ruth never enjoyed the level of respect normally given to the daughter of respectable parents. It was generally known that after the graveyard incident, her mother used to check on her from time to time during the night. Her parents knew she occasionally slipped out of bed to meet up with different boys, usually much older than herself.

Cleveland, the fast bowler, star cricketer, and handsome son of Mr. Carlisle, was the main one. It didn't matter who else was serving. If Cleveland was in the shop and Ruth entered, it was always Cleveland who served her, and she was guaranteed to get back more money than she had paid. The thing about this situation was that there was no need for Ruth to go to the shop—her parents had a maid to do that for them—but they found that no amount of talking would stop her from going there and buying things they did not need. Starving her of pocket money was out of the question, as they feared she would get it from admiring young men.

Mrs. Golding sometimes complained to her husband that their daughter was ruining the family name. When challenged by his wife to chastise their daughter, Mr. Golding would simply grunt to denote he'd heard what she had said. Mrs. Golding, on the other hand, confronted Ruth about her absence from bed some nights. She never once let her husband know, and though he was aware of his wife leaving the room and guessed that she was checking on their daughter, he never once asked her the result. Later, rumour had it that it was because of what the folks called her "loose behaviour" that Ruth was sent off to an aunt in Kingston before it was time for her to leave school. Not too long after that, the Goldings left Plummers.

Just over a year or so after the Goldings left, news reached the district that Mrs. Golding had died a few days after getting the news that Mr. Golding had failed to return from an early morning swim. His body was never found, and some people felt he simply went away, perhaps left the island, though there was no explanation as to why he might have done that.

The local people felt sadness for the family and were pleased when in 1948 the Golding's home was restored to its former glory. Until Mrs. Green arrived, Mr. Marshall, who was overseeing the work, would not confirm who he was preparing the house for. Nobody had expected Ruth to return to Plummers.

The courtship between Jean and Kenny Sanderson was carried out through correspondence. Major Fitzsimons, a somewhat eccentric man with a waxed moustache, was a friend who served with her husband in the same regiment. Because he had not yet remarried, the major was Jean's first target as a husband. He, however, wrote to her in no uncertain terms that he was done with settling down for the time being and was looking to move to another hot place in the colonies at the end of his tour of duty in Singapore, but definitely not Australia. He added that if she cared to wait for him to be sure he wanted to marry again, he would keep in touch. When she wrote back that she wanted to get away from a suitor in Australia and also get back to Singapore, it was he who suggested that she contact Kenny, who he described as a pushover. "You would be set up for life with him if you manage to pull it off," he advised. Jean, who was twelve years older than Kenny, was not at first keen on him, thinking him too young and inexperienced. She was also mindful of what the ladies who knew her would think of such a union. In the end, she began correspondence as the major suggested. He coached each of them in what to say to the other without either knowing.

As far as Kenny was concerned, the letter from Jean that set things in motion, enquiring about how things were going and what changes had occurred since she'd left Singapore, was a letter from someone who was missing a great social life and wanted to return to it. He was convinced that his letter-writing skills were at least equal to the major's ability to sweet-talk the ladies, as the exchanges over the next eighteen months led to his wedding.

He wondered how the major was getting on in Kenya, managing the beginnings of a coffee plantation. Kenny was sure that, unlike himself, the major would have full charge of the reins. It made him think whether he would have had a different management style if he had managed to serve. He thought, *If only. If only they knew how much I envied them. How much I envied being properly addressed as 'sir,' military-style, instead of the lazy mouthing I had to put up with from the servants on a daily basis and from the guests when they wanted a favour, such as a matter dealt with ahead of someone else.* He imagined the crisp "Yes, sir," and "No, sir" said with gusto, with pride because he was the monarch's proxy. It was the Queen's commission that was being addressed through him. It was Queen Victoria who was being saluted, through him, as he understood it. He recalled how he was often mocked that a century or so earlier, he would have been sent off to become a minister of religion because he couldn't do much else. He recalled that he was never angry in comparison to the other male Sandersons; he knew he was not as bright or as focused as to what he wanted to do. Then he corrected himself and recalled also that he wanted to join the army, but they told him his eyesight was too poor. He started wearing glasses because of that but discarded them after a few months, realizing he could see and read as easily without them. It left him wondering whether other forces were at hand to prevent him joining.

Unfortunately, he accepted that such longing would remain a dream. For a moment he wondered why a Scot should have such yearnings. Then he returned to reality, savouring the cool hillside breeze and the serenity of the evening as God's other daytime creatures prepared to slumber. He would sit on the veranda and continue to reflect. It helped to pass the time.

By the time Kenny left Singapore, he had accepted that Jean might not follow, as she was not sure being a plantation owner's wife would give her enough to do. The fact that she was a seasoned traveller helped Kenny in his decision to make the trip alone to Jamaica.

Sometimes in his early days in Jamaica, he laughed to himself, *"If only they knew just how much I hated the socializing I was forced into as manager of that hotel."* He recalled that he was older than many of the army officers, who enjoyed undermining his authority by giving instructions to his staff, especially when they knew he had told them otherwise. They spent a lot in the hotel bars, and the advice from the older Sandersons was to grin and bear it. Apart from that, he considered them reasonable gentlemen, who, like himself, were in a situation forced upon them by duty. They might not have necessarily liked what they were doing or where they were doing it, but they made the best of the situation. But his situation, he thought at the time, was permanent whilst the officers' were temporary.

Although he liked the officers, he hated their wives, especially those who wore their husbands' ranks embarrassingly, demanding service and attention above others because of the higher rank of their husbands. When he discussed this with his wife, she would simply say, "The senior officers' wives spend the money. They also show off and invite others to do likewise, especially if the invited have never been here before. Remember, the Ross is a business, Ken."

He had no answer to that. After all, without any real work experience, she was the power behind the successful running of the Ross. He didn't care that his family members were unhappy with the power he handed over to her. She was the perfect hostess, and because of her, foreign government officials and professionals chose to stay at the Ross as Singapore headed full steam ahead in its rebuilding programme following the war.

He remembered the breakneck busy periods and the lazy days when he had to find things for the staff to do: painting walls and whitewashing stones in the driveway that didn't yet need a fresh coat. He thought about the free accommodations, food, and drink he gave to those in the know concerning troop movements so he could plan for the newcomers without having to be overly polite to those soon to leave. In that, he told himself, he was smarter than his family gave him credit for.

One guest who got his full attention was Major Fitzsimons, a captain on his arrival but promoted soon after. He didn't seem to have many friends, and they spent many hours talking. He remembered an incident when the major, a burly widower with no children, a keen badminton player, and a bit of a ladies man, came close to having a fist fight with fellow officers who decided to tease him that badminton was a ladies' game.

Kenny smiled at times when he recalled how, in her quiet moments in the hotel and usually with a drink, Jean delighted in telling stories about her past, ensuring that the officers' wives, especially, understood that she had some real class in her own right. She spoke about when Captain Sutcliffe died from malaria and her decision to go to Australia, where she had friends, instead of returning to the United Kingdom. She made sure they knew she was from a well-off family from the north of England who felt she had married below her station, and so she had no wish to be near them, even though she knew she would want for nothing if she returned. She emphasised that she stayed for three years in Australia before returning to become Jean Sanderson, wife of the hotel owner and manager. As most of the wives she knew before had by then moved on to India, other parts of the Commonwealth, or back to the United Kingdom, her story seemed plausible enough to listeners.

FOUR

It was a weekend in late 1935, and most of the guests had left. Kenny had gone to bed, sedated by the tablets Morag had slipped into his night-time cocoa. Morag, in her red blouse and blue skirt asked May to take a drink to the butterfly room—so called because of paintings of butterflies that hung on the walls—the instructions were specific: "Not now. In twenty minutes," she said as she nodded towards the little round table with a clock on it. "It is for the soldier who will be there." She smiled and gave May a slight nod. May smiled back, admiring the elegance of her boss as she glided away towards the room. She had delivered drinks to the room before, usually to anxious men awaiting "action" or those who were half asleep after such action. She had not bargained for what was to follow.

May came face-to-face with Morag at the door. Morag continued to tuck her blouse into the waist of her skirt before walking ahead of a soldier out of the room. May was just about to turn back when Morag signalled that she should continue into the room. Expecting to leave the drink in the room, she was surprised to find another soldier sitting in the far corner, beside the round table. His hat was on the nearby bed. May was unsure what to do. Sensing her awkwardness, the soldier said, "I'll have it here, thank you."

"Yes, sir," she replied.

Rather than having to squeeze past the soldier to rest the drink on the table, she decided to hand him the glass of rum and coconut water.

"No. Rest it on the floor. Here. At my feet. I will manage." When May hesitated, the soldier continued, "That's okay. At my feet. I will manage, I said."

May thought it an odd request, and with a degree of nervousness, she did as she was told. She recognized the handsome, clean-shaven soldier with a dimpled chin as one who had been smiling at her most of the evening. She enjoyed the admiration, but as Morag had warned the soldiers not to fraternize with her staff, she thought no more about the admiring glances. Special girls were provided for their fun. Something about the unspoken words that passed between her and the soldier told her something was different with this particular soldier and that Morag had a part to play in it.

"So you are May."

"Yes, sir."

"You say the 'sir' better than some of the squaddies do," he laughed. May did not know what *squaddie* meant, but she laughed nonetheless as she went to put the glass at the soldier's feet. As she stooped, the soldier got up, removed his hat from the bed, and made his way to the doorway. He closed the door so silently, it hardly made a sound.

May had not even reached the floor with the glass by then, and she stopped, wondering what was happening behind her. The room was silent, as the soldier had not started walking back. May gently put the glass on the floor and, just as slowly, stood up and turned around. She saw the soldier, leaning on the closed door, his arms folded. He was smiling. For her to get out, he would have had to move.

She looked alternately at the door handle and the soldier's smiling face, and before she realized what was happening, she found herself smiling as well. After a few tense moments, she took a few steps towards the door, keeping her eyes lowered. As she approached where he was standing, the soldier moved, allowing May to open the door if she wished.

At the same time, he pleaded, "No—don't go. Not yet. Please… please don't go." May stopped with an arm partially outstretched to grab the door handle. As if ordered to do so, the hand dropped slowly and came to rest by her side. "Do come and sit down for a moment," stammered the soldier. May's hand met his, and they walked slowly towards the bed. "Please turn down the lamp," he whispered. May wondered why he was whispering.

"Yes, sir."

"For God's sake, stop saying *sir*...at least not now." May was a bit startled by the aggressive tone, and she found herself laughing nervously. She sensed that the soldier was himself nervous, and she wondered whether he was inexperienced in dealing with women. She thought that if he was as young as he looked, she might just as well leave. However, seeing that Morag had just left the room with another soldier and had obviously given the young man the OK to wait for her, she decided to stay.

The soldier took another step towards her, right up close so that there was just air between them. He put his hands gently on her shoulder and fiddled with the starched collar of her white blouse before turning her slightly. He controlled her body in a very slow fall onto the bed. May lay quite still, her fingers entwined and resting gently on her stomach. The soldier propped himself up on one arm and leaned over her. She closed her eyes and began to breathe in the soldier's rum-laced breath. After a few moments of inaction, she opened her eyes to see the soldier looking at her, smiling. She melted into a smile, which turned into a giggle.

The soldier got up and put the chair behind the door, jamming it against the handle. May got up into a sitting position. She watched him walk towards her, unbuttoning his shirt and undoing his belt as he approached. In the dimmed light, she could see he was smiling. She watched the tall, handsome young man get nearer with slow, shuffling, short steps, his trousers at his feet. He then eased her down slowly on the bed and lay beside her, both on their sides, not a muscle moving between them.

To her surprise, the silence was broken by the soldier talking about himself. He told her he was new to Jamaica and was pleased that he had taken to the the Jamaican cuisine. He reeled of names of foodstuff to emphasise the point: Avocado (locally known as "pear"), sweet potato, breadfruit, callaloo, cassava, chocho. He went on to talk about the dishes he really loved and how pleased he was when she served him cow foot, yam and fried plantain earlier. She was surprised when he did not mention ackee and saltfish, and rice and peas, but she said nothing. Just when she thought he would go on to talk about drinks like sorrel and ginger beer, he told her it was his first time in the countryside and asked her what she knew about the history of the Dalbeattie estate, which was very little. He then went on to tell her how the name of the place and the names of the owners meant they were from Scotland. He told her that he knew her last name was McIntosh and that it was a Scottish name. He also gave her a short lecture about the difference between Scotland and England, ending with the claim that he was a descendant of the Sandersons. May didn't believe him, thinking that if it were so, Morag would have told her. As the young man talked, May became more relaxed, but never so relaxed as to be familiar in speech. She just listened. This annoyed the soldier a little, as he was keen on a conversation. He even insisted that May refer to him as Alex. Just at the point of getting bored, he lifted May like a baby with his strong arms and gently placed her in the middle of the bed. Before she could settle, May felt the soldier pulling at the elastic waist of her skirt. She was unsure whether to raise her hips to let it slide off easily. Before she could reach a decision, Alex had given up and began to lift the skirt from around her ankles. It was then that she decided to assist him, and she raised her hips and pulled her skirt down herself. She listened in the half light as the soldier's breathing became quicker and heavier, and she realized she'd better assist him in the final stages. She gave a little laugh as he thanked her before thrusting his body down in quick succession. May wanted to slow him down, but she didn't know what to say. Soon afterwards, she found herself holding the young man in a tight embrace with her arms and legs until his thrusting stopped and his breathing slowly returned to normal.

The following day, May was a bit nervous facing Morag. She was unsure whether it was because of her own actions or because, yet again, she was holding a secret for her boss. As it turned out, the matter was never discussed. May did, however, notice that Morag was very kind to her, letting her off work early if there was not much to do and giving her little presents like perfume and handkerchiefs. She was also aware that Miss Agnes was not at all pleased when that was done.

May became pregnant shortly afterwards and thought about the encounter many times and was pleased that Morag never mentioned anything about it to her. She never saw Alex again and often wondered what would have happened if the baby had been his. Would he have been like so many other soldiers and simply moved on, or would he have acknowledged and supported his child? She also wondered whether she would have asked Morag if Alex was in fact related to the Sandersons as he had said.

When the heavy rainfall began in the summer of 1936, the people of Plummers were not concerned because being in the mountainous eastern part of the island, they were not only accustomed to heavy rain and wind, but they knew how to handle it. When the storm arrived, however, things were different. They and the surrounding districts were among those who suffered the most damage.

People were slow to make their way to the church or to neighbours or relatives with sturdier homes. In fact, people only moved out when their homes began to crumble around them. Some who were in the fields just managed to get home before rivers were too swollen to cross, and those who lived on the sea side of the road that ran through the district suffered most, as all the houses collapsed around them. People lost livestock. The banana crop was wiped out. Many of the thatched roofs that were so endearing in the way they kept the little houses cool were nowhere to be seen. Sturdy houses were bereft of their shingles or corrugated zinc roofs whilst less sturdy ones defied logic by remaining totally free of any damage.

Two of those who died were fishermen. They were trying to get their boat further from the beach when they were swept away by a huge wave. Another was the wife of one of the fishermen; she decided to return home to collect items, only to have the house to collapse on her. She died the next day from her injuries. Daisy was born the following day.

For weeks after the storm, people sang at the top of their voices anywhere and anytime the spirit took them, praising and thanking

God for taking them safely through and asking for continued protection. Attendance at church soared. Whereas previously the vast majority of the congregation had been women, many men started to attend. A few marriages took place between folks who'd been living together for years, as if such a formalization of their union would bring them protection from God's wrath.

For most people, the height of what they endearingly called the *breeze-blow* was a signal that the end of the world was nigh. Nobody among them could recall such winds and rainfall. Whenever they talked about it, they spoke of the noise that accompanied the wind, the sting of the raindrops on their bodies, the noise of the objects flying through the air and knocking against one another as they passed overhead or close to them. They talked of their fright. They remembered how the rain seemed to come at them from the side instead of from above. They noted how the wind blew from one side at first, and then, like a miracle, it started to blow from the opposite side. They did not try to hide their fears from their crying children. They simply cried with them. They were not ashamed to let their children know that they, too, were helpless and scared to death.

Some folks said they saw very little because they'd kept their eyes closed for much of the time. It was a natural instinct—lower the head and keep the eyes closed. They also talked about the suddenness of the end, which they said was unlike the beginning.

Part of the road was washed away by the surf, which provided work for the men who did the digging to widen and create a new road as well as for the women who broke up the stone for the public works department.

The mission house was badly damaged, and the church folks gave priority to seeing that the English parson and his children were safe and secure. They would have done a great deal more before seeing to their own needs but for the intervention of Mr. Carlisle. He was very vocal about the need to "look after yourself first." His stance was seen by some as being that of an independent spirit. Many also felt that because of his relative affluence, he could take such a view. Unlike him, many in the district wanted to keep in the good books of the churchgoers and the parson. They felt that Mr. Carlisle, whose oversized head made him look a bit like a dwarf, and who never went to church, was hell bound and was clearly laying the foundations by making such statements. They were also aware that he had often complained that the parson, who drove to Bramley, the nearest town, to do his household shopping, did not support the locals.

In the end, the people worked hard and put the parson's home back together quickly. They were convinced it was the right thing to do. It was what God wanted them to do. Moreover, to them, the parson was a visitor, and all they were doing was treating him and his family as visitors should be treated. It was an argument that ran for some time. The breeze-blow had made its mark.

After the storm had passed, the layout of the district changed. Those who had lived on the sea side of the road were rehoused behind the protective wall of trees on the other side of the road, some two hundred yards or so from the sea on the gently sloping hillside.

A meeting was held at the church to decide what could be done for the fishermen and their families, and not too long afterwards, the parson announced he'd been granted permission to part with a piece of the land to offer the fishermen. A select few from the congregation suddenly found themselves in favour and were the first to be offered fish whenever the fishermen came ashore.

Clearing the ground and identifying the boundaries was a speedy affair, with the villagers engaged in "pardner" working—many people getting together to work for a meal instead of for cash. It was a system that had worked extremely well for the construction of the mission house. It was also a custom used for clearing and preparing land for planting.

Those who previously lived on the sea side and did no farming because the sea spray burned the crops were compensated despite their lack of farm foodstuffs by developing a successful bartering system with some shopkeepers and households: foodstuffs for fish. After the breeze-blow, their lives were transformed a little, as they were now able to do a little farming of crops like tomatoes and sweet potatoes.

Also, on moving further from the sea, they took the opportunity to split up into smaller, more individual families.

To outsiders, the recovery after the storm must have seemed miraculous. But they would not have known that many of the residents in Plummers were related, which meant that getting a new house spot after the breeze-blow was not a problem. Also, the houses were basic, built mainly to accommodate night-time sleeping arrangements and provide shelter from rain. The elderly and the very sick would be the only ones expected to be indoors during daylight hours. There was no such thing in the residents' minds as overcrowding, so the houses were tiny, most consisting of two or three rooms. Since the majority of the occupants were children, all they had to do was to move a little closer to one another at night-time.

People like James and Ginal, both fishermen, soon became everybody's best friends—heroes, even. They were the ones who owned the huge saw with handles at each end for slicing through the large tree trunks to make the boards and shingles for house building. They were accustomed to doing their work in private, deep in the wooded areas from daybreak till about midday. It was lonesome, back-breaking work. The only company they were accustomed to were the women who provided them with food and drink.

The breeze-blow changed all that. The men found themselves working in public with gusto, putting on a display for the onlookers who marvelled at the rhythm they developed as they pulled and pushed the huge saw through the logs. There was no question of leaving the wood to dry out or to season. Green boards were quickly snapped up, and houses were built or repaired in no time. Tree trunks that some wanted cut up for house boards had to give way for boatbuilding because that was what James said.

It was not long before the lanes were cleared so that the mules and donkeys could get to and from the farms. The river crossing was more troublesome, as huge boulders and deeper water made it difficult for the animals to cross in some of their usual places. In the end, new crossing points were created for the animals.

As the clearing up and rebuilding got underway, bottles filled with kerosene and plugged with cloth for a wick were lit to provide light. They flickered in the houses in the bushes for brief periods at nighttime where previously there had been total darkness. The wildlife that had been disturbed by the smoke, the crying children, and other noises brought by those who had moved up from the coastline simply moved further into the bush. It was not a gradual process because of the immediate demands of the breeze-blow devastation.

The storm also created a switch in the status of some families. Most notable was the lowering of the status of many of the church people. People like Miss Gertrude and Miss Liza, who used to have people standing at their gates and shouting their business to them, suddenly began inviting folks into their front yards to speak to them. They knew that the scarcity of some farm items meant money no longer had the power it once had. They also knew that the shortage of shop food put a greater demand on locally grown produce.

The many self-sufficient farmers sold their produce to the folks in the other districts. They saw themselves as being different from those of the neighbouring districts. They had good boatmen who ensured they were also self-sufficient in fish. In contrast, the surrounding districts were more dependent on the Dalbeattie property for work, and so the young men from OutaBridge tended to have more cash, newer, shinier bicycles, box cameras, and all the trappings to attract the girls from Plummers. This added to the friction that already existed.

Following the breeze-blow, the government instituted a drive to replant bananas quickly and aid their growth and development with fertilizer, the cost of which was subsidized. It was the government's way of helping the small farmers get back on their feet with a quick cash crop following the losses suffered by the breeze-blow. The government also started a grafting programme of citrus trees.

Jamaica, like most of the Caribbean islands, offered a programme whereby young, fit men could go to work on farms in the United States under contract. Most of the young men in Plummers looked forward to the opportunity to get a ticket. After a few short months, many would return with American accents, sleek, straightened hair, fake gold watches, and enough money to get the girls. The smarter and, usually, older ones spent their money on providing a better standard of living for their families.

By the December 1944 general election, many of the fit young men were in the Royal Air Force or the army, fighting for the British motherland. On the face of it, competition for the farm work should have been less fierce. However, the competition for the few places became partisan, with selection being determined according to the support given to the winning political party. The election results also caused friction between families as people in Plummers became more and more involved with national politics. People who were thought to be illiterate became great speech-makers and persuaders of their party's views.

For the first time, the church people found they were no longer the sole influence: previously quiet, reserved farmers who had travelled and worked in the tobacco and sugar cane fields of Cuba, helped in the building of the Panama Canal, or fought in the First World War successfully, exaggerated their experiences to give a sense of authority to what they were saying. They used big words, talked in long, rambling sentences, chopped their fists in the palms of their hands for emphasis, smiled broadly, and laughed loudly at their own jokes. Plummers came alive in a way that surprised everybody and gave them all a sense of purpose, evoking memories of the past. Different reasons were given for the change in how the work tickets were issued. These ranged from the hardships caused by the war effort in terms of the reduction of overseas help coming to the island from Britain to a realization of the people that they could benefit materially if they were seen to be a part of the winning team. The fact that the losers could suffer did not seem too much of a concern. It seemed they felt family ties would overcome any such disadvantage.

In general, political awareness and party allegiance surprised many of the older folks, who were not accustomed to seeing families at war, cursing each other over politics. The old were especially keen to vote. They ambled to the polling stations and proudly cast their votes, dipped their finger in the indelible ink, and then walked home proudly with that stained finger stuck out for all to see.

As a result of the changing circumstances, the drift of Jamaicans to work in the United States continued, and Plummers had its fair share of leavers. Remittances were slow at first, but things began to improve for those left at home. The apparent good fortune abroad encouraged many to join the exodus to Cuba and the United States to improve their lives and engage in an adventure.

FIVE

Geoffrey Marshall, sometimes referred to as "the high school boy," was from one of the prominent families in Top Ground and Plummers as a whole. His father, the only white person who lived in the electoral district of Plummers (barring the Sandersons and the visiting parsons), farmed many acres on the edge of Plummers. According to the older folks, he just turned up in the district one day, and within a short space of time, he'd built his house about a quarter of a mile from the road with a stone wall bordering the road. It was rich and fertile land, and it afforded him a decent living with a resident labourer and additional workers when the work demanded it. He ended up being a popular supplier of foodstuffs to the higglers, who sold them in the Kingston markets.

Not long after the house was completed, Marshall married Inez Grant, a beautiful dark-skinned young lady who dabbled in hairdressing and whose parents, strangers to the area, taught at the elementary school.

The proceeds of the farm allowed the Marshalls to provide their son with a high school education at a boarding school. Living a little way up the hill away from the rest of the district, Marshall senior was the proud owner of the only horse-drawn buggy in the area. He surrounded himself with many dogs and was never seen out after dark. How he and Inez met was a mystery.

It was a great surprise to everybody when Marshall senior joined the many that went off to Cuba. Those with decent jobs or a higher standard of living usually stayed on the island, as life for them was already good. Also with his being white, the folks couldn't make sense of it. As soon as he left, Inez moved down to the district, building another house for herself and her son. Mr. Marshall never returned. Through the postmistress, they knew he kept in touch with his wife right up to the breeze-blow. After that, nothing further was heard from him, and the house slowly decayed following the damage. The local people freely reaped the fruits and foodstuffs that grew wildly before the area was overcome by bramble and weeds. Mrs. Marshall continued to live well from a private source of income, and as far as folks were aware, neither she nor her son ever went back to the house or even set foot on the land again.

Miss Inez, as she was generally called, ran the only basic school available in the district. The children packed into her house in bad weather but stayed outdoors in good, which was most of the time. She provided a head start to a few children ahead of their entry to elementary school at age seven. Not surprisingly, they were mostly children of the church folks, although she only attended church on special occasions.

As a boy, Geoffrey was clearly privileged. He was aloof from the rest of the children in elementary school. He was one of the rare ones who did not play cricket as most boys did then. Though he was allowed to play with boys from the church, he was never allowed to go to their homes. Above all, he was never allowed to accept a meal from anyone outside the home. He was a studious boy and the only boy to have music lessons from the church organist.

Things were not too different at high school. He was again studious and did very well, his classmates saying that it was mostly because he had more time to study than those who took part in sports. In addition, instead of spending his holidays in Plummers, Geoffrey was sent off to Kingston, where he had cousins. It seemed his mother did not want him to mix with the youngsters from Plummers. It was a surprise, therefore, when upon graduating from high school, he returned to work in the area, becoming the bookkeeper at Dalbeattie.

A pleasant, good-looking man of medium height, Geoffrey was conscious that he was a rarity in the district, being a wavy-haired, light-skinned young man with a good local job. When most country high school boys had to head to Kingston to find work to suit their education, mostly in the civil service, he was in a powerful position. He was responsible for giving out work, and he favoured the people of Plummers even when overwhelmed with demand from the people from OutaBridge.

Sunday afternoons, Geoffrey went off to the neighbouring districts to see his many newfound girlfriends. There was no secret as to what he was up to: each girlfriend knew about the others. His time for the Plummers girls was during the week. It was then he would give them the occasional lift, enjoying the feeling as they clasped their arms around his waist and pressed their breasts into his back. He loved that. The Plummers men hated him. From time to time, his mother, who was aware of her son's goings-on, would scold him, telling him that she didn't want "any and any gal pickney" coming to her with a baby saying it was her grandchild. Her concern grew as the girls her son gave lifts to became younger and younger. She later persuaded him to get a car instead, even though she had no interest in a car ride. She never went anywhere out of Plummers, except for Christmas shopping in Kingston on a day trip by bus to buy the many little presents she would give to the pupils of her school.

Although it was an uncomfortable few early years for Geoffrey, as he did his best to mix with the folks he had been seen to shun in his younger days, life was made easier for him because the young people liked him, and the older ones warmed to him on account of his position at Dalbeattie. Plus, he seemed a genuinely nice person. He disappointed them when he went away again. A year later he returned with a wife, Eva, and went back to work for Dalbeattie.

Eva Marshall was never made welcome in Plummers. Even the churchgoers made her feel uncomfortable by hardly speaking to her in the short time she was in the district before she went off to the United States. The story was that she had left him despite his saying that he would be following soon. In the seven years that followed, Geoffrey only received two letters from Eva. Although everybody knew the story, nobody talked about it to him. He had always been a quiet man, generally, and he became even more reclusive, choosing to live with his mother instead of with one of his teacher-girlfriends. He seemed to be pretending he still had a wife, though they knew better.

Plummers was looking up, and the people were prospering. Geoffrey, though, was still a bit of a recluse. As time went by, Geoffrey and the parson were the only car owners in the district. Another vehicle owner had a truck that carried people and produce from Plummers and surrounding districts to the market in Kingston. At other times it carried bananas to the wharf.

Then one day, as if woken from a dream, Geoffrey bought a motorbike—a gleaming silver beauty that had all the ladies from OutaBridge clamouring for a ride. It was the icing on the cake: he had just been handed the job of manager of Dalbeattie following Mr. Sanderson's decision to give up the reins.

Daisy agonized over whether to pass on the message from her aunt to her mother. It was not like her to even think of not delivering a message; it was just that she somehow recognized the importance of it and was not sure if she liked Ruth. She knew about the Golding family and that they were teachers from OutaBridge and that her father was a Golding. Her information came from Martha and what she picked up from comments some of the women made for her to hear, without addressing her directly.

Having heard enough about those who went to the United States, Daisy knew it offered a better life than what she saw around her. She found herself thinking about Jennifer who used to live with Martha and imagined herself in New York like her. She saw herself in some of the shoes she'd seen at Ruth's house. She imagined walking in them. She tried to imagine the places she would be walking, but her imagination failed her. She would look in some of Martha's magazines for help.

Brought back to reality by the braying of a donkey, Daisy quickened her steps. Within a short while, her mind was on the message and the possible outcome. She was bothered because she could not imagine life without her mother, irrespective of how important getting away from Soldier would be or how great a life she could have with Ruth, though she was still unable to think of the woman as her aunt. Then she realized that Ruth had said nothing about going back to New York or even taking her with her if she did so. It was that realization that caused Daisy to shed a tear. In the end, she did not know whether she consciously decided not to give her mother the message or if she just fell asleep before doing so.

The Parson preached the first and third Sundays of each month. May and Daisy, like so many others, normally attended church service only on the first Sunday when the parson served holy communion, and Sunday school had a special meaning for the children as the parson's wife told them biblical stories. Despite it not being a first Sunday, it was going to be a special Sunday for May nonetheless, even with a lay-preacher, because it could turn out to be the day when her Daisy could be given hope for a better future.

It was not that she wanted to be rid of her daughter. But in recent years, she'd been plagued by the memory of Oliver every time she looked at the girl. Her daughter's smile reminded her of the smile she'd seen on Oliver's face as she looked up, the sun beating down through the leaves, the special smile she'd been sure was for her alone despite his record with other girls. She could still feel his sweat dripping onto her face in their special place among the guava trees, with their tiny leaves that allowed the light and shadows to dance on them. She remembered the time they made love in the gentle drizzle, causing her to recall it so many times whenever there was gentle rainfall whilst the sun shone at the same time. It was on land belonging to the Dalbeattie property, and although she'd managed to get him to join her at her home a few times whilst her mother was at work, he was not at all comfortable about doing it there.

She remembered how it started. She was heading to the shop one day when he walked up to her. "May," he'd said, "it's time me and you get together, you know. What you think?"

She remembered being flattered and the way the words *get together* kept ringing in her ears. She genuinely did not know what to say, so she chuckled and went on her way. She was surprised when, on her way back, she found him waiting for her just a short walk from her home—but around the bend so they couldn't be seen.

"Look," he said. "I'll wait for you round the back of the house after you go to bed. Don't let me down now."

May did not answer, but they both knew that she would be there. She did not disappoint him. They spent quite a while talking before he led her by the hand further away from the house to the ackee tree that grew in a V shape. He sat in the V with May sitting on one of his legs.

"You know that I like you long time, right?"

"How would I know that?" she replied.

"You mean you never see how I smile with you, special like?"

"You smile at all the girls like that. I hear about you from I was little, you know. They even warn me about you."

"Well, you were too young, and, I mean, you couldn't expect a man like me to wait till you grow up. That would be like...like torture. I mean, look how you nice now."

"Bet you say the same thing to *all* the other girls," she said. "And what about teacher Elaine?"

"What about her? Look, don't spoil things now because all these things are way before you come of age, so to speak."

Before May could say another word, she felt his hands rubbing her breasts and his lips making loud noises as he kissed her neck, her face, and her lips. This type of behaviour was new to her. With the others, she was always in a hurry, trying to get back before she was missed from her bed or before her mother or father returned from wherever they went or before somebody passed by. Now she felt herself anticipating the touches and found them appearing where she least expected them. She was twisting and turning on his leg. She stood up, sat down, and stood up again. She did not know what to do with herself. She was not accustomed to such a preamble to what she was certain was going to happen that night. This was different, and she was enjoying it. She had never heard such loud kisses before. She had never felt such tingling sensations. She had never felt such warmth inside her. She felt a hand sliding up the inner side of her thighs, and she moved her legs apart. The hand moved up farther and stopped suddenly.

"Nice, you come prepared. Good. You want it just like me. You want it bad!" Oliver said.

May didn't answer. She knew that by being naked down there, she was sending the message he had just received. She found herself hurrying him to drop his trousers. She was out of control and was a bit embarrassed at being so, but she couldn't stop herself, and so it was that they had sex for the first time, with her sitting on him in the V of the ackee tree.

Oliver was not a hurtful memory for May because he had left her for another woman. No, it was hurtful because of what she called her "mistake." Now she was being punished by having to look at Oliver's face every day through their daughter, the living proof of her having hurt the only man she had truly loved. She knew she and Oliver had an on-off relationship, and each had sex with others over the years. But whilst others were pleased to do it with her at night-time and then walk by her in the daytime as if they did not know her, Oliver was different. Even though they did not socialize or sit together in church, he brought her gifts from Kingston, things like perfume, material for dresses, and a straightening comb. She still didn't know why she'd stayed in the room with the soldier when she'd had the opportunity to leave.

May knew it was her honesty about not being sure who the father was that was her undoing, and she wondered whether she had hoped the soldier was the father. Even more so, she wondered whether it was her hoping that he was really a Sanderson that led her to succumb to his advances. She accepted that she was responsible for her own hardship, to such an extent that she had not even received a tin of condensed milk or a packet of crackers from Oliver for their daughter. She also accepted that she was in the same boat as other women in the district who were bringing up their children without a father's help, but that did not make her plight any easier.

Morag was not as good a hostess as Jean, and without her being aware of it, Old Sanderson began to see her more as a fussing nurse than a concerned wife. He no longer had his views sought about styles and colours. He missed the opportunities to suggest daring deviations to what was evident, as he had sometimes done with Jean, and marvel at the surprisingly good results that appeared in her watercolours. He also missed watching the little girls who sometimes found it difficult to accept that the paintings were indeed a true reflection of themselves, being so different from the images of photographs.

He developed a routine of going for gentle horseback rides, sometimes with Soldier, other times alone. It was mostly a silent journey but for the odd question to Soldier about names of plants he had forgotten since Jean passed away. Those were the evenings when, like the nights when Morag used her medical knowledge, he would go to bed early and sleep soundly throughout the night.

When not out riding, Kenny would read, mostly American magazines, especially FBI stories. He did not have the patience for novels. He lamented the fact that the soldiers and foreign visitors no longer stopped by.

Morag had an admirable devotion to her husband, and she did all she could to give him a sense of life. As far as many of the folks were concerned, she was still a young enough woman who was deserving of company. It was therefore no surprise when the soldiers began visiting again.

Morag liked May because she seemed to have the traits of trustworthiness, patience, and politeness—all the attributes that would have made her suitable to work in a similar establishment in England. She also found that she never had to talk much to May: a nod here and there, a smile, a quick movement of a hand or finger not discernible by others present. Yet there was never a moment when the invisible boundary between mistress and servant was broken. That was, until the special weekend.

SIX

It was time to meet Ruth, and May, dressed in a yellow dress with her white hat and handbag, walked slowly towards the church. Although she was disappointed that Martha had chosen to walk with her friend Mrs. Preston as usual, instead of giving her a little comfort by walking with her. May, her hair swept forward, partly covering her face, took advantage of the situation by walking as slowly as she could in the cloudless heat of the morning, so as not to have her face shine through the thin layer of makeup she wore. She knew she couldn't match Martha or Ruth but she didn't have to show herself up.

The regular churchgoers noticed her approaching. Some quickened their steps, and others simply ignored her. One or two said a polite good morning, and May returned the greetings in a pleasant manner. She had thought about bringing Daisy with her but decided against it.

Not wanting to upset the regular worshippers and have anyone stand over her in a silent demand for her regular seat, May stood at the back until most of the regulars were seated before she sat. During the service, she stole glances at Ruth from time to time and was sure that Ruth never once returned her glance.

At the end of the service, May was of two minds: should she wait in the church to have a chat in private, or should she go outside and wait for Ruth to approach her at her leisure? She really had no idea what to do. In the end, she waited just outside the church door, being one of the first to exit.

The ladies (there were only a handful of men in the thirty or so who were in church) seemed to take forever saying their goodbyes. Many did not speak to her. She was sure some of them looked at her with knotted brows and a vexed countenance, as if she was guilty of something terrible or even that she was soiling their holy building with her presence. When that happened, she simply looked away or down at her feet. For much of the time, she stood with her back to the church, arms folded, staring in the direction of the graves but not looking at anything in particular. Finally, Ruth, immaculately dressed in a beige suite with very wide lapels topped by a matching hat that made her look like a sailor, wore less makeup than May had expected to see. Her very high heels seemed a bit out of place for the walk on the dirt road but May knew such a walk was no problem for her. Her permanent smile did not change as she approached May and spoke in a whisper.

"I get the impression you expect us to be having a chat here...at church. Am I right?" Ruth enquired.

"Yes, ma'am. That is the message."

"Well, that is wrong. I am sorry. I did say after church, but I want to talk to you at my house. So, can you stop by later?"

"Yes, ma'am. What time?"

"Time?" asked Ruth, wondering if people in Plummers were now doing things by the clock, not realizing that May had learned to do so because that was how the Sandersons functioned. When May didn't respond, Ruth added, "Give me time to sort myself out...and bring Daisy with you. In an hour or so. That all right with you?"

"Yes, ma'am. I will bring her."

"You tell her about her father?"

"Her father, ma'am?"

"Never mind. You just bring her along with you." She turned, smiled at a church sister, and walked away before May could say anything more.

Both ladies noticed that several of the other ladies had stopped in the road outside the church, chatting and looking across at them from time to time. Ruth smiled at them as she headed home alone. May quickened her steps to join Martha, who was also walking along slowly on her own, presumably waiting for May to catch up with her so she could hear what had gone on between her and Ruth.

The two women walked slowly together towards home in silence, stealing a glance at each other from time with a smile. Once in the yard and just before parting for their own homes, Martha said, "You look nice you know."

"Thank you," replied May, before saying. "I wish I could sew a nice dress like you. How you get the pleats so…so even?"

"I guess it's just down to practice. Well, training and practice." As if putting a stop to any further questions, Martha continued: "Things going to change for Daisy now?"

"What you mean?"

"Well…you know. Her aunt must know what is happening, and if she tell her brother…you know."

May shrugged, turned, and walked away and across to her house. She suspected Daisy of messing about with some of the boys and so did not want to push the matter too far. Keeping her cool seemed her best option.

May had not told Soldier about her planned meeting with Ruth because she did not know how he would react. Now she hoped he would be glad to have Daisy out of the house. She also knew Soldier had never said anything nice about Oliver after hearing from others how he'd left the district without owning up to being Daisy's father. Nobody in the district knew the full story. There was praise, however, for Ruth, who, since she'd returned, made efforts to ascertain with May whether her brother was indeed Daisy's father, adding that if it was so, regardless of Oliver's attitude, she was prepared to help with bringing up Daisy.

May genuinely did not know for sure who Daisy's father was. She had not told anybody but Oliver that there could be doubt. To this day she did not know why she'd told him. She noted, however, that as far as she knew, he had always told people he was not sure, not that he was not the father. She accepted that the problem was of her own making. Also, to her surprise, Morag had once told her that if the baby belonged to the soldier, she would make sure the baby had some help. They had not spoken about it since, and May believed the kindness she'd received from Morag over the years was due to the fact that either she held her secrets or she had at first believed Alex to be the father.

Although May had been agreeable to taking Daisy with her to see her aunt, she changed her mind. She decided to tell Martha about the message and about the chat Ruth had had with her daughter. As she did so, she looked for signs that Martha knew already, but there was no such hint from Martha's expression.

May changed from her church clothes and left home in good time for her meeting with Ruth. When she was about fifty yards from her destination and out of sight of Ruth's veranda, she stopped to fix her hat and straighten her clothes. Arriving at the gate, she felt an eerie silence, as if something catastrophic was about to happen. On seeing May, Ruth stood and smiled as before. The ladies' eyes were locked for the few seconds it took May to walk the few feet from the road, up the two steps, and onto the veranda.

When May was within a few feet of her, Ruth, now casually dressed in a polka dot dress and slippers, turned and said, "Come. Follow me." This surprised May. She had expected to be seated on the veranda. She hesitated before following Ruth into the living room, which was directly off the veranda.

They sat opposite each other around a small table covered with a starched white embroidered covering. A Bible and a thimble were the only things on the table. Ruth excused herself for a moment, and May, a little uncomfortable when she saw a tray of life-size lizards carved out of wood, began to look around the floor to see what else might be there. Once she looked up, she eyed the room and noticed that it was smaller than she had expected. She paid particular attention to the framed landscape pictures, a couple of them snow scenes that hung from the walls.

The discussion between the two women started well, with Ruth trying to put May at ease by telling her to stop saying "Yes, ma'am" and

"No, ma'am" all the time. May tried, but she lapsed occasionally. Ruth got to the point quickly: her mother had told her of her discussion with May some years ago, and had said that if it was true that Daisy was her granddaughter, she would help to support her, irrespective of what Oliver said, because most people knew Oliver and May were "doing things." Ruth said she was on a mission to see that that was done. May didn't believe her, believing that if that was the case, Ruth would have had a chat with her a long time ago.

As for her own return to Jamaica, Ruth said she was originally from OutaBridge. Through her parents, two of the few outsiders the folks sold land to, she had a foothold in the district. She had come back to make her home in Plummers.

May was surprised to hear herself ask Ruth what she planned to do in Plummers. She was equally surprised when Ruth calmly answered that she planned to buy and sell "things." May asked if she thought her parents would be happy with that for a Golding and was surprised when Ruth smiled and explained that she would be dealing with arts and crafts. May asked her to explain a bit more.

Ruth explained that the tourist trade was developing well and creating a growing demand for items like carvings, brightly coloured items like fans and aprons, and crocheted items for centre tables. She went so far as to point out that she had identified people in Plummers who carved lizards out of wood and stone, wove baskets, and made fans and had been told about people in OutaBridge who carved more intricate wooden figures. She was sure she could develop a good market for their products and planned to do just that.

Suddenly both ladies seemed to become aware of the lightheartedness of the conversation and fell silent.

"Look," said Ruth finally. "I have bun and cheese and lemonade prepared already." Without waiting for a reply, she disappeared towards the dining room, which was at the back of the house.

May had a good look around the room. She noticed the sewing machine and the cabinet with the light-blue wine glasses. Two larger-than-life wood carvings of lizards on a box made her feel uncomfortable. She knew it was a three-bedroom house and was yearning to see where her daughter would sleep. She sighed loudly when she realized that if she agreed for Daisy to live with her aunt, the girl would have a proper bed at last. She would be well taken care of because they were blood. She would go to school regularly. She would learn how to be a lady. She consoled herself that it was an easy arrangement: if Ruth started to take advantage of her, she could easily take her back.

After surprising May with a tour of the house and spending some time in what would be Daisy's room, Ruth asked, "So what you think?"

May finished chewing whilst thinking of what to say. "Well, you are her aunt, and it seems a good idea to me. I think she would like it here with you. Yes…she would like it. But what about your children?" Then she put a hand over her mouth as if to stop the words from coming out. She wanted to say sorry or something to show that she did not want to appear forward. To her surprise, she saw Ruth smiling.

"That's all right. That's all right. I am glad you asked. I know that people have been wondering who Ruth Green is, where are the children they hear I have, and so on. I know. I will tell you." She went to her bedroom and returned with a brown paper bag, from which she pulled out some newspaper clippings. She spread them out, the way one would a deck of cards, and asked May to pick one, any one. May did as she was instructed. The headline read "Fatal Merry-Go-Round Accident." Instead of reading it, she handed it to Ruth. There was a moment of silence. May looked at Ruth and saw the tears running down her face.

May noticed that Ruth did not mention her husband, but she said nothing. She watched as Ruth dabbed at her eyes with her handkerchief. She then asked where it had happened. Ruth explained that it was at a beach and amusement park in New York. She explained how her husband and daughters went on the funfair ride and how a boat-shaped carriage broke away and killed an onlooker, her husband, and her daughters. She did not tell about the anxious days that followed the accident, when the girls used every drop of their strength fighting to stay alive, giving false hope to their mother.

After a period of silence, the ladies returned to discuss Daisy and the benefits of her living with her aunt. May was sure Ruth had her own idea about Soldier and Daisy. She vowed not to introduce the subject in their conversation, but she would put her right if Ruth did. She was disappointed when Ruth did not mention it either.

Throughout the latter part of the discussion, the word *aunt* was used many times. May felt uneasy walking away without taking the opportunity to explain that despite what Ruth might have heard about Daisy and Soldier, much of it was untrue. She hoped she would get the opportunity another time. In the end, May said she would talk to Daisy and reach a decision. By the end of the evening, the ladies were talking and laughing like old friends.

On the way home, May reflected on how she had handled matters. She had told Ruth that she had only told Daisy that her father had gone away to America and that he was not supporting her. She admitted to wanting to say more but being unable to bring herself to do it. The matter wasn't dead, however; she would just have to wait for the right time to deal with it. She knew she couldn't let Ruth think the way others in the district thought about her and her relationship with Soldier and how it affected Daisy.

That night, as they lay together in bed, May told Soldier she was considering letting her daughter go and live with her aunt. He grunted. When the statement sunk in, he raised himself on his elbow and asked if he had heard her correctly. May confirmed in a more forceful voice and waited for his reaction.

Soldier slowly lowered himself on his back. "I hope you don't regret it," he said.

When pressed for further explanation, he fell silent. May was a bit troubled by this but went ahead with her decision. Soldier never once asked about how Daisy was getting on once she left, and May never discussed her daughter with him again.

In the months that followed, May often thought about how well her daughter looked since going to live with her aunt. She attended school often, wore shoes and a brassiere, dressed smartly, and travelled out sometimes. Her fears that Daisy might be used to do all the housework did not materialize, as Ruth continued to have someone come in on Saturdays to clean and polish the floors. May sometimes said a

"Thank you, Lord" out loud for the new, better life her daughter was experiencing.

Daisy still visited Martha to learn to sew, even though Ruth had a sewing machine. She secretly looked forward to the day when she would get the chance to show her aunt what she could do and to the day when her aunt would allow her to use her sewing machine.

The people in the district watched Daisy's development with interest, and the ladies in particular chatted among themselves about it. The general feeling was that Ruth was a saviour for Daisy, and most, silently wished the little girl well.

Agnes did not believe that Soldier was interfering with Daisy. She had asked him outright, and he told her he had never and would never do such a thing, and she believed him. She also asked him if he knew that there was a rumour that he did that sort of thing. He replied he was aware but that he would deal with it in his own way and his own time. Agnes did not like that reply; she feared violence was in the air. She told Morag about her discussion with Soldier, and Morag told her that as far as she was concerned, it was not a matter that required any action by the Sandersons. Agnes was not at all pleased with the response and feared that Morag would tell May about their conversation. She did not know that Morag was already aware and was unhappy about it.

Later that day, May was in the ironing room when Agnes entered and sat on a chair. May could see she looked a bit worried.

"What's the matter, Miss Agnes?"

"You mean to say me showing it strong, strong?"

"Yes, Miss Agnes. You look really worried."

"Look, May, I better come to the point. You know there's a rumour that Soldier…Lawd, I don't even know how to say it."

"You talking 'bout my Daisy?"

"Yes."

"It's not true. I am her mother. I would know, and I would protect my daughter if what people say was true."

"I know. I know that, and I believe you. I believe Soldier as well because him say it's not true."

"You mean to say you ask him about it? You ask him about something like that?"

"Don't know what get into me."

May stopped her ironing and sat on a stool with her head in her hands. There was a deafening silence. Neither lady looked at the other. "What would happen if he said it was true?"

Agnes kept her head bowed and did not reply.

"Who else you talk to about this, Miss Agnes?"

Agnes got up and walked out of the room without answering. May stared at the vacant chair.

SEVEN

Geoffrey and Ruth became quite good friends. Although not one of those involved in political debates, Geoffrey used politics as the opener for his first night-time visit to Ruth's home. It didn't matter that she was not interested in politics. The fact is, they learned a lot about each other through their conversations, which did not dwell on politics for long. Their relationship moved from being a business one—his stewardship in rebuilding the house for her—to quite a friendly one, whereby he could be seen by the light of the lamp, sitting inside the house after just two visits of being entertained on the veranda.

Geoffrey, ever the neat dresser, his hairy chest taking a peep out of the top of his shirt, spoke of his disappointment in not joining his wife in the United States and said it was just one of those things. He admitted that though it had taken him a long time to accept that his marriage was over, he was glad it had finally happened, adding that it was a blessing in disguise. He also mentioned that his mother did not like the idea of him spending so much time visiting Ruth. Ruth told him she was aware that his mother did not like her, but she was a grown woman now and was not disposed to being bothered by others.

Unlike in her conversation with May, Ruth volunteered the stark facts about losing her husband and daughters and moved on to other matters. She was aware Geoffrey was taken aback, but that was how she planned it, and that was how it would remain. No questions. No further discussions. Geoffrey sensed it, too, and though he wanted to ask a few questions, he did not.

With his contacts at Dalbeattie and his rubbing of shoulders with the English soldiers, Geoffrey brought Ruth gifts of ginger wine from time to time. His visits soon became the talk of the district. Some felt they were well suited to each other. Others were happy that the young girls would be safe from him since he had an interest in Ruth, but in the same breath, they feared for Daisy, who would invariably be around him. Everybody wanted someone else to warn Ruth. In the meantime, they watched and waited for signs of trouble.

When night-time came, it was never easy for Daisy to know when it was time for bed. When she'd lived with her mother, bedtime was simply as soon as it got dark. With her aunt, it seemed to depend on how much company her aunt needed. It did not matter to Daisy that her aunt kept her up late, reading to her or reading with her. She just concentrated on trying to please her aunt by making fewer mistakes each night.

Daisy liked Geoffrey, who sometimes brought her candy, though he always handed it to Ruth instead of giving it directly to her, and it was not long before both Ruth and Daisy got used to the special sound of Geoffrey's footsteps approaching the yard, one heavier than the other. Whenever Daisy heard them, she would look at her aunt, who would return a gentle nod, the signal for her to go off to her room and to bed. Once when Miss Martha asked Daisy if Geoffrey slept in the house with her aunt, Daisy said she did not know. Although she was not believed, Daisy was content she was telling the truth because whenever she went to her comfortable bed, she fell asleep soon afterwards.

As the friendship between Geoffrey and Ruth developed, May was not concerned about how it might affect her daughter. She once told Martha, "Daisy and her aunt are blood, so she will take care of her niece." Though she was tempted to ask Daisy about the frequency of Geoffrey's visits and whether he stayed there at night, she never did. Then one day she nearly fell out with Martha when Martha suggested that she talk to Ruth because she was sure Ruth knew what the people of the district already knew about Geoffrey and young girls. May responded that they could be wrong about Geoffrey just as they were wrong about Soldier. That statement troubled Martha. She felt May was being stupid, pretending not to know what everybody else knew about Soldier and Daisy and Geoffrey's reputation.

Ruth's business was going well. The lizard sculptors were popular with the tourists, and the weavers couldn't keep up with the demand for straw hats. Daisy was learning to crochet the little hats for the one-foot-high ladies carved out of wood, and Ruth herself sewed colourful kitchen aprons that were also popular with the tourists.

Ruth's weekly goods were packed neatly in boxes and travelled with her on the morning bus to Kingston on Thursdays. It was just not right for a lady of her social standing to travel in the market truck overnight, arriving at daybreak on Friday, even if she was travelling in the front with the driver. The higglers themselves would not think it right for her to do so. Travelling early Thursday morning also gave her time to meet up with her secret Kingstonian friend, John J. Hunter.

Called JJ by his friends, he was a tall, thin man and a tax officer. He was divorced, and his wife had remarried a police sergeant. JJ's only child, a son, lived with his mother. After the divorce, JJ had sold the family house and moved into a two-bedroom rented house in a nice area of Half Way Tree. His friends were all from the professional class, and he had enough money to indulge his favourite pastime, horse racing, becoming a regular at Knutsford Park racecourse. He knew the trainers, many of the owners, and the jockeys, and he provided useful information to the young racing sportswriter. People warmed to JJ as a means of getting to know others. He was a regular at church and came into contact with politicians and radio personalities. Although the English parson chided him from time to time about his gambling, they remained friends as well.

Ruth was impressed when at the bank, the post office, Times store, or the Cross Roads police station, JJ was greeted with politeness and respect. She often wondered why he found an excuse to drag her with him to visit at least one of the locations with her every time she was in town, always saying he had to pop in to speak to this or that person, invariably someone in a position of authority. He never seemed to be at work when she was in town. She assumed he was just showing her off to his friends and colleagues. She was also delighted that she could visit him without notice and that he was happy with her doing so. She could stay with him for longer if she chose, and he would be OK with that, too. She felt safe with JJ and felt that even if he wasn't being faithful to her when she was not there, at least he treated her with respect whenever she was.

Ruth looked forward to her Kingston trips and being taken out to Carib Theatre to see the latest films. She enjoyed her trip the previous Christmas to a pantomime at Ward Theatre, and she also enjoyed her waterfront walks with him, especially when, mistaking her for a tourist, local sellers approached her with the type of handicraft she herself sold. She was sure some of the sellers knew JJ, and that made her feel she was probably seen as just another of his conquests, out for a stroll. Sometimes she felt JJ was just a little too sure of himself, and she thought of doing something to jolt him once in a while. Then she thought of Geoffrey and wondered what would happen if they came face-to-face, say, at her house. She was amused by the thought.

Though she was sure that JJ had serious thoughts about her, Ruth was not sure how far things would go since she was uncertain as to whether he had gotten over his divorce. She wondered if he was using horse racing to help him cope with his loneliness. Ruth also wondered why JJ had not told her about this hobby, which she'd found out about from a conversation between him and a friend. Was it just a pastime or was he a serious gambler? she wondered. Then, just as quickly, she threw the thought out of her head. She was grateful to him for getting her into the arts and crafts business. He had said that she was running a business, a craft business, and that she should see herself as a business owner. He also advised her to sell to hotels or to the higglers, as he saw her as a class above and believed she owed it to herself to project herself likewise.

Ruth was not as flattered as JJ had hoped. She saw herself as just the person JJ described, but she kept quiet because she wanted to think about his idea of selling directly to the hotels. As expected, he made a hotel connection for her. She had her price, and the hotel was free to sell at any price it could. It was an arrangement that worked well for both parties. As a safeguard, she also sold a few items, usually those with minor flaws, to a few ladies who sold outside Times Store, along King Street, or at South Parade—the busy areas.

It was also JJ who had helped Ruth recover from her sadness on her return to the island. She was so, so grateful she'd accepted his assistance when she struggled that day to convince the bank clerk to deal with her before the others so that she would not miss the evening bus back to the country, where she was staying with her late husband's relatives. How glad she was for his intervention and how impressed she was with the softness in his voice and the bank clerk's immediate surrender, either to the authority of his voice or because they knew each other. It did not matter then. However, she recently felt a need to ask JJ if he knew the lady and, if so, how well he knew her. She had not done so because she found she was not as brave as she thought in that regard. She was content with her bravery in not letting JJ and Geoffrey know about each other. She was unaware, however, that the two knew each other in another capacity.

JJ had been introduced to Kenny Sanderson a few years earlier by a horse-racing friend. He later gave him unofficial advice concerning his tax affairs. He knew he shouldn't offer such advice, but he also knew that if he didn't, someone else would. Although Geoffrey and JJ had never met, JJ knew about Geoffrey from his visits to Dalbeattie. Those visits stopped when JJ was promoted to senior management, but he still kept in touch with Kenny.

Manny was a quiet, good-looking young man from OutaBridge. He had what people called 'good hair,' a mixture of African and Indian or mixture of other wavy haired race. The people from Plummers took quite a liking to him because he was very helpful and caring, especially to the elderly, who he would help in any way he could without seeking a reward. He also had a few admirers among the girls, but because he was very obviously poor with little to offer the ladies, those relationships never went beyond admiration. They knew, however, that on some nights, he shared his hut with Lala. They thought that even Lala deserved some male company from time to time.

The cricket team also benefited from having Manny among them. Not even his habit of not wanting to leave the crease when given out by an umpire's decision would make them want to leave him out of the team, however much he embarrassed them at times. He was a key player, opening the batting and keeping wicket. His lazy batting style also meant that he was usually in for most of the innings, scoring his ones and twos whilst others came and went. He was an example of how someone from OutaBridge could become a Plummers man.

After a couple of years, Manny fell from grace and was forced to leave Plummers after beating up Lala one night, forcing her to walk to her parents' home in the pouring rain. Neither would say what had led to the argument and the fight that left Lala's face bruised and her thumb dislocated. However, Mr. Warren, one of the local preachers and the district constable, took it upon himself to make the incident an item for a sermon, much to the disgust of some of his flock, who feared that their own domestic business could one day suffer the same fate. They showed their distaste with loud clearing of their throats and unnecessary coughing during his sermon. Afterwards, they were at pains to point out that they were not unsympathetic to Lala but that some things were just not appropriate for a sermon.

On being told about the sermon, Manny publicly swore to teach Mr. Warren a lesson one day. Mr. Warren confronted him in the presence of others, for safety, and made it plain to him that threatening a law officer was a serious offence for which he could spend time in prison. Mr. Warren hoped the threat would be enough to make him feel safe from an assault from Manny. Not long after that, Manny felt the temptation for revenge was too strong for him to control himself, and so he left Plummers. A few weeks later, some of the Plummers higglers reported meeting up with him at Coronation Street market in Kingston. He was scraping a living by loading and unloading trucks at the market. As far as anyone knew, he had not set foot back in Plummers.

Everybody in Plummers noticed that Soldier had been extraordinarily quiet over the past couple of weeks. Some said he was pining for Daisy. Others joked that Marshall better watch himself. What the folks did not know was that Soldier had other problems to contend with.

Soldier was once nearly fired from Dalbeattie but was saved by Old Sanderson. Soldier knew he would not be so lucky next time. He knew it wasn't his fault and that he had Morag to thank for being truthful that she had accidentally backed into him when his erect penis struck her bottom. She said that she did not know he was standing there, but that he must have been watching her for quite a while. She also said that he did not move or attempt to move and that he had a pleased look on his face. Her story made no difference to Old Sanderson, who scolded his wife for not dressing appropriately around the servants and assured her that she had nothing to fear from Soldier or any of the people who worked for him because of the special relationship that existed between the people of the district and the Sanderson family. But since the incident, Morag had never really been comfortable being alone around Soldier. That incident had come back to haunt Soldier because he'd had another uncomfortable encounter with Morag recently.

Soldier had gone off with some soldiers to get fruits and jelly coconuts, but, forgetting the bags, he had to return to Dalbeattie. He knew he should not have left the soldiers alone away from the house. In his haste, instead of entering the yard by the usual track, he galloped through the fence that took him by where Mrs. Sanderson and a female visitor were lying naked in the sun, giving them no time to cover up. The fact that Morag had so far said nothing bothered him.

Smudge was a dapper dresser and 'trigger man.' So when he was told to meet at the racecourse, he knew it had to be a good job, a well-paid one that would fit in with his skills and reputation to leave no link with the paymaster. Still, he was always nervous because he knew any meeting could be a revenge meeting, with him as the target. For that reason, he always had a backup man watching the man he was meeting.

As agreed, Smudge, built like a bodybuilder and bow-legged like a jockey, made his way a few yards past the winning post and waited near the public toilets. He preferred an area where his back was to a wall. His military training in the war had prepared him well for such a rendezvous. The instructions were said just once, in a slow, precise voice. He noted that the person was now two minutes late, and he began to get nervous. Then the figure of a boy approached with an envelope.

"De man say to give you dis, sah." It was not what Smudge had expected, and he was even more nervous as the boy dashed off into the twilight shadows. He moved his squat, muscular frame quickly to the side of the building and crouched.

After a minute or so, he heard, "All clear, boss. All clear." He knew the voice of his trusted backup. He stood proudly like a soldier on parade and pulled at his collars as if to make himself presentable before walking towards his backup. He didn't know he and Manny had the same target, by different paymasters.

It was a much brighter night at OutaBridge, but not as bright as the previous night because of a thin layer of clouds. Just as it turned dark, about the same time that Smudge was leaving the racecourse, Manny dragged the boat by the rope as he walked along the bank around Duppy Point and headed a short distance upriver. He knew the path well. He tied off the rope and sat under the almond trees just below the level of the road. The only sound was made by the flow of the river against the bow of the boat. There was a gentle breeze. Every now and then, he broke the monotony by throwing a little pebble in the water and listening for the sound as it landed. Then he would go back to listen for the car approaching.

Finally, a car stopped a few yards from where he was. He followed the instructions and crept slowly up the bank and coughed three times. He listened as the car door closed with a gentle click. He heard the slow footsteps coming closer and louder towards him. Then he heard the clearing of a throat. After a few seconds, the man was right up close to him.

"Turn around," commanded a male voice. Nervous, Manny did as he was told. He had not bargained for this. He listened keenly to the briefing: Soldier would do his patrol early afternoon. He would take one or two routes, but he would eventually pass under the big pear tree. Manny would be able to see him on the far ridge and would have about fifteen minutes before he reached the pear tree.

Manny had been chosen for the task because he knew the area better than anyone else, especially in the dark. After all, he used to steal foodstuffs from the farms in the dead of night after surveying the crops in the daytime. The time he had been away would not harm his knowledge of the tracks.

He rehearsed in his mind what he had to do. He should start his approach from far out, keeping the lantern light on the Dalbeattie veranda between the two big logwood trees. It didn't matter too much if he wavered a little on either side of the logwood trees, but the final approach from about 150 yards out had to be right; otherwise he could run aground.

The instructions were strict. He should pile rocks into the boat with him, as many as it was safe to carry. After he came ashore, he was to take out his rope and whatever else he brought in his crocus bag, leave it all on the beach, and wade back out to sea with the boat till the water was up to his chin. That was when he should use the axe to chop a hole in the side of the boat at the waterline and stay with it until it filled with water and sank. The rocks would help keep it down for some time. He had nothing to worry about as long as he went out to sea as told. That far out, the waves would drown out the chopping sound. He would then wade back to the shore and either bury the oar or get rid of it in the bush later. Then, he would gather his things and make his way to his spot.

Manny thought he recognized the voice of the man giving him the instructions, but he was not sure. He put the envelope with the money into his pocket and smiled to himself. Unknown to the man, this was something he might have done for nothing. After all, it was because of Soldier that he had to leave Dalbeattie. For all he knew, nobody wanted much to do with Lala. She was neither ugly nor beautiful. She had a nice body, but not even her own family had the patience to wait for her words as she struggled to deliver them through her horrific stammer, something that meant she had hardly any schooling. As far as Manny was aware, it was not until he'd started giving Lala a good time that Soldier thought he should do likewise. Worse still, Lala had the nerve to tell him that Soldier was better than he. He remembered clearly how he'd waited ages for the word *better* to be delivered and how he anticipated it so much so that its delivery and the first punch he delivered coincided.

Having obeyed the instructions not to turn around until after the car had driven away, Manny was angry when the man stuck the point of his pistol into his ribs to make the point. He felt there was no need for that, but he was also afraid. He obeyed and did not move a muscle until after the car had gone. He suddenly felt a great urge to do a good job.

EIGHT

The sea was calm, even with the light breeze. The full moon had passed a few days earlier, so Manny knew he would have the darkness for the time he wanted. He had a makeshift oar just in case the fishermen had removed theirs from their boats. He waited till it was dark and quiet enough before pushing out the boat laden with his crocus bags of stones. He let the gentle flow of the river help push the boat out to sea before dipping his oar into the water.

Manny paddled a bit out to sea so that he could line up properly with the light on the Dalbeattie veranda. He fixed his eyes on the light but could not see the two lines that were the borders of the two trees. He rowed in towards the shore, crisscrossing, searching for the marker that would bring him in safely to the beach. He began to wish he had taken the land route he had in mind. He was, however, a good boatman, like many of the folks from OutaBridge.

He began to panic. He thought he might be too far out and began to paddle towards the beach, keeping an eye on the lights of the houses on his left on the land that jutted out to sea, creating the bay. He knew he was going in the right direction. He suddenly realized he was hardly moving and thought it must be because of the tide. He doubled his effort and was relieved when the lights started to fall behind him, suggesting he was making progress towards the beach. Not long after that, he saw the outline of the logwood trees, and he paddled further to his right to line up his boat. He put in one last effort to get to the beach before he was totally exhausted. He just about made it.

It was at this point, lying of the beach from exhaustion and holding the rope to ensure the boat did not drift out to sea, that Manny began to have doubts about what he was about to do. He knew, however, that he could not turn back. He had been paid in advance. He did not know by whom, but he was sure that they would find him if he took their money and did not deliver.

After regaining his strength, Manny continued to do as instructed and waited for the boat to sink. "So far so good," he told himself. Still, he would have preferred simply making his way by foot to Plummers. Instead, for some reason, his paymaster seemed to want someone to find the boat the next day or as soon as possible, likely so that the investigation would concentrate on the people from Clover Hill.

After making his way into Top Ground by the routes he knew quite well, Manny was extremely careful not to cause the dogs to go berserk with their barking, even though he knew that when they did so, it was because they themselves were scared. He settled down for the night under an ackee tree on the edge of the Dalbeattie yard. It gave him a little comfort, being close enough to see the lights of Dalbeattie yet far enough for the dogs to not create a fuss.

Just before daybreak, Manny's internal clock woke him up as he had hoped. He made his way close to where the action would take place.

Geoffrey was a little late and sweating when he arrived. Ruth was angry as she watched him repeatedly wiping his face, forehead and neck. He offered no explanation or apology. For the last few weeks, Tuesday had been their special night. That's when they would talk and laugh more and drink more ginger wine than at any other time. And that is when he would return to his own bed a few doors away later than at any other time.

Ruth knew she could not prepare a proper meal for Geoffrey because he said he had to eat with his mother. Tonight she planned to tell him that he would have to change that arrangement on Tuesday nights. She wanted a more wholesome relationship. She had a choice, and she was going to exercise it. He did not know that she was struggling to keep JJ from visiting her in Plummers. He did not know that she feared losing them both, even if he did not at the moment think of her in a serious way. Tonight she was going to make sure she understood just where she stood. After all, having explained JJ's presence in her house last time by calling him the adviser to her craft business, she had to use all her ingenuity to prevent him from spending the night and causing her a problem.

Following JJ's visit, Ruth realized she had to make a decision soon. She had weighed her choices: live in Kingston with JJ or try to make a life with Geoffrey in Plummers, or wherever they saw fit. She did not think the decision was too difficult. After all, she knew she could trust Geoffrey because of how he managed her affairs, rebuilding the house for her whilst she was planning to return despite her having mixed feelings as to whether it was a wise thing to do. She had watched him closely over the past months and felt he would make a good life partner. She knew it was something of a gamble, but she felt she had to take that first step. The biggest obstacle with him would be his mother.

When Geoffrey arrived later than usual, he noticed a smell more akin to rum than the ginger wine they had grown accustomed to sharing. He noticed Ruth was laughing a lot, and she was also speaking in her cultivated American accent rather than in the Jamaican twang she had quickly gone back to. After a while, he gave up trying to have a discussion because she was not hearing him, often asking him to repeat himself. Also, when he waited for a response, she was quiet, although smiling a lot. He was confused and a little worried. Then, without saying a word, she rested her head on his shoulder, putting her full weight on him. He rocked back, using the wall to support them both. After many minutes of silence, he eased her head from his shoulder and began leading her to the bedroom. Once inside the bedroom, as if waking from a dream, Ruth stopped suddenly, pushed him gently backwards out of the bedroom, said goodnight, and asked him to close the door to the veranda as he left. She stood by her bedroom door and listened as his footsteps faded away.

Daisy was not quite sure what was happening. First, she was fighting for breath. Then she felt the weight on top of her, followed by a feeling of the air in her body being forced out. Next she felt a hand between her legs and a voice that whispered, "Take it easy. Take it easy, girl. Keep still."

It was an order that Daisy was clearly expected to obey. She became still for a few seconds before trying to shift from under the weight whilst trying to keep her legs together, trapping the hand in the process. The hand moved from between her legs, and she felt a gentle slap across her face, the other hand still covering her mouth to stop her from making a noise, if she dared. Then the hand was back, trying to force itself between her legs again. Daisy kept her legs together tighter than before.

"What happen? You only give it to Soldier? Open up."

Daisy did not flinch. She was glad she could not see what was happening. Then she felt the warm, sweaty, hairy legs pressing down and sliding across her own. She felt a sudden pain as the inner side of a leg was pinched just below her crotch. She squeezed her legs together even tighter in a reflex action before giving in to the force. Suddenly she realized she was breathing freely, as the hand over her mouth was removed. She thought of calling out to her aunt, but she was scared. The air was being forced out of her body by Geoffrey's weight, and a sharp pain brought her close to crying out. Instead, she clenched her teeth and went rigid. When she realized she had not breathed for a while, she took a deep breath.

During that act of brief relaxation, Geoffrey put his hand over her mouth once more and forced himself into her without any regard for her groans and feeble blows with her fists. He kept up a relentless motion as Daisy's body stiffened again and again in a fruitless attempt to move herself from the thrusting inside her. His deep, throaty groan frightened her as he came to a stop. She didn't remember much after that.

Ruth was a bit more sluggish than usual. She blamed it on the rum the night before and scolded herself for not sticking to the ginger wine. Then she noticed that Daisy was likewise sluggish. She thought the girl must have jumped out of bed the moment her eyes had opened. That was before she saw the little spot of blood on Daisy's nightdress. Before speaking to her, Ruth went and examined Daisy's bed.

She pointed to the sheet and said, "But Daisy, it's not time yet."

"Is not me monthly, Auntie."

"What?"

"Is Mr. Marshall…him—him…"

"Mr. Marshall? What you mean *is Mr. Marshall?*"

"Him come inna me bed last night, Auntie."

"What? You telling me him come back here last night?"

"Yes, Auntie."

"You make plan wid him?"

"No, Auntie. Him force me—"

Daisy reeled from the slap her aunt delivered across her face.

"Auntie," she screamed, drawing out the last syllable.

"You tell lie as well, girl? You mean to tell me you miss Soldier that bad? You miss him so bad that you—" She delivered another slap to the other side of her face. Daisy pressed both hands to her face as she found the energy to scream back at her aunt.

"No, Auntie! Me not lying, Auntie! Soldier, I mean Papa, never do dat to me, Auntie! Him never do dat to me! Him beat me up, but—"

Before Daisy could finish her sentence, she felt another slap, coinciding with an accusation of lying.

"Me not lying, Auntie," she sobbed. "Me first time, Auntie. Never do it before, Auntie."

Ruth delivered another slap, this time deliberately on the side of the girl's head. "Trying to play innocent with me? You like big men?"

"Is me first time, Auntie. Papa never do dat to me. Him never trouble me, Auntie. Papa never do dat."

As if hearing her niece for the first time, Ruth held Daisy at arm's length, looking directly into her eyes. "You telling me the truth, girl?"

"Yes, Auntie. Papa never…him never…"

"But everybody say you and him…"

"Not true, Auntie. Him never trouble me."

Ruth shifted her hands to Daisy's shoulders and stared straight into her eyes. "You telling me the truth, girl—I mean, Daisy?"

"Yes, ma'am. Me not lying." Ruth hugged her. Soon they were both sobbing.

After a few moments, Ruth said, "Daisy, I think you telling me the truth because…" She trailed off, resuming with, "How you feeling?" Without giving Daisy a chance to answer, she pressed Daisy's face into her bosom and continued crying. A few moments later, she said, "If him leave you with a baby, him not going to get away with it."

Daisy watched her auntie attempt to say more, but words would not come out. She thought her aunt was about to explain what she meant by "He is not going to get away with it." Instead she heard her aunt say, "Lord, have mercy on us. I don't know what to do. I don't know what to do." Again Ruth held Daisy gently by the shoulders, attempting to say something. Judging by the rocking of the head, Daisy thought her aunt wanted to say she was sorry, but again, no words came. Daisy knew her aunt was sorry for doubting her, sorry for hitting her, sorry for all that had happened to her. It was just that, for some reason, she couldn't bring herself to say it.

It was not normal for Agnes to run errands for the Sandersons. That was left to the other servants. This message, however, was too important to be left to any of the others, and it was not something Morag wanted to put in writing.

Agnes had heard about Ruth's fledging craft business and wanted to discuss how she could become a part of it through her love for crocheting. She watched the rain clouds on the horizon and decided to make an early visit and get back before the rain came. As she approached the veranda, she realized something was up. Although Ruth was known for her loud, strong voice since returning from the United States, the noise coming from the house indicated real anger. Ruth was in a rage, and the girl was crying. The shouting and screaming and the words *lying* and *Mr. Marshall* were enough to make Agnes withdraw. She shook her head from side to side and looked around to see if anyone was watching her. Satisfied she was alone, she descended the steps as if she was leaving the house normally.

Manny snuggled down in his chosen spot by Criss Cross, the river crossing. He ate his fill of roast corn and roast breadfruit in coconut oil. He picked and ate guava and mangoes, then finished his meal with sugar and water mixed by the riverside. He settled into his favourite spot to watch the ladies bathe at daybreak. He was not concerned about being seen because the noise of the water running over the rocks as it flowed down to the silence of the pool below would drown out even a sneeze.

He watched the ladies as they faced the bank to protect their modesty, not knowing they were turning towards him. Where he sat was known to be full of nettles and sometimes wasps. Manny had his way of handling such things, and he smiled to himself as he watched the ladies. It was like old times for him. He checked the position of the sun in the sky from time to time during what was a long wait. When it was time, he would make his way to the cluster of pear trees, from where he would launch his attack on Soldier as he came by at a gentle trot.

Just as he was preparing to leave for the rendezvous with Soldier, Manny saw a group walking slowly upriver. He watched downstream with wide-eyed amazement as Jake, who did odd jobs around Dalbeattie, led a group of three people upstream. After a few moments, he realized they were two white soldiers in white shirts and shorts, one tanned and the other very pale, and Morag, in slacks, rolled up to her knees. They were all walking in the middle of the wide, shallow stream. He knew that although Dalbeattie was not far away, such walks from the house were normally done only if Soldier was with them. He was sure they were expecting to meet up with Soldier. He squinted and stared. He couldn't understand why they were walking in the middle of the stream instead of along the path by the riverbank. He noticed that the men's shoes were slung across their shoulders with the laces tied together. Morag was wearing her white crepes whilst Jake, barefoot as usual, had his hands in his pockets. They were walking slowly, breaking into smiles from time to time.

He watched the group until they got to the edge of the deeper area in front of him that formed a pool, left the river, and walked a little farther on the far bank. He continued to watch as they sat on the two big rocks that had been deposited by the raging waters during the storm. He noticed that the shorter of the men, the well-tanned one, carried a pistol in a hip holster. His mind flashed back to his briefing. *Was that the man who put the pistol to my ribs?* he wondered. Then he recalled that the man had talked with a cultured Jamaican accent, and this was a white soldier.

He watched transfixed as they chatted and smiled. He wondered what they were talking about to include Jake in the conversation. He wanted to get away, but each time he thought of moving, his eyes focused on the soldier's pistol, and he stayed put. He noticed Morag did most of the talking, pointing out different aspects of the landscape, picking different leaves, and passing them to the soldiers, who smelled some of them.

After a while, the soldiers put their shoes back on, and they all left, walking slowly as they headed back downstream, this time sticking to the track beside the river.

As soon as they were out of sight, Manny went across the river to where the group had been sitting. He kept looking at the ground, upstream and then downstream. His expression was quizzical as he tried to figure out why they had been there. Just as he was about to cross back to his hiding place, he heard the sound of someone walking towards him along the track, downstream from the direction of Top Ground. He realized he could not get back across the river without being seen, so he crouched behind the rocks.

He watched as Luvvy, the long-haired half African, half Indian beauty from OutaBridge, came into view. He watched her approach where he was and noticed that she was all dressed up. His eyes locked on the bottom of the deep-cut V neck blouse. It was not yet midday, so he figured she must be on her way to Dalbeattie. As she passed where he was, she stopped and looked around as if she was expecting to meet someone. She stood, arms folded, and looked downriver, then across to the track on the other side.

The first Luvvy knew of Manny's presence was when he grabbed her from behind with a hand over her mouth, her head and upper body pressing hard against his chest. In a flash, he ripped at her clothes, and her skirt fell to her feet. She was naked underneath. He was surprised that Luvvy did not struggle and instinctively eased his grip. Luvvy turned around slowly, eyes popping out of her head with rage. Manny was breathing heavily. He stepped back, his eyes staring at her crotch as he licked his lips. Sweat poured from his head and face. He did not see the punch Luvvy landed on his mouth, but the sight of his own blood on the back of his hand made him wild with rage. He grabbed Luvvy by the throat, squeezing with both hands held out straight in front of him. Luvvy kicked out at Manny, trying desperately to loosen his grip. Her feet, tangled by her skirt, made her lose her balance, but she did not fall because he held her upright and straight out in front of him. Such was his fury. Such was his strength. Even when her body went limp and wanted to fall to the ground, he still held her up and straight out in front of him, his eyes bulging out of their sockets. He finally let her body down slowly and dashed back across the river. He grabbed his crocus bag and dashed off to carry out his task.

Manny arrived by the pear trees with less time than he had hoped. Seeing Soldier in the distance, he climbed the tree and watched as Soldier kept the horse on a tight rein at walking pace, looking at the ground from side to side, the way the American Indian trackers did in movies. He hoped Soldier would not look up.

When the horse was about two strides from being in the perfect place, it stopped, and despite Soldier's urging, it would not move. Manny began to tremble with fright. The horse needed to take just two more strides to be in the perfect place for him to drop the noose. He decided he had to act there and then. He had to take a chance even though the horse was not perfectly placed. He was sure Soldier would look up any moment, and he would be in big trouble. Just as the rope was falling through the air, Soldier looked up. Manny pulled quickly on the rope as the horse was spooked and moved forward. Soldier slipped off the horse backwards as he tried to jump to the ground, and the rope began to tighten around his neck. He grabbed on to the rope above his head, his eyes staring as he tried to pull Manny out of the tree. Manny had the length right, and Soldier found himself swinging in midair, his toes brushing the ground with each pass as the rope began to tighten, choking him. His lips moved in a vain attempt to shout for help or to curse Manny, but he had no voice.

Slowly, his hands began to lose their grip as the strain became too much for them. Despite the men staring at each other, not a word was exchanged. Manny sighed with relief and looked around to see if anyone was watching. He then jumped down, gathered his things, and headed back to his hiding place, leaving Soldier suspended from the pear tree.

NINE

Papa Sam was well known for leaving home for his farm plot when it was still dark. He was adept at judging when to leave so that he would always arrive just as it was light enough to start work. Thus his workday usually ended about midday, leaving his compatriots still working for a couple of hours more in the heat. He was taking his usual shortcut home when, as he came around the bend, he either couldn't quite make out what he was seeing or didn't want to believe his eyes. He walked slowly up to the lifeless body dangling from the tree. He put his crocus bag of foodstuffs by his feet and looked up with a frown. Then he ran, screaming, "Ah! Ah!" It took him fifteen minutes or so to get to the shop, where he told the story of what he'd seen. The older men, who were as usual enjoying their domino game, sat looking at one another, nobody willing to be the first to speak.

"What? Nobody believe me? Me say Soldier heng himself down by Baggy Bush." Again, there was no response. Realizing he'd left his bag with his produce by Soldier's feet, he asked one of the young men to accompany him to get it. As soon as he walked out of the shop, everybody started talking at the same time. Their statements ranged from, "It look like he couldn't take losing Daisy to Marshall" to "I wonder what him do that is so bad over at Dalbeattie?" Nobody seemed to care much. Nobody wanted to go and see for himself. Nobody mentioned getting the police. It was as if something they'd wanted to happen had finally happened, and they were glad it had.

Ruth spent the whole day agonizing about how she would approach Geoffrey about his rape of her niece. She finally got the courage to head over to his house to see his mother. She had no idea what she would say to her, as like most of the women around, she feared the woman's abrupt manner and piercing stare. She stopped at the gate for a moment, holding Daisy's hand in a strong grip. She took a couple of deep breaths and marched purposefully straight into the yard, dragging Daisy by the hand as if she had done some wrong and was being brought to be punished. She stopped suddenly by the side of the house. She huffed and puffed in silence and then took a peep around the corner of the house. Mrs. Marshall, a burly woman who always dressed in dark clothes, was bent over her washtub. It was a rare sight, as she usually had someone doing such chores for her. Ruth whispered to Daisy to return home before plucking up enough courage to march towards Mrs. Marshall.

Speaking whilst in motion, she said, "Miss Inez. Miss Inez, I want a word with you." Before she could say another word, Mrs. Marshall raised herself abruptly from the washtub and set her wet hands akimbo. Her stare stopped Ruth in her tracks. After a moment of silence, she said, "You washing, Miss Inez? How come? What happen to…"

The increased stare from Mrs. Marshall was translated by Ruth as, *"You are out of order to be speaking to me like that."* Ruth was still angry, however, and was determined to let Mrs. Marshall know of her anger and the reason for it.

"That look like the pants Geoffrey was wearing last night. Why you washing it, Miss Inez?"

"I see you lose you manners."

"Nothing to do with manners now. Must be something special for you to be washing instead of Helen. And so late in the day as well."

Before she could respond, Mrs. Marshall cocked her head just at the sound of a car approaching. Both ladies stood looking silently at each other. They heard the car door slam, and they waited silently, still staring. After a few seconds, Geoffrey approached from behind Ruth, at the side of the house. He walked towards the ladies, hands in his pockets, brow knitted, his eyes moving from one lady to the other.

When it was obvious that neither lady wished to speak in his presence, he asked, "You heard the news?"

"What news?" asked Ruth fiercely.

"Well, first they find Soldier hanging from a tree, then they find Luvvy dead, naked nearby at Criss Cross. So putting two and two together…"

"Well, the two of them come from OutaBridge. They better not bury them here. Take them back to where they come from," said Mrs. Marshall, her arms still akimbo. Ruth looked troubled.

"When did this happen?" she asked.

Geoffrey replied, "Must be just after midday because it was Papa Sam who found Soldier's body on his way home. Well, I better leave you ladies to carry on with your business."

The ladies looked quizzically at each other but said nothing. Geoffrey did not see the looks, as he had already turned and headed to the house. Ruth walked away and headed home. Geoffrey, seeing what he regarded as a quick exit by Ruth, went to his mother.

"What she doing here? I thought you did not like her." His mother did not answer.

"What's the matter, Mama? Why you look so vex? And why you washing?"

"You injure yourself?"

"No. Why you ask?"

"You want somebody else to wash you pants with bloodstain on it?" Geoffrey did not answer. His mother continued, "All I will say is, if it was that little girl over at you know where, I warn you, I am not accepting any grand pickney from them." Without waiting for a response, she returned to her washing.

Geoffrey stood for a moment in silence before walking away. He hesitated at the doorway, not knowing whether to go inside or to go over to Ruth. But what would he say? Had he arrived in time to stop a discussion? Had Daisy told her aunt about what happened? If she had, did Ruth blame Daisy or him? Did Ruth tell his mother what Daisy may have told her? If Daisy talked, could he get away with saying she'd invited him? With her being so young, what sort of excuse would that be? It had been dark—could he get away with denying it? He decided that unless Ruth said something to him about it, he would carry on as if nothing had happened. He would begin by going over there at nightfall.

The news of the deaths travelled quickly. After all, nothing like that had happened in Plummers in living memory. It was Soldier, the Dalbeattie ranger. It was Luvvy, regarded as the most beautiful of all the girls around.

Two policemen, accompanied by the soldiers and Jake, were down by the river before dark. It was Morag's idea for the soldiers and Jake to volunteer immediately that they had been in the area earlier. After all, she knew it was possible that they'd been seen, so they had to show they had nothing to do with the incidents and nothing to hide, even though it was generally agreed that it was a murder followed by suicide of the murderer. It was not uncommon for murderers to take their own lives rather than face the gallows.

The police spoke with the soldiers again over at Dalbeattie over drinks. They repeated their story about the walk by the river before the incident took place. Such a walk was not uncommon for city folks who visited the countryside. And such visits by city folks to Dalbeattie were well known by the police.

The police learned that Luvvy had told a couple of her friends that she was going to meet Soldier by Criss Cross and would be going over to Dalbeattie with him. It was also common knowledge that Luvvy had been over to Dalbeattie before on social occasions and that Soldier and Luvvy joked from time to time, with Luvvy telling him that despite his reputation, she was sure he couldn't manage her. Some thought Soldier planned to put Luvvy to the test. So once the bodies were identified, there was consensus that Soldier had raped or tried to rape Luvvy before hanging himself. The matter was settled as far as the police were concerned. The official line was murder then suicide.

May learned about the incident by someone shouting out to her from the road. Martha had expected May to talk with her first. She was therefore put out when she found out that May had gone to see Agnes instead of her to receive words of support and comfort. When the ladies finally saw each other that night, May was confused by Martha's somewhat aloof attitude. She wondered whether it was because she was glad that Soldier was gone out of their lives.

Feeling grieved, May felt that those who had believed that Soldier was molesting Daisy would see the rape and suicide as proof of his behaviour and conclude that they had been right all along. She secretly wondered if they thought she had changed her mind, too. She, however, felt sure that Soldier had never troubled her daughter. She wanted to scream out that whatever he may have done, he had never sexually molested her little Daisy. She was convinced she was right, though she was uncertain she would be able to convince anyone of it.

Geoffrey spent the evening in his room contemplating what he would do concerning Ruth's visit to his mother. He did not know what had been said between the ladies before he arrived. His mother's tone told him she knew something, but what was that something? Would Ruth have had the nerve to accuse him before talking to him about it first? He wanted to ask his mother outright what Ruth had come over for or specifically ask her what they'd been talking about before he arrived, but he couldn't. Not even at his age could he ask his mother such questions, especially with her comments about washing his trousers and Ruth seeing her over a washtub as well. This was one occasion he did not want to face his mother. If she had been told about last night, he would be her little boy now, in need of her support, in need of her protection. He was sure he would get it.

Although Ruth did not expect Geoffrey to come over that night, she felt herself looking out and listening for his footsteps. At the same time, she felt herself keeping close to Daisy, squeezing her shoulder from time to time, as if to reassure her or to simply say how

sorry she was about what happened. She wanted to talk to Daisy but found she could not. She wanted to tell her again not to mention it to anyone—that she, the adult, would handle it. But she was afraid that doing so would impress on Daisy her responsibility for what had happened. She finally begged her not to tell her mother, as she would be seen to have failed in protecting her as she was supposed to. She resigned herself to the fact that she had indeed failed to protect Daisy. She decided that she would tell Daisy about the deaths of her own daughters, and she did. Neither showed any emotion at the time.

Just before bedtime, Ruth found herself thinking about her brother and how she would break the news if Daisy became pregnant. She reminded herself that she was the only one who knew how to get in touch with him and decided not worry about that unless it became absolutely necessary. Instead, she watched Daisy rocking herself gently in the rocking chair, even though she was ready for bed. She then heard herself tell Daisy that she should go and sleep in her bed. She thought it was too soon for the girl to get back into her own bed. Daisy made her way to her aunt's bedroom. Ruth followed, dragging the rocking chair. Daisy moved over to the corner of the bed, expecting her auntie to climb into the bed as well. Instead, Ruth rocked herself gently to sleep by the side of the bed, leaving Daisy awake.

The following morning, Morag called her staff together and told them that because of what she called "the incidents," her guests would be returning to Kingston immediately.

May, who was silent for the two days following Soldier's death, refused to go back to work at Dalbeattie, despite the pleadings of Morag and Agnes. What folks did not know was that May blamed herself for being a party to providing "girl company" to Dalbeattie for the visiting soldiers. Despite what others may have thought, she was content that she had only had sex with one soldier on one occasion whilst at Dalbeattie. She had also never told anyone about it. Since it had happened before she'd teamed up with Soldier, she was confident that Morag would never tell anyone about that night. Nobody asked Daisy how she felt about her stepfather's passing, and she never shared her thoughts with anyone.

The following evening, the day before Soldier's funeral, Martha and May were sitting indoors by Martha's sewing machine. May had been there for nearly two hours, talking about Daisy and contemplating her own life after Soldier whilst many women and children were in the yard, chatting among themselves. May was in no mood to receive condolences, and Martha was not going to let anyone into her house. May confided that she would be leaving the district immediately, not even staying for the funeral the following day. Morag had arranged it all.

Martha thought Morag was getting rid of May because of what Soldier had done. May explained, however, that Morag wanted her to stay and had even offered her one of the nice beds from one of the spare rooms and told her she could have her baby boy with her in the days. She added that Morag also offered to take on one of the girls from Plummers to do little chores, which would include looking after her little boy. She said she thought about the offer a great deal, but in the end she decided she could not continue living in the house, in the district, among people who really didn't like her, and now that Daisy was all right, it was best to leave.

May didn't tell the full story. She didn't tell her that Morag had told her she felt she was losing a friend, something May found strange. She didn't tell her that Morag also told her that she felt she would have a better life ahead now that Soldier was gone, another thing she felt strange about. She felt Morag didn't appreciate that in Plummers—in all of Jamaica—at such times, being honest was not superior to expressing feelings of sympathy, real or not. At the same time, she admitted to herself that Morag might be right.

Still, Martha tried to get May to change her mind. She told her that in a short time, everybody would forget about Soldier, and just as the words left her lips, she began to apologize, saying she did not mean it like that. Her efforts didn't stop there. She pointed out that May had a job others craved. She would be near to her daughter and would get a lot of sympathy from the people in the district.

"And what about Daisy?" May asked. "Won't people say what Soldier did was proof that him trouble Daisy?"

"Not necessarily," replied Martha. "Anyway, Daisy is safe now. You don't have anything to worry about anymore. Think about it," she said, as she poured lemonade for the both of them.

Martha tried very hard to get May to see the tragedy as something that was none of her doing. As far as Martha was concerned, Soldier was clearly one of those men who could not control himself, and as he had lost his access to his little Daisy, he took out his frustration on Luvvy, who must have put up a bit of a fight for him to kill her. Martha secretly wished she had put up a fight in her youth when a teacher forced her to become a woman before her time.

Ruth was not aware of May's decision. She did not think much about Soldier and Luvvy either. She was totally focused on Daisy's situation and what she would do if Geoffrey made the girl pregnant. She realized that the next few weeks were going to be agony. She wanted to ask Daisy some details about how the sex act had ended, but she just could not talk about it. She was angry with herself and wished there was someone she could share her concerns with. She even thought of talking to Geoffrey. She wanted to tell May that her daughter had come to her a virgin, that despite what had happened between Luvvy and Soldier, she had been right all along—Soldier had never interfered sexually with her daughter. These remained ideas Ruth could not bring to reality. Daisy, on the other hand, went about life as usual, though she was aware of the torture her aunt was going through. If she was worried about being pregnant, she did not show it.

Ruth decided she would get out of Plummers whether or not Daisy became pregnant. She was also determined to confront Geoffrey and his mother if it did happen. Her anger was so strong that at times she found herself wishing Daisy was pregnant. When she caught herself thinking that way, she asked for forgiveness. She prayed more often in those anxious weeks than at any time before in her life. She wondered what would happen if Geoffrey denied he was the father and suggested that Soldier was—that that was one of the reasons Soldier had done what he did, especially hanging himself, knowing he would be kicked out of Dalbeattie and shunned by the people of Plummers. At the same time, she thought that such action would have been viewed as a bit dramatic for something like that, especially as such actions were not that uncommon for stepfathers. How she would explain things to May became her greatest worry, especially as abortion was dismissed as soon as it came to mind.

TEN

It was twilight, and within a few minutes of leaving to tell Ruth and Daisy of her decision to leave the district, May returned and asked Martha to accompany her. Noticing the questioning look on Martha's face, May said, "It will be dark when I am coming back. Come with me. Come with me, man."

Despite her dislike for walking in the dark, Martha agreed. The two ladies walked slowly, arm in arm, but hardly exchanged a word. Instead of calling out from the roadside, they walked straight up to Ruth's veranda and tapped on the door. Ruth, with a storybook in hand, was surprised to see them. Before they exchanged greetings, Ruth called out to Daisy to come to the veranda before inviting the ladies in.

Daisy hesitated when she saw them, and her aunt gave her a gentle push towards her mother, who cupped her daughter's chin in both hands and kissed her on the forehead. Daisy turned and buried her head in Martha's bosom. Martha cherished the demonstration of affection, a gesture that was not lost on the other ladies.

"How you bearing up?" asked Ruth.

"I am all right. I am all right," responded May.

"And how are you, Miss Martha?"

"Could be better, I suppose," she replied, still smiling. Ruth watched the two ladies looking at each other as if wanting the other to speak first.

"Can I get you a drink? Some ginger wine?" asked Ruth, breaking the deadlock.

"Yes. Yes," said Martha, hurriedly, surprising May with her eagerness.

"Lord, I didn't even offer you a seat. Forgive me. I am sorry."

With that, Ruth offered seats to the ladies, and although May had not answered about the drink, Ruth poured her one as well. When Martha kept looking at Daisy, widening her eyes and knitting her brow and making Daisy smile, Ruth began to get a bit jealous. She told Daisy to take the book to her room and come out when called.

Martha led the conversation, explaining what May had decided. She spoke softly and quickly, as if she had a brief time to speak on May's behalf. Ruth looked towards May from time to time for some sort of agreement to some of the points Martha was making. May, however, kept her eyes lowered and remained silent.

At the end of what seemed like a sermon, Ruth began asking questions and found herself addressing those questions to Martha. Martha looked to May for her to answer, but May continued her silence. Martha reluctantly began dealing with the questions, basing her answers on what May had told her, assuming that if she got anything wrong, May would step in. May recognized that Martha had already provided the answers—Ruth just wanted her to talk. She kept her silence.

The meeting was also a welcome opportunity for Ruth to tell the ladies of her plan to move to Kingston with Daisy. She immediately became visibly nervous when she realized that the move had been, up to that point, only an idea; now she was putting herself in a position of no return. She knew she had to do whatever she could to make the idea a reality.

"The best thing to do," said May. Martha agreed. An onlooker would have been hard-pressed to say who was Daisy's mother, such was the forcefulness of Martha against the meekness of May.

A brief silence was broken by Ruth who, for the first time, mentioned Soldier by name. Martha, who had been doing the talking for May, fell silent and looked at May in a quiet order to speak. May hesitated.

Ruth said, "I know it must be hard for you. You going before or after the funeral?"

"Before," said Martha immediately. "It's better that way. Mrs. Sanderson sort everything out already. They taking care of the funeral as well."

"Where they burying him?" asked Ruth.

"Down by the big breadfruit tree," replied Martha. Then she added, "Nobody going to use the short cut to Chalk Bottom anymore. I think that's why they putting him there. Spiteful. They don't want people passing too close to the house, seeing and hearing what going on over there."

May suddenly came to life with, "What you talking about? Nothing going on over there. Can anybody tell you who you can or can't invite to your house? People too wicked. That is one thing I won't miss."

Her sudden rebuke of Martha surprised Ruth, who immediately looked towards Martha, silently inviting her to respond. Martha said nothing. Ruth looked towards May, who was staring straight ahead. She then called out, "Daisy, come here." Daisy trotted into the room, and Ruth continued, "You mother has something to tell you."

May sat up in surprise. Neither of the women came to her aid. She had to deal with it herself. She started by telling Daisy that she was glad to see that she was happy with her aunt and that she wanted her to know that all she wanted was what was best for her. Because of that, she was going back to her own district with Daisy's little brother, leaving her with her aunt. She assured her daughter that she would write to her, and she made Daisy promise that she would write as well. May could feel tears welling, so she stood abruptly and said goodbye before they came.

Later that night, Ruth told herself that pregnancy or no pregnancy, on her next visit to Kingston she would talk to JJ about moving in with him. She would approach it as if it was a done deal: she was coming to live with him at last. He'd always wanted her to, and she had finally decided to do it. She wondered whether she was jumping out of the frying pan into the fire, but she was so sure that JJ was a decent man. He would be a father to Daisy; he was different. She then wondered at the possibility of JJ objecting to her bringing Daisy. She thought of renting a place for herself to start with so as to not impose on JJ for the first couple of months, taking things one step at a time. She soon abandoned that for having made all her plans on the basis that Daisy would not become pregnant. She felt she had nothing to lose.

Ruth found herself thinking of the day she and JJ met in the bank and how sure she'd felt that JJ and the bank clerk knew each other very well. "Maybe he even know everything about my account," she told herself. Still, it didn't matter. That might help JJ decide she could bring Daisy with her, as it would not be a cost to him. She agonized so much that her head began to ache. She cried herself to sleep and hoped things would be clearer in the morning.

Daisy got up before her aunt, a rare thing for her. Ruth was concerned. "What happen? You couldn't sleep? You feeling all right? Come, come. Come to Auntie." Daisy made no attempt to answer any of the questions, and it seemed her aunt did not expect an answer.

"How would you like it if we moved to Kingston? Let's get out of this place. You can go to the pictures. Go to school by bus. Have nice friends..."

"But what about Thelma?"

"Oh, you will see her again. It is not forever. We will visit Plummers from time to time. I will still do business with the people here. And you won't have to see that bad man. What you say?"

Daisy hugged her aunt, who had watched the girl getting used to being hugged, something she'd been uncomfortable with at first. Ruth hugged her niece and assured her that they were both going to live a better life in Kingston. She also asked her not to say anything to anyone. She knew she was taking a risk, but she felt she had no choice.

Having told Daisy about Kingston, Ruth began to torture herself about whether she could really trust JJ with Daisy, given what had happened with Geoffrey. Still, she felt she had to take a chance. She hoped Daisy was smart enough to keep her promise not to say anything to anyone about what Geoffrey had done, and she decided to take a gamble. She realized this was quite a burden to put on Daisy, but she was going to do it anyway. She would spend the next few days discussing things with JJ.

Soldier's funeral was not well attended, as was usually the case in Plummers. First, Morag made it known that there would be no feast over at Dalbeattie, though food would be provided, as was the custom among the locals, managed by the church sisters. As far as she was concerned, Soldier's burial was not a celebratory event. Also, being that the grave was going to be on the Dalbeattie property—something that surprised the locals—the folks knew they could not wander at will at the graveside. In the end, a few of the Dalbeattie workers and their partners—no children—were present. The minister said a prayer based on forgiveness, and soon afterwards, the grave was filled in, and everybody went off to the churchyard for the feast. There was an abundance of food. They were treated to macaroni and cheese which was avoided by most of the men who stuck to their traditional dishes of rice and peas, curry goat and rice, jerk and boiled pork, dumplings, yam, sweet potato, pear, corn, tomato and a variety of green vegetables. Though there was ample supply of soft drink, the men were disappointed with the meagre supply of rum.

Luvvy, on the other hand, had a well-attended funeral the following day in Clover Hill. It followed the tradition of feasting and rum drinking. The folks from Plummers and Clover Hill came together for the occasion. There was no representation from Dalbeattie, as Morag did not want to be linked with Luvvy in any way. As far as she was concerned, all matters between the girls who visited were between them and Soldier, the middleman. Again, the food was plenty: curry goat, plain rice, rice and peas, chicken, jerk pork and an array of different cakes. There was an abundance of the everyday foodstuff, including yam, corn, plantain and banana. Three ram goats were killed for the occasion. It was the first time that a funeral in the area was like a street party. It was all done by donations from the folks from Plummers and Clover Hill.

The following morning, Ruth looking tired from her hurried walk, arrived at Martha's house without warning. Instead of sitting on the veranda, Martha immediately invited inside before excusing herself for a moment to put a headscarf on. Martha decided that the matter must be an important one to cause the visit, and nobody else was going to hear a word of what passed between them.

Ruth looked around the room, which doubled as a living room and a sewing parlour. She noticed the many different pieces of material folded and placed neatly one on top of the other in a corner. After a little chitchat, Ruth got to the point. She told Martha that she had decided to leave Plummers and would arrange for her house to be rented. She then told her that her plans to move to Kingston were linked to the fact that she might be getting married and that she would continue to develop her craft business and so still have links with the people in Plummers. She added that she would like her to reconsider her decision and make some of the aprons for her.

Martha replied, "What you mean, 'might be getting married'? That don't make any sense to me. *Might* be? What foolishness that?"

"It's…it's a little complicated. The point is, will you make the aprons for me?"

"So you not answering me question?"

"I'll explain another time. What about the apron?"

"I am a dressmaker. Those things are just basic stitching. A waste of time for me."

"But that is it. Easy money for you."

"Money isn't everything. Don't ask me again."

Ruth smiled at the abruptness of the response, which she saw as Martha trying to appear cross when she was not.

Martha was thinking that the move to Kingston would be a positive one for Daisy, but she also knew she would miss the girl. She wanted to continue teaching her to sew. Proper sewing, she called it. She would prefer to have Daisy around. She felt that she was the right person to care for her, but she hadn't wanted to upset May at the meeting with Ruth and so gave her support to Daisy's staying with her aunt. She had no such restraint alone with Ruth. She could say how she felt.

Martha told Ruth that it was God who'd sent her but that sewing aprons was not what God wanted them to talk about. She wanted Ruth to know that she felt confident that she would let Daisy visit her from time to time, but she was not happy that she was taking Daisy to another man. Soldier was bad enough, and she'd witnessed the way he'd manhandled the girl. She was not happy. Ruth listened in silence, bursting to speak out in defence of Soldier, but knowing she could not do so without saying how she knew.

Martha talked about the pains she was now suffering in her hips and how having Daisy around would be good for both of them. She emphasized that she was not looking for a servant but just a little help in return for teaching her a good trade, a trade the girl had already displayed talent for and one that would set her up for life.

Ruth listened in silence as Martha rubbed her side and contorted her face to emphasize the pain. Martha took on the role of mother again and asked detailed questions about Daisy's schooling. Ruth thought enough was enough—she already had May's blessing. However, being in Martha's house, uninvited no less, she would bite her tongue instead of reminding her that she was talking about her niece and not just some motherless girl.

When Martha said, "So which man you taking Daisy to now?" Ruth gave her a stern lecture about her relationship with Daisy, reminding her that she was her aunt and that although she appreciated what Martha had done for Daisy in the past, she must remember that "blood thicker than water." She went on to tell her that the matter was really between her and May, and it was out of courtesy and a recognition for what she had done for Daisy that she even discussed the matter in her presence. Martha huffed and puffed and threw her hands in the air before resting them on her hips. She went into a tirade at Ruth, telling her that she obviously did not know what she had done for Daisy, ending with, "Ruth Golding, I regret the day I waste me time defending you 'gainst the people in the district."

"Defending me? Defending me against what? Against who?"

"You think the people here have short memory? Get outa a mi house. Leave me property! Now! Right now! To tell you the truth, Miss Golding, I don't trust you one bit. I don't trust you. I don't trust you at all. Come outa me house! Now! Right now!"

Ruth was startled by the outburst, and she left in a hurry, Martha slamming the door at her heels.

After a short while, she reopened it and shouted, "You think I don't remember you, Ruth Golding? You come back here playing big shot. Think I don't know how you used to jump outa you bed at night time fi go look man. You was a disgrace. Bring shame on you parents. Respectable parents, too. You behaviour kill them with shame. You have no shame to come back here, you wicked, nasty woman. What is de truth about your own pickney, dem? Where you get so much money from to come build big house? A whole heap of tings don't make sense. And since you come here…" She stopped speaking when she realized that the only people listening to her were her neighbours because Ruth had hurried out of earshot.

"What you looking at? Who talking to you?" she shouted to nobody in particular before slamming her door and slowly sinking to her knees, hands clasped in prayer, looking to the heavens, saying, "May God have mercy on that child."

Two weeks after the funerals, Oliver was visiting his friend Paul DeMar in New York. Paul worked for Pan Am and made frequent trips to Jamaica. He had the know-how and connections to bring back lots of bottles of the real stuff—Jamaican white rum. Oliver would be taking his haul back to Atlanta with him after the short visit.

"So tell me, Paul, what I pay for?" Paul brushed his hair back with both hands before replying.

"I tell you, man. I don't understand. I don't understand. It was supposed to be a trigger man. That's why it cost so much."

"So, what? I pay for a suicide?"

"Look—I don't deal with the trigger man. Anyway, you get what you want. So what's the problem?"

"Money. My money is the problem. Just think how they must be laughing at you."

"Look—you wanted him dead, and him dead. So what's the problem?"

Oliver tapped his fingers on the table. "I don't like it. I don't like it. Doesn't seem real. Doesn't seem real at all. You comfortable with it?"

"Yeah. I am comfortable. That's the end of the matter as far as I am concerned."

"I still have a bad, bad feeling about it."

PART 2

ELEVEN

(Kingston)

One of the startling things about Kingston for Daisy was how late the sun shone in the mornings after it had made its way over the mountains. She just could not get used to seeing it for the first time when it was high in the sky, when all her previous life the sunrise had been very early, with the sun seeming to rise from the sea directly in front of Plummers. She also found that unlike the houses in Plummers, many of the Kingston houses did not have much outside space. They seemed quite close to one another in comparison.

Although JJ's veranda lay just a few feet back from the road, it had a gate to the side that led to another house behind it. The yard was fairly big, and just like in Plummers, there were no boundary markings between JJ's and the house behind it. When she asked about where she could play, she was a little surprised that she was not allowed to wander into the yard area at will. The reason Ruth gave at the time was that they didn't know the people living at the back well enough, and one had to be careful. That was one of Daisy's lessons about being a girl in town.

Looking at the house from the roadside, two evenly sized rooms lay at each end with a veranda in the middle, the width giving the false impression of a huge house. The room on the left was Ruth's bedroom, and the one to the right was Daisy's. Behind Ruth's was the only bathroom. Behind the veranda was a tiny dining room, and behind Daisy's room was the kitchen.

The only regular duty Daisy had was to keep her room clean and tidy. Ruth told her that it was important that she learned to take pride in keeping it that way. A cleaner came in twice a week, but she was under strict instructions never to clean Daisy's room.

Daisy was grateful for the way Ruth and JJ treated her. She was grateful, too, for the way JJ taught her, in a fun way, to use a knife and fork properly. Later he took her to hotel restaurants with Ruth and generally showed her off. They made sure she went to Ward Theatre and was able to engage in conversation with her friends about the pantomime, ballet, or contemporary dancing. She was particularly happy about being exposed to the cultural side of Jamaican life, some of which she had been unaware of just a short time before.

Daisy's new friends included a couple of schoolmates who lived close by. She would be seeing less of them as soon as they left school at fifteen, but for now they often travelled to school together. Her first year was a bit embarrassing. She struggled to keep up with the work, which was too advanced for her despite the extra instruction she received from Ruth and JJ. Some of the children teased her because of what they referred to as her country accent. She also had a tendency to shout. They didn't know that such was the normal speech volume in Plummers. It was not long before Daisy began speaking less and more softly, becoming "one of them."

Things were great at home for Daisy. She enjoyed the luxury of having her own room and a double bed, a dressing table to put her comb and other things on, and a big mirror all to herself. Living in Kingston, the capital, was like being in heaven. She spent much of her first night smiling to herself as she changed her hairstyle over and over again. She was so pleased and confident that when her aunt popped in to check if she was OK, Daisy didn't stop combing her thick hair. It was as if she knew her aunt would want her to continue doing what she was doing. When her aunt left the room, Daisy spent some time rolling about in the bed, enjoying the space and the softness. She slept very well that night.

It was JJ who insisted that with special tuition Daisy could make it to secondary school, though she would be a bit late and therefore probably the oldest in her class. When Ruth doubted she could do it, JJ reminded her that most students started high school at age twelve and graduated with their Senior Cambridge certificate at seventeen. A select few would then go to the sixth form for an additional two years for the Higher School certificate and then on to university. He was confident that with the right assistance, Daisy could persevere and do the Senior Cambridge at nineteen.

Daisy found it difficult to contemplate being the oldest in her class by up to two years for a period of three years. She also wondered how she would cope in the one-to-one teaching environment she would have to face when she left elementary school. It was a challenge she was not looking forward to.

Throughout her period of private lessons, Daisy was aware of the looks that passed between JJ and Miss Prentice on the occasions he dropped her off or picked her up from her lessons. His routine was always the same: he would have his head down in the racing page of the newspaper, then occasionally exchange a smile with a little shake of the head. Daisy followed the golden rule of children—not to be involved in "big people business." She was pleased when she later learned through a conversation she overheard that her aunt knew Prentice was an ex-girlfriend of JJ but that she regarded them as just friends now. She remembered the caution she heard her aunt give JJ: "Just don't do anything to make that girl lose respect for you."

When Daisy applied to take the test to get into secondary school, she knew that if she did well, she would be allowed to start in the third form. The school confirmed what Ruth had said about her being the eldest girl in the class at seventeen, as the majority were fifteen or under, and that subject choices for the Senior Cambridge certificate would be made at the start of the third year. They also explained that the test would cover all the subjects she would have learned had she been in the second form.

Because of JJ's easy-going attitude, assuring her not to worry and just do her best, Daisy was determined not to let him down. She worked hard but did not do as well as she had hoped. However, the school still allowed her to start secondary school because she did exceptionally well in English, chemistry, and mathematics. She was even thought to be gifted in the latter two. The headmistress told JJ she felt Daisy could be an asset to them, as they were trying to improve their Senior Cambridge results. She also stressed that Daisy needed to work at the other subjects, as being brilliant at those three was not enough.

Daisy started secondary school and found it very hard going in the first term, largely due to difficulty concentrating following her period of one-to-one tutoring. She also found it hard to make friends, as friendships seemed to have been cemented in the earlier years, and nobody seemed willing to help her break into her circle. Even helping others with their chemistry and mathematics homework did not change that. She also found it difficult to plan her homework properly, and unlike some of the others, she did not have a friend with whom she could check her understanding of anything. JJ decided to pay his friend Prentice another visit to help Daisy through her first year.

The arrangement for additional private tutoring caused a bit of friction between JJ and Ruth, who was convinced JJ was only doing it so he could continue to see Prentice. JJ denied that and told Ruth that he was committed to helping Daisy achieve her best, and if she did not want him to do it, she should simply say so. Ruth was taken aback by the statement and vowed never to say anything again that could be construed as a lack of support for her niece.

As time went by, Daisy and Prentice became good friends, talking about personal affairs, much to the surprise of both. Prentice talked about some very personal aspects of her life growing up in Clarendon and her eventual move to Kingston after going to teacher training college, including how she'd struggled to make friends with other teachers and professionals. She even said she was not quite sure how she ended up at teacher training college, as she never wanted to be a teacher.

On graduating, Prentice did not go into teaching as planned but instead went to work in the prison service, having been encouraged to do so by a family friend in the probation service. She told Daisy how she was seen as a failure by the rest of her family, who accused her of lacking ambition. She said she stuck with the prison service job for six years before finally going into teaching for two years before becoming a private tutor. The change came about after she read in an American magazine about a woman who'd made a business out of teaching adults, mostly those who were working and studying. Although the same facilities for work and study did not exist in Jamaica, Prentice felt there was enough demand to make a business of it. As she had some savings, she decided to give it a try, and now she was in the position of having to refuse clients. She also explained to Daisy that JJ helped her run the business with his special tax knowledge and contacts for students. Overall, the work had proved to be a nice way to meet some interesting professional people. Her only disappointment was that she had more high school clients than she preferred.

Daisy learned that Prentice and JJ had met through a mutual friend and that they were never really boyfriend and girlfriend, perhaps because of the age gap between them. Although the two liked each other, they realized it would not work. Prentice also told Daisy that she had met quite a few nice fellows through JJ and offered to introduce her to one or two of the younger ones, those in their early twenties. Daisy laughed rather than replying.

It dawned on Daisy that she needed to talk to someone about her experiences. She needed to offload, but there was nobody she felt she could speak to without it getting back to her aunt or JJ. She began to consider Prentice. It seemed a bad idea to her, yet she couldn't get it out of her head. She decided to take the chance.

One day, in the middle of a lesson, she said, "Miss P, I want to talk to you about something. Something very personal. Can I?" Prentice looked over her glasses without answering. Daisy took it as a command to carry on. She told her about being beaten up by her stepfather from a young age and being raped at the age of thirteen. She did not say who had raped her, but she made it plain it was not Soldier.

After moments of silence, disappointed that Prentice just stared at her in silence with a knitted brow, Daisy went on to confess that the experience made her fear sexual intercourse even though she had a strong urge to have a good experience.

She was surprised when, in a matter-of-fact way, Prentice said, "I can fix you up. I can arrange that for you. You need to overcome your fears early. Otherwise it could be a bit of a problem for you later on."

Daisy was shocked by the no-holds-barred approach, and it showed in her facial expression, to such an extent that Prentice apologized. Not believing the apology to be sincere, Daisy wondered if her aunt had told JJ the details and he in turn had told Prentice. She thought long and hard about trying to find out but decided to let the matter rest. She needed Prentice's help, and prior knowledge of what she had been through might be a good thing. It would, however, not come from her lips. "You would do that for me?" she asked. Then, after a period of silence, she continued, "I didn't seem to take you by surprise. How come?"

"How come what?"

"Never mind."

Richard Ventura and Daisy came face-to-face for the first time when they bumped into each other on Prentice's veranda on arrival at the next lesson. Daisy noticed that the young man didn't have any books with him. At the start of the lesson, Daisy asked, "Who is he?"

"Who you asking about?"

"You know who I am talking about."

Prentice smiled. She was disarmed by Daisy's forwardness. They were becoming more relaxed with each other, but the boundary between teacher and pupil was getting too blurred for her liking.

"Let's just concentrate on the lesson today. Now, have you done the homework?"

"I just know you arranged for me to see him. I just know it. I can see it in your face now as well."

"Daisy, will you—"

"Is he one of yours?"

"I think you are overstepping the mark now, young lady. You really must just concentrate on what you are here for."

"He is. Isn't he?"

"Daisy McIntosh!"

"OK, Miss P. OK. He's nice, though, and more for me than for you."

"Now, look here, young lady. The fact that I agreed to help you with your…your situation does not mean you can disrespect me. So, let's just get on with the lesson." Daisy frowned but got on with the work.

Just before the end of the lesson, Prentice volunteered that Richard was the son of her travel agent and that she acted as a go-between for a few people who wanted to travel but did not have the full fare. She helped them out. She explained that it was a little business she ran on the side, and so the tickets had to be delivered to her for the travellers to collect from her. Daisy was impressed with her business acumen.

Daisy spent a lot of time scrutinizing Prentice. She could see why JJ would fall for her. She was bright, very dark and beautiful with short cropped hair that suited her long face with wide, bright eyes that were hidden by glasses whenever she was reading. She rarely smiled but when she did, it was heartwarming and real. Daisy wondered how someone like Prentice was not married with so many nice, single men around her.

For many days afterwards, Daisy thought about what Prentice had said, and she spent many nights imagining doing it with Richard. Then she heard herself say, "Miss P, I am ready. I am ready to get this—this *thing* over with. I think the sooner the better."

Prentice smiled. "Leave it to me."

The following Monday, Richard and Daisy met briefly at Prentice's home, and both admitted to Prentice that they liked each other.

Two days later, Ruth was travelling home by taxi after a visit to the hairdresser. Just a short way from home, the driver stopped alongside another taxi to talk with the driver. Ruth noticed a young lady in the back seat of the other taxi, looking out the window to the other side. She thought the person looked very much like Daisy. She turned her head away but kept her eyes on the young lady, trying to be sure one way or the other. At the same time, she fixed her headscarf in such a way that the person would not see her staring. As the taxis began to pull away, the young lady turned and looked straight ahead. Ruth was now sure it was Daisy, and the taxi was going in the direction away from home. She was angry and thought about ordering her taxi to turn around and follow the other, but she resisted. She was not sure whether she was angry with Daisy or angry with herself for being so trusting. She looked at her watch and realized Daisy should still be in school.

On arriving home, Ruth thought of phoning the taxi driver, her regular, to find out where his friend had dropped off the passenger, but she decided against that, too. She dashed into Daisy's room and noticed that her uniform was pressed and hung up, ready for school the next day. Her school bag was missing, but she did not have a lesson with Prentice because it was Wednesday. The room was tidy. She sniffed the pillow, then the sheets. She went into the bathroom and the kitchen and looked around. She wandered around the rest of the house as if looking to see if anything was missing. Then she sat down at the table, and, with her hand under her chin, she just stared.

Ruth contemplated telephoning the school to find out why Daisy was not there, but she just as quickly dismissed the idea. After a minute or so, she walked towards the telephone table and reached to pick up the telephone, but she decided against it. She returned and sat at the dining table, staring into space. She was confused.

As the taxi pulled up, Daisy got out. She quickly walked up the steps, turned, and headed towards the door at the end of the veranda. As she approached the door, it opened, and she was greeted by a big grin from Richard, a handsome, athletic-looking young man of medium height. As he closed the door, she dropped her bag on the floor. She giggled as Richard reached out and grabbed her by the shoulders to stop her from rushing at him. She forced herself forward against his arms in a playful game of strength before giving up, allowing herself to be guided slowly backwards until the back of her thighs came into contact with the bed. Richard pushed her gently, forcing her backwards until she fell on the bed. She never stopped giggling.

Richard looked down on Daisy with a smile as he began taking his shirt off. Daisy watched him. She stopped giggling and was now smiling.

He threw the shirt on the floor and said, "Soon come."

He left the room. Daisy sat up and looked around the room admiringly before undressing. Richard returned to find her lying naked, face down on the bed. She was giggling again. He startled her by flipping her onto her back and pinning her down by the shoulders. Daisy pushed at him hard with her feet against his stomach. The look on her face told him she was not joking. He let go of her shoulders, and she wagged a finger.

"No rough stuff. Any of that foolishness, and I am out of here," she said sternly. "You not roughing me up."

Richard froze. His expression asked a thousand questions. He was not accustomed to being spoken to like that. In such situations, he was usually the one in control. *He* decided what happened, when, and how. It was always like that, even with the mature ladies—teachers, bankers, and housewives who regularly sought his service. He remembered Prentice telling him to be gentle with this one, but he hadn't taken her seriously. He wasn't going to be dictated to by a seventeen-year-old school girl. Just as he was contemplating his next move, he noticed Daisy breaking into a gentle smile, her eyes focused on his now limp penis. He told himself she was pleased he was wearing a condom. He decided to take control, as he was accustomed to doing. He stared at her as his brain got into gear and his erection returned.

"Just turn over and go 'pon you knee," he said, as sternly as Daisy had spoken to him. He was surprised when she obeyed. Before she could settle herself on the bed, she felt his hands on her hips and her body being pulled backwards as he began forcing himself into her. She clenched her teeth and grabbed the sheets with both hands, her forehead resting on the bed. It was not what she was expecting. She moved her hips forward, away from him, but found his arm under her stomach, pulling her back as he continued to try to enter her. For a moment, she felt she was going through what Geoffrey had done to her, and her body stiffened. She pushed herself up from the bed.

"No!" she said, raising a hand. Richard did not understand that she really meant no. He immediately pulled her back towards his groin and went deep into her. Her head pitched forward to rest on the bed as she let out a muffled sound. She began to breathe heavily, hoping it would get easier and be more fun in a moment, as Prentice had said it would.

It was still light when Daisy arrived home.

"Evening, Auntie."

"Evening. How was lessons today?"

"Forget say today is Wednesday?"

"You right. So, where you coming from so late?"

"Well, we didn't have any lessons last two periods because they still repairing the lab. So I went to do some work with one of the girls. Her mother is a friend of Miss Prentice."

Ruth wanted to ask a few questions about the friend and where she lived, but she didn't. "I see. Wash your hands, and come and eat." Ruth looked around to see if there was any unusual reaction from Daisy. Daisy, however, had turned and was already on her way to the bathroom.

Daisy's answer made sense to Ruth. She knew about the work being done in the lab, but she was still uneasy about the taxi. She was sure it was Daisy she had seen.

"Which bus did you take?" she asked.

"Went by taxi because they live near Matilda's Corner. Papa said I should take the taxi."

Ruth created as many opportunities as she could to walk close to Daisy, and she sniffed the air as she did so, trying to catch the odour of a man or of sexual activity to suggest that Daisy was not telling her the truth. There was no such evidence.

Daisy's relationship with Richard lasted several weeks. It ended when, despite liking Richard, she soon realized that he was getting bored with her, wanting her to leave as soon as possible after their sex sessions. She wanted a little more than that, so she simply ended the relationship, never giving him an explanation. Prentice never asked, either. Daisy vowed to seek out her sex partners herself in the future and be like some of her classmates, whose parents thought they were good girls whilst they did what they wanted to do.

TWELVE

(1953)

It was the night of a visit to the theatre that Daisy cried herself to sleep just thinking about the life she'd left behind in Plummers and the joys she was experiencing in Kingston. However, when she later spoke about her country life, she found that some of her classmates wished they'd had the childhood she'd had and the freedom to wander about in the open spaces as she described to them. She vowed never to break their hearts with the other side—the dangers of being a little girl among some of the men that had been around when she was growing up. She never gave a thought to the fact that the same dangers existed in the town.

When the young Queen Elizabeth II of England visited Jamaica near the end of the year, Daisy went down to the wharf to see the Royal Yacht *Britannia* decked out with its lights. It was a joyous time. She also went to school events to mark the visit and wondered what would have happened had she been in Plummers.

Daisy's comfort was interrupted when she found she had to share her bed with JJ's sister, Pansy, whenever she visited. She didn't mind the sharing. What she didn't like was that she had to sleep in the corner side of the bed and be afraid of disturbing Pansy if she wanted to get up during the night. She also hated the fact that Pansy took control of her room, moving her things, using her hair oil, deciding what should be placed where on the dressing table, and insisting that if she decided to go to bed a bit early, then Daisy had to do likewise so as not to disturb her. It did not matter to Pansy that Daisy was allowed to listen to the American radio station WINZ, broadcasting from Florida, for a little while before bedtime, and since neither JJ nor Ruth was aware of what was going on, Daisy felt helpless. That was a piece of injustice as far as Daisy was concerned.

Pansy, of course, had no idea what was going on in Daisy's head. She did not realize that Daisy, despite her early classroom backwardness, had made great strides, and not just in her schoolwork. She had also become conscious of the injustices present within a family environment. The latter was something she wished she could talk about freely, but she knew she had to show manners to grown-ups, whatever the circumstance.

JJ was very protective of Daisy, coming to her rescue many times when it came to household chores. He felt she should do less housework and more schoolwork, and she noticed that her aunt would give in quickly to his suggestions, seeming almost afraid to differ from him in anything relating to Daisy's education. JJ would also allow her to spend more time with her friends than her aunt would. Not surprisingly, he was stricter with her when it came to her studies.

As time went by, Daisy was not automatically sent to her room when Ruth's and JJ's friends stopped by, and she soon developed a fondness for Johnny Rogers, one of JJ's friends. He was a good-looking portly man, many years younger than JJ. Daisy knew that she could always count on a nice smile from Mr. Rogers and was happy that he gave his smile in full view of JJ, who never seemed to disapprove. She was also aware that it never happened in her aunt's presence. Once she surprised herself by asking her Uncle JJ how come he had such a good friend who was so much younger than himself. Just when she was about to put her hand over her mouth for asking such a question, JJ replied without lifting his head from the horse-racing results.

"He drives, and I do not. In fact, his late father was really my friend." Daisy thought about asking more questions but let it stop there.

Rogers was in fact a kind, gentle young man. He was aware that he lacked the education many of his counterparts had; he was more interested in business and felt too much classroom work was not necessary for that. He had a habit of pretending to be a bit naïve about certain things, and he would watch for others' reactions. Those who corrected him, especially in a gentle, straightforward manner, were likely to get into in his good books. Those who sniggered or whispered would have to work very hard to gain his trust, if they ever did.

Having been introduced to sex at an early age by a young maid, he soon developed a reputation as a bit of a wild boy. Along with his good looks, he'd inherited a great deal of money from his father, who sold his rental properties shortly before he died. The family-owned nursing home was the only business Rogers had to focus on.

From the time Daisy arrived in Kingston, she was under strict instructions about what she should and should not say about her previous life. The tale she was to tell was a simple one: her mother had died, and her aunt, her father's brother, was now looking after her. Nothing more. Daisy understood. She settled well into the Kingston lifestyle and did not go back to Plummers for the first three years.

When the folks in Plummers saw her, they were pleasantly surprised to see a lovely young lady. Daisy did not allow the rift between her aunt and Martha to get in the way, and she spent time with Martha on that first visit. She also spent time with her friend Thelma, who had had a baby.

Her friend Gladys was welcoming, and she invited Daisy to sit with her on her veranda. The two sat and chatted as if it was something they had done before. Gladys's mother even said a polite hello, and Daisy was relieved when she did not question her about her life in Kingston.

News about Daisy and her development filtered through to the district as Ruth continued doing business with folks there and in the surrounding areas for her craft business, which was doing well. It was noticeable that in those three years, Ruth never once saw Martha. She never once asked anyone about her. She even stopped close by to Martha's house and talked to others she would not normally pass the time of day with just so that Martha could see her. Martha, for her part, never gave her the pleasure of seeing her looking on. Many of the people, mostly the churchgoers, tried their best to get the ladies to heal their wounds, but with no success.

Martha had not changed her opinion over time. As far as she was concerned, she was the one who should have Daisy. She had shown that she could be trusted to see all was well with the girl. She was the one who could be trusted to heal the little girl's wounds now that Soldier was gone. She did not think Daisy would be safe with her aunt, especially in a place like Kingston—the den of iniquity, as she called it—and she saw Daisy's long absence as pure spite on the part of Ruth Green, now Mrs. Ruth Hunter. Ruth, on the other hand, thought Miss Martha was outright rude and malicious and was not worth her time.

Though the two had not returned to Plummers earlier, the people got news about what Daisy was up to from her friend Thelma, who visited Daisy with her baby each Christmas. The visits were carefully orchestrated—early morning arrival, a bit of shopping, then back home on the evening bus. Daisy would have loved to have spent more time with her friend, but at the same time, she was thankful just for the opportunity to meet up with Thelma. She was pleased that they cemented their friendship through correspondence.

Daisy wrote more or less only positive things because she knew her letters could land in anybody's hands. She wrote about her new friends and her big room and how she was getting on in school. She also told Thelma how much she missed the fresh fruits and, sometimes, the sound of the waves dashing against the rocks. She avoided other details that could be interpreted as boasting.

Ruth was planning a business trip to New York the following year. She planned to take Daisy with her as an eighteenth birthday present, as it would be the summer holidays. In the end, however, she explained she could not take her: her plans had changed, and she would be dashing about a bit more than she had originally expected.

Daisy was content with the change and happy that her friend Margaret was going to keep her company for the few days her aunt would be away. She also had the added comfort of knowing that Margaret's mother would be popping in from time to time. Ruth and JJ both thought Margaret was a good choice because although she was a couple years younger than Daisy, she was a devout Christian like her mother and a good example.

Ruth arrived at the restaurant by taxi and was immediately greeted by a grey-haired man who asked if she was Mrs. Hunter. She grunted in the affirmative.

"I have been advised to show you to your seat, madam, and you will be joined by Mr. Watson in a moment." His accent was more English than American. As the waiter hurried ahead, Ruth walked deliberately slower than usual, enjoying the admiring glances from the other diners as she walked upright, chest out, her handbag hanging elegantly on her arm. She told herself that they must think she is some well known singer or other such person and she was going to play the part.

Ruth was uncomfortable about being shown to a seat in the darkest area of the restaurant when there were several empty seats in a more brightly lit area. It was not the first time her brother had done that, and she'd told him she didn't like it. She spent the few minutes she waited fiddling with her purse, her collar, her sleeves. Just when she was about to lose her composure, Oliver, now Oliver Watson, appeared from the shadows and sat down beside her without even a greeting. They just looked at each other and smiled.

After a few moments, she whispered, "You have been watching too many movies. Nobody is following you—or me, for that matter." Oliver patted his sister on the arm and continued smiling.

"That's a very nice suit. I like the tie as well. I am sure it's a woman who dressed you."

"You still have that thing about a man not being able to choose colours?"

"But it's a fact."

"I should know better than to argue with you."

"Just as well I had admiring glances when I came in, otherwise I would think I look a mess."

"Oh…sorry. You look nice sis. Really, you do."

"Too late now. You not going to ask about your daughter?" she added.

"I know you will tell me," he said in a hushed voice.

"So, how are you?"

"OK. Things are fine. Business is good. I just can't stop him gambling on the horses, though."

"You managing to keep him away from you money?"

"I have no problem with that. He is a good man. He doesn't ask me anything, and he knows it's insurance money...my husband...my children."

"You coping all right with that? You know—the memories?"

"I am all right now. I have a lot to thank Daisy for."

"I feel kinda jealous."

"Well, you know what to do."

"Kinda tricky. Anyway, about JJ..."

"So far, so good. I am a bit worried, though. He has a lot of contacts in the right places. He knows a lot about some people and their tax business, and I feel there is some dodgy business going on between him and some of them."

"How dodgy?"

"Don't know, really. But I have a feeling things are not on the level between him and some of them. I wonder sometimes if he owe them money. Anyway, where's your friend?"

"Visiting family in Brooklyn."

"How come I never see him? How come you never once introduced him to your little sis? I think something funny is going on that you want to keep away from me. If I am right, I am happy with that."

'Look at it this way—sometimes it's better you don't know some things." He patted his sister's arm reassuringly as the waiter approached.

Oliver told his sister to choose a steak meal, emphasising on it being 'rare'. Ruth replied:

"People in Jamaica don't eat raw meat and as you Jamaicans step off the plane you start talking about rare steak. What happen...it make you feel American?"

Oliver did not answer and to his sister's surprise, he changed to a well done steak, just as she had ordered."

Ruth and her brother spent a pleasant evening in the Manhattan restaurant, in hushed conversation for much of the time. He told her that he and his friend had shared the driving up from Georgia and that they'd done the trip nonstop apart from stopping for gas. They would begin the return trip as soon as he left the restaurant. She told him how proud she was of him that he'd finally accepted Daisy as his own and how happy it made both her and Daisy feel. She thanked him for agreeing to send money to his daughter from time to time, including Christmas and her birthday. She also told him he should make the effort to meet her. Oliver did not comment.

Oliver was a little angry when Ruth admitted to telling Daisy things she had agreed she would not reveal. This included his skipping his work contract, the fact that he had a new name and identity—although she said she had not revealed any details—that his wife was American, and that Daisy had siblings.

Ruth explained that Daisy was intelligent enough to understand why he could not travel freely and that she was also asking so many questions about him that she was finding it difficult to hide things from his daughter. She did not admit that she volunteered a lot of information in an effort to win Daisy's confidence and to make their relationship a bit closer. She was not sure she had succeeded. Still, she had no regrets about sharing the information; in fact, each time she did, she felt a load was taken off her shoulders.

In answer to a question, Ruth told her brother that she was not in any way worried that Daisy would pass on the information. As far as Ruth was concerned, many people had broken their contracts and in spite of what he thought, he was not important enough for the US government to waste its time looking for him. She went on to make the point that all he needed to do was to ensure he kept out of trouble so as to not give the authorities the opportunity to do any checks on him. Oliver, who had listened in silence to his sister, did not know that she'd seen a worried look on his face when she talked about keeping out of trouble.

"You know, if I was in your wife's place, I would want my children to be aware of their big sister. It's not fair, you know."

Oliver was pensive for a moment. "I can understand that. I am not heartless. But how do I explain it after all these years? Go on—tell me what I should say."

Ruth thought for a moment before saying, "I will have to get back to you on that."

When the silence seemed too long, Oliver clicked his fingers and said, "Tell me something—how much about your own situation have you told her? After all, she is just like your own daughter now."

"A lot. In fact, everything about the accident and the girls. If your wife was Jamaican, would you have told her about Daisy?"

"I suppose so." He then changed the mood with, "How come you never tie up with Marshall?"

A long silence followed before Ruth replied. "I am happy with JJ. Daisy is happy with JJ. That's what matters."

The siblings continued chatting throughout the meal. Onlookers would have thought they were clandestine lovers, the way Oliver kept looking around as they chatted in hushed voices and the way they laughed and touched each other's hands affectionately. Ruth updated her brother on what she'd learned from her occasional visits to Plummers, knowing that her brother had no other contact in the district. He asked about the family house and said that if he were to return to Jamaica, that's where he would live.

After a further period of silence, Oliver said, "So you still believe Soldier heng himself?"

"Don't want to talk about that again. What's done is done."

"Look, you can't hide from reality, you know."

"Stop. And promise me you won't talk to me about it again."

"All right. All right—no more. But you have to admit that if he didn't heng himself, it was a brilliant idea."

Ruth did not answer, and she did not lift her head, either. Finally she asked, "So why you get youself stuck into this security job? You can do a whole lot better."

"You looking down on me now?"

"No. I just know you can do a whole lot better."

"Status-wise, yes. But this job keep me away from a lot of people, as I mainly work on my own. I earn enough for the family, and it's a secure job."

"Well, at least you seem happy."

"I am. I am." There was a longer period of silence between the siblings again, and it seemed to be noticed by some of the other patrons, who were looking at them, the only black couple in the restaurant.

The silence was broken by Oliver. "Soldier get what he deserved. He was a nasty, wicked man. I wish I did it meself."

"What you talking about? Anyway, thought you promised you wouldn't mention it again."

"Look…you think it easy for a father to know that a grown man like Soldier doing them sort of things with his little girl? He should have been castrated."

"Keep you voice down. Where you think you are? And what if Soldier didn't do what they say he did?"

"Come on, sis. Don't tell me you taking up for him now. You know the man was a beast."

"But you don't know him."

"Know enough about him, though."

"Let's stop it. He's gone now. Daisy has put him behind her, and she is going to be someone great, though a bit late—oh, it rhymes," she laughed.

Nothing more was said about Soldier. They chatted and laughed throughout the rest of their meal. Just before he asked for the bill, Oliver began to fumble in his jacket pocket.

Ruth said, "Give me the envelope in the open. None of this cloak-and-dagger business. You draw more attention to yourself that way."

Oliver did as asked, and Ruth put the envelope into her purse. Ruth would be banking a part of the cash for him in Jamaica and using the rest for looking after Daisy. The pair remained in the restaurant for another fifteen minutes or so. Ruth asked a lot of questions about Oliver's family, and Oliver asked how Daisy was getting on. Later, when the cab pulled up by the restaurant entrance, Ruth got in.

"To the Lightbourne Hotel," said Oliver.

"The Lightbourne Hotel," the driver repeated as the cab pulled away. Another taxi rolled up in its place, and Oliver got in.

On the third evening following Ruth's departure, JJ arrived home with Rogers. It was the first time Daisy had seen her papa JJ drunk. He slumped into the couch, and Rogers turned to leave. Daisy got up and began to loosen JJ's shoelaces, but she stopped suddenly. Her jaw clenched, her lips pouted, and her eyes widened. Both Rogers and Margaret realized something was wrong, and they looked at each other questioningly.

"What's the matter?" asked Rogers.

"Nothing. Nothing," said Daisy, regaining her composure and continuing to take JJ's shoes off before returning to sit at the little table.

Instead of leaving, Rogers took a second look at Margaret, who was sitting in the chair, and said, "You Mr. Clemence girl?"

"Yes," replied Margaret.

"You don't remember me?"

"No."

"I am Mr. Rogers. I own the nursing home."

"Oh…yes. I remember." She picked up a book and began reading.

"What's the matter with you? You have no manners at all. Here I am talking to you, and you bury you head in a book. Must tell your father about it." With that, he smiled his usual smile at Daisy and left.

The door had barely closed when Margaret said, "He is one of those nasty men, always putting his hand up girls' skirt. Staff can't stay at the nursing home because of him."

"How you know all that? Him do it to you?"

"I work at the nursing home?"

"How you know that, I say?"

"Because my mother used to manage the nursing home for his father, and once the father died, my mother decided she wouldn't take on the job of trying to protect the young girls."

"You still didn't answer me. Him ever do it to you?"

"Me? My father would kill him."

"Tell me something—you mean your mother know about it when the father was alive but didn't do anything about it?"

"She talk to the father about it all the time. But the son is just one of them rich young men who is spoiled by their parents. No responsibility. No training."

"You sound like an old woman. It's like listening to your mother. Not calling your mother old, you understand."

"You watch yourself."

"What about his mother?"

"She is worse. When Mr. Rogers died, she take off to go and live with her daughter in Canada. She had enough money stashed away, and she was getting embarrassed by her son's antics, so she just pick up herself and fly away."

"How you know so much?"

"Uncle JJ know more."

"You don't like him, do you? I mean Mr. Rogers."

"You better not like him, too. And remember I said that."

"I am going to make sure Papa JJ all right."

"Just remember what I said," Margaret repeated more forcefully.

"I'm going to see to Papa."

"I am sure Mr. Rogers know that I know all about him," Margaret added. Daisy didn't reply. She went to check on JJ, and Margaret went to the bedroom.

Daisy forced cushions under JJ's head and stretched his feet out on the couch. Satisfied that he was comfortable, she switched off the main lights, leaving the table lamp on, and went into the bedroom.

Margaret did not lift her head from her Bible as Daisy entered the room. Daisy sat on the chair at the foot of the bed. She was disappointed to hear what Margaret had said about Rogers, and she began to think of the times she had been close to him. She thought of the little hugs she used to get from him, the little treats she received and the butterfly brooch he'd given her a year earlier for her seventeenth birthday, which JJ had taken credit for so as not to upset her aunt. Most of all, she remembered the day she'd stopped by his house with JJ. She recalled how he had walked naked from his room on the way to the bathroom before apologizing that he had forgotten she was there. She didn't believe him.

After a few minutes of reflection, Daisy and Margaret discussed what to do about JJ. They agreed that leaving him in the chair was best. "I'm going to bed now," said Margaret. Her tone was not pleasant.

"Why so early?"

"Just seeing Mr. Rogers and seeing you smiling with him like that, I don't feel nice."

"What? You think me and him…?"

"I never said that. Anyway, JJ would kill him."

"How you like talking about killing so much? For a Christian, and one who just put down her Bible…"

"The Bible is full of stories about killing. Jesus himself was killed."

"Oh no. I am not going to get into any of that sort of chat with you tonight. Not tonight. No. Not tonight."

"Take it from me, Daisy. The way he was looking at you, I know him have plans for you. You mark my words."

Daisy did not reply. After a while, she began to understand why her aunt readily agreed that Margaret, her friend who attended a different school, could stay with her whilst she was in America.

Instead of relaxing and falling asleep, Daisy thought about what had made her hesitate when taking off JJ's shoes. The events of that day—the day she felt had changed her life—had come back to haunt her. She saw the piercing look from Soldier's eyes, the screwing-up of his face, the pouting of his lips, and his words: "Is what you call dis? You not learnin' a ting." She remembered the khaki shirt he held by the shoulders, pinched between the fingers and thumb of both hands. She still couldn't recall seeing the blow coming.

She had no idea how long she had been on the ground. She could recall Martha's voice and see her face staring down into hers. She remembered the words very clearly. "Daisy, can you hear me? Can you hear me, girl? Are you all right, Daisy?" The memory of the incident made her cry. Margaret, asleep, was unaware of Daisy's torment.

For the next few days, Margaret's words of warning about Rogers were like a challenge to Daisy. Every time she thought of getting to know Rogers better, she backed off because she felt she might one day run into Richard with him, and she didn't have the experience to deal with situations like that. She could not, however, get the idea out of her head. What she did not know was that Margaret had spoken to her mother about her suspicions and that her mother had spoken to JJ, hoping that JJ would warn off Rogers.

It was JJ rather than Ruth who encouraged Daisy to accept invitations to go to the cinema with her new friends, despite never openly taking credit for it. It was JJ who encouraged her father to play a role in her life, and although there was seemingly no emotional attachment, Daisy was content with the knowledge that she was accepted by her father and was now considered a Golding.

Grateful for the extra tuition she received, Daisy made very good progress. As she grew older, she appreciated that neither she nor her aunt ever mentioned the rape. She recalled having come close one Sunday afternoon on the way home from the cinema.

They had their arms locked as friends or sisters. Suddenly her aunt said, "You know something? I was thinking that I and Mr. Marshall could have…you know…could have had a life together." Daisy did not respond. "How strange life can be," her aunt added. They looked at each other and smiled. Daisy appreciated that life in Kingston was a good one for her and that she had every reason to smile.

As to her silence, Daisy wasn't sure whether it was because she did not know what to say or if she could not say what she wanted to say. She felt she knew why her aunt smiled. After all, she had married a well-respected man who held a good government job, and he was being courted by many of the businessmen.

Since the marriage, JJ put much more time and effort into Ruth's craft business. Daisy once heard Ruth complain to JJ that the business was creating too much work for her. Because of that, JJ involved Daisy more and more, and she proved to be a quick learner. She was happy with that because it meant she went out more with her aunt on visits to the hotels and helped with the basic bookkeeping that would be eventually handed over to JJ to tidy up. She also enjoyed the praise for the neatness and accuracy of her work.

THIRTEEN

(1955)

From the main road, the Dalbeattie house didn't seem that far away. The road, however, had so many twists and turns with parallel tracks that it took a while to get there. One could not enjoy the breathtaking view of the sea and the skyline without stopping. Such was the danger of going off track on the narrow roadway. From the house, the mass of the sea's different shades of blue was a sight to behold. At times it was as if the sea's lights were permanently switched on to flicker intermittently, differing in size and intensity as the distant waves broke at will.

Few would have known what was going on in Morag's head when the parties ceased. Unlike Jean Sanderson, she had no watercolour painting to occupy her time. She no longer read much, as there was no one for her to show off her understanding of the latest political and financial news, which now came to her a bit late anyway. She had at first put a lot of effort into understanding the herbal scene, paying attention to the remedies for colds and fevers and what would help wounds to heal. She even experimented a little, pounding lime leaves before boiling them to make tea in order to improve the flavour. She persisted for as long as her stomach could cope with it before giving up, accepting that the taste was just a little too harsh for enjoyment. She adjusted to the fact every hot drink was called a tea: bush tea from a variety of local plants, ginger tea, coffee tea, cocoa tea, and, of course, green tea. She was baffled when there was no explanation as to why Ovaltine was simply Ovaltine, without the word *tea* attached to it.

Having lost touch with all her relatives, her reaction to questions about them was met with the same answer: "You choose your friends. Your relatives are not always your relatives, so you are best rid of those you don't get on with." She used to have a longer version but found she often misquoted it, and so she settled for her own shortened version. She couldn't help thinking about her Aunt Eileen, her mother's only sister, at such times. Eileen had told her about the folly of thinking she could move into the middle- or upper-class society without being bruised. In her quiet moments when she should have been sleeping, Morag often thought about how nobody from her side of the family had been invited to her wedding. She'd sent Eileen a letter telling her about the wedding, making it quite clear that it was information and not an invitation.

When Morag began settling down in Jamaica, she wrote to her aunt, explaining how grand a life she was living. The reply was short and to the point: "You cannot saunter your way into the middle and upper classes like that. You have been on the other side of the fence. They all know that. It will not work. You will not be happy. You cannot be happy. You are on your own with no one to watch your back in that far-off place. You will regret it."

What irked Morag was, first, that her aunt did not start the letter with a salutation or even bother to sign her name at the end, even though the sender's name was clearly written on the back of the envelope and Morag knew her aunt's handwriting. Second, she had written to her aunt after the wedding, explaining that the letter about the wedding had been sent by her husband's family. She had a soft spot for Eileen, a teacher in the Scottish Highlands who had helped her draft her early job application letters. She had a sense of gratitude towards her. She was hurt.

Eileen was a prolific letter writer, and her views on any subject were respected by the rest of the family. Once Eileen took that stance with her, Morag knew it was curtains as far as the rest of the family was concerned. She vowed to make her stay in Jamaica a success. She would never, under any circumstances, return home with her tail between her legs.

By year's end, the extra lessons Daisy was having with Prentice came to an end. The craft business was not as profitable as it had been, and Ruth thought JJ was beginning to neglect his responsibilities towards Daisy. When challenged on the latter, JJ just shrugged it off with words that suggested that Daisy was a big enough girl now to take on responsibilities of her own, especially getting around and planning her study periods. He also reminded his wife that Daisy was never short of money for a taxi if things got difficult. As far as he was concerned, he was being responsible in teaching Daisy to be responsible.

JJ did not seem at all concerned that in recent weeks Daisy, like himself, had been coming home late more often than before and that she sometimes went back out without saying where she was headed or who she would be seeing. He was also unaware that on her return, Daisy smelled as if she had just taken a shower, leading her aunt to conclude that she had been spending time with male company. This speculation was compounded when, on those occasions, Daisy did not take her usual night-time shower before going to bed. When Ruth finally couldn't take much more, she cornered JJ and let loose.

"This girl is brazen. She clearly doesn't care what I think. She has no respect for me. She has no respect for you, either. You have given up on her. She has exams coming up, and instead of studying, she is out spending time with some no-good man from God knows where. She is a disappointment. She is reckless, totally reckless. God knows what's going to become of her. Why don't you talk to her? You scared of her? Be a man, for God's sake."

JJ did not respond, and that made Ruth even angrier. She was in torment. She wondered whether Daisy's late evenings were linked to JJ's late nights, but she was scared to ask a direct question, fearing that if the answer turned out to be yes, she would have no idea what to do. She even thought of getting someone to spy on Daisy from the moment she left school in the afternoons, but again she was scared of the possible result. She thought of doing the same to JJ when he left work, but she knew she couldn't do that either. She couldn't sleep. She ate nonstop. She stayed in more often than she was accustomed to. She cancelled appointments with her hairdresser without good reason. She was not supervising the business as she ought. She felt she was going off her head.

Ruth wondered whether adopting a more aggressive tone towards Daisy would get an answer—any answer. It was most annoying that Daisy never engaged in an argument with her, despite her pleas. "Just say something, Daisy," she would beg. "Say something. Anything. Talk to me. Why you treating me like this? Don't I have a right to know? Suppose anything happen to you—what do I tell my brother?" She regretted not saying "your father" and felt that everything she said ended up giving Daisy the upper hand.

Because of the rape, for which she still had a great sense of guilt, Ruth was afraid of driving Daisy to the point where the child might tell her outright that it was all her fault. Ruth had prepared herself for such a confrontation for years, but it had not yet happened. She had also prepared her answer, a simple, "Yes. I take the blame for it, and I am sure you know how sorry I am." She knew that it might not be enough, but she felt there was nothing else she could do to make amends. She was grateful that, so far, there had been no need for it.

She knew she should have been much stricter with Daisy, perhaps even threatening to send her back to Plummers. Instead, she was now doomed to a life of constant torture by this girl who she had set out to save from a life of pain and suffering. It made her think God was punishing her. She felt overwhelmed by what she saw as God's punishment and would ask out loud when she was alone, "What have I done to deserve this? You took my husband. You took my girls. I try to do good for this girl, and you find another way to punish me. Why? Why? Why?"

After these outbursts, she would head to the liquor cabinet and help herself to JJ's whiskey, despite her hatred of the smell. It was an impossible situation, and sometimes she just wanted to run away.

Ruth often wanted to shake up Daisy by telling her how, despite all she and JJ had done for her, she was just plain ungrateful, disrespectful, and behaving just as the people of Plummers would expect her to. She wanted to tell her that nothing would become of her if she continued to neglect her schoolwork and behave in that way. However, it was as if a clamp had been placed on her tongue so that her thoughts could not be transferred into words. She wondered whether Prentice could shed light on Daisy's whereabouts. Then, as suddenly as they began, Daisy's evening absences ended.

Instead of spending the time on her studies, however, Daisy began to take an interest in the craft business. She surprised JJ one day by doing an audit of what was selling well and suggesting they carry fewer items but more of those that sold best. As it turned out, the top two were the fan and the apron, both of which had high profit margins. When questioned about how the idea came about, she admitted she had been reading the economics books JJ had been assigned in his correspondence courses. JJ was impressed. One result of this new interest was that Daisy interacted more with Rogers, and in her conversations with him, she learned that JJ had been trying to get him to further his studies so he could contribute more to the management of the nursing home.

Travelling back from a night out of drinks, JJ made the mistake of telling Rogers about his recent gambling losses. Rogers took the statement as a cry for help. It was not the first time JJ had mentioned losing to him; it was, however, the first time he had said it with such a sense of dejection. To Rogers, it was the difference between hearing things were bad, and, "Bwoy, me mash up, you know." He knew his friend needed help. Since JJ had helped to prepare the accounts and knew the company's finances were sound, Rogers was content to advance him funds to cover his gambling debts, confident of getting the loan back.

"Anything I can do to tide you over?"

"No, man. I have a whole heap of people I can call on before I would need to call on you."

"Well, as you say—I am here. You know where to find me if I can help." JJ shrugged his shoulders but said nothing. Then Rogers changed the subject: "So tell me something—how come you let me down so with Daisy?"

"What you mean, 'let you down'?"

"You forget you promise?"

"What you talking about?"

"You say, 'When she turn nineteen, I won't mind, but you not meeting up with her in my house.' Well, she nineteen now, and every time I try to come by, you find excuse for me either not to come, or if I come, you fly outa de house same time. Even when I come early, you dress up ready long time, and you dash outa de house jus' so me no have reason to come in. I know you missus don't like me much. She jus' tolerate me because I am you friend. I think she have a ting against young men who have money, as if it is some kinda sin. You get me? I am on de right track, right?"

"Look, things and times change, all right? Daisy is more and more like my own daughter, and as a friend...too much complication, man. But don't you fool yourself that I don't know you sort things out yourself. It's just that, well, better you than..."

Rogers ignored the last comment and responded, "Ah. So you remember now. That's all right. That make sense. Look, not because I not educated like you, you going to try and make a fool out of me. That's all."

"I notice you didn't comment on the last bit of what I said," observed JJ.

"Now, what you expect me to say. I can't lie to you, and I can't, well, like, you know..."

"Just let's agree not to talk about it again."

Rogers made a fist and thumped JJ playfully on his arm without responding. JJ was stony-faced; he was regretting that he had started the entire conversation. Instead of being dropped off at his gate as usual, JJ decided that he would stop by Bruce's, his favourite patty shop, and then walk the short distance home.

JJ arrived home late, and both Ruth and Daisy were asleep. He walked aimlessly around the kitchen and the living room before sitting and eating a patty with a drink. After a half hour or so, he felt sleepy and gingerly opened Daisy's bedroom door. The light from the living room shone on her covered torso, and he stood looking at her sleeping form for a moment before going back to the living room. Then, leaving the door ajar, he returned to the living room, picked up a cushion, lay it on the floor just inside Daisy's room, closed the door, and was soon asleep.

Just before daybreak, Ruth stretched out an arm, expecting to find JJ beside her. She did not think too much of it when he was not there. She had grown accustomed to his coming in late in recent months, sometimes drunk, at which times he would sleep on the couch. She had assured herself that no other woman was involved. It was just that he could not walk away from a drink, and his friends had enough money to keep the drinks coming.

"Mr. Rogers, is JJ with you?" It was a call she hated making, letting Rogers know JJ had not come home the night before.

"No. I drop him off at Bruce's. Said he would walk home."

"I see."

"I will call you back in a couple of minutes," Rogers replied.

Ruth decided to alert Daisy before the girl found out about JJ's absence in some other way. She gingerly tried to open Daisy's door, rather than knocking as she would normally do. The edge of the door pushed into JJ's leg, and he let out a groan. Ruth kept forcing the door whilst calling out Daisy's name, thinking that Daisy had collapsed behind the door. The commotion woke both Daisy and JJ. Daisy was immediately aware that her aunt was at the door, but she couldn't understand why she could not get in. Then both realized that it was because of JJ.

It took a little while for JJ to get himself together and offer an explanation. He said he had felt he should be a guardian angel to his "little Daisy" that night, and so he had done just that. Ruth thought it was drunk talk and was angry with him for shaming himself in front of Daisy. JJ insisted he was quite sober and repeated very slowly that he felt he should be a guardian angel for Daisy. He added that he did not care if Ruth thought it was drunken talk.

In the meantime, Rogers had phoned a couple of friends who he felt would be able to locate JJ, that is, if he hadn't been robbed or worse. Before he could call Ruth back, she phoned him to say JJ was home and had fallen asleep in the bathroom, where she had not looked before reporting him missing. She did not expect Rogers to believe her, but she also knew he dared not ask her any questions.

There was a very angry silence that morning between JJ and Ruth, as neither wished to engage in an argument in front of Daisy. Daisy, on the other hand, was intrigued as to why JJ had felt the need to guard her on that particular night. Did he believe that she was somehow at risk? And, if so, from whom?

Later in the silence at the breakfast table, Daisy felt compelled to act. Rising from the table, she said, "Papa, can I have a word?"

It was said in such a demanding tone that Ruth sat up as a child being told to do so by a teacher. Daisy left the table abruptly and headed to her room.

"Excuse me. I have to see what she wants." JJ rose and followed Daisy to her room.

Daisy left the door open for him and stood by her bed, arms folded, her body swaying from side to side. JJ entered and stood just inside the open door.

"You can close it."

"But…but…"

"Close it, Papa. Please."

JJ closed the door slowly and stood by it, his hand resting on the doorknob.

"So, what and who were you protecting me from, Papa?" Daisy asked, smiling.

"What you talking about?" Daisy said nothing. The silence forced JJ to continue speaking. "Look, I had a few drinks too many and, you know, I just decided not to wake up you auntie. I just make up the story about guardian angel. That's all."

"So why you didn't sleep on the couch like before? Papa, you know I know that nothing no go so. Something happened last night, yesterday, to make you feel you want to protect me. Thank you. Thank you." Then she added, "Is it your nursing home friend?"

JJ did not want to give any indication that he was discussing her with Rogers and so did not respond. He turned to open the door.

When he opened it, Ruth was standing there, barring his way. She had been listening. JJ looked her straight in the eyes and pushed past her. Daisy walked briskly to the door and shouted down the hallway after him, "Papa, I am going to study real, real hard. I am not going to let you down." She looked at her aunt and closed the door without a word.

Ruth was incensed. She spat out the words in a low voice. "Ungrateful wretch. Papa this, Papa that." Then, when the frustration got too much for her, she wrenched the door open and shouted at the top of her voice, "I won't let you down, Papa? It was my idea! To have you here in Kingston was *my* idea. I won't let you down, Papa? What about me? Who cares about me? What thanks do I get? The idea to save you from them big dirty men in Plummers was *my* idea! I won't let you down, Papa? So what? You feel it's OK to let *me* down? Ungrateful wretch!"

Daisy walked towards the door, and Ruth backed away hurriedly. Daisy closed the door without saying a word. Ruth turned, sobbing, both hands covering her face as she walked away.

Lying in bed that night, Daisy reproached herself many times over for having kept quiet over the years about the fact that Soldier had never sexually molested her even though she'd had many opportunities to set the record straight. She knew no matter how much she tried in her younger years, she would not have been able to convince anyone just how much she feared Soldier.

Often in her lonely, reflective moments, Daisy was convinced life had been unfair to her. After all, she was a victim of circumstances beyond her control, yet she was still experiencing bouts of emotional suffering. Was the physical torment she had endured not enough? She told herself over and over to stop punishing herself and accept that she did not have the ability to deal with a situation that she had learned was not unique in Plummers.

Some days she wished her mother was still alive so she could see how well she had turned out. She knew her mother would have been proud of her. On other days, she wished she could challenge her mother as to why she had not done more to protect her from the beatings she suffered from Soldier, because Geoffrey had made it plain to her that fateful night that he, like others, believed she was "doing it" with Soldier. Nobody knew how many times she had cried herself to sleep over the years.

Lying on her back with her Bible clutched to her chest and her eyes covered by a towel to block out the light, Daisy stretched out her legs and rocked her heels inwards and outwards, tapping out a rhythm with her big toes. It was a habit she'd developed to comfort herself over the years. She began humming her favourite hymn to the beat before falling asleep.

The following morning, JJ joined the many who wandered down to the wharf to see the ship *that was in port to pick up passengers immigrating to England. He had done this before, watching and mingling with the crowd, picking out those who would be going aboard later: the men in their hats and ties and broad smiles, the women in their crinoline skirts with handbags and white gloves.* On this occasion, however, he was wondering whether he had made a mistake in not making the trip years earlier. He was in a confused state of mind.

The Hamilton staff was ecstatic when Daisy achieved a Grade 1 pass in the Senior Cambridge examination. For a private institution that was known to accept students who failed to get into the major high schools, it was a ready-made advertising opportunity. In addition to her Grade 1 result, Daisy received the Mason Barratt prize for excellence in chemistry. Again, the school knew it could capitalize on her achievement.

Winning the prize brought Daisy her first real rebuke from JJ for causing a rift between himself and the interviewer after she was interviewed on the radio about the award. Unknown to her, JJ had set up the interview through a contact at the radio station. She felt the interviewer was trying to diminish her achievement by mentioning that she was a couple of years older than the majority of students who took the exam. That was a bit too much for her. As far as she was concerned, the honour was rightfully hers due to the hard work she'd put in. She felt that the interviewer's attitude was based on the fact that she was from Hamilton instead of one of the more prominent schools. In retaliation, she gave a big thank you to the company for providing the scholarship to the island—putting emphasis on the word *island*—and for giving her the opportunity to become the first winner of the scholarship. She said she hoped the company would retain its links with Jamaica for years to come.

Her statement embarrassed the interviewer, whose closing remarks, prepared by JJ, contained the exact words that Daisy had spoken, words she'd overheard JJ saying when he was discussing the matter with Ruth. They were both suspicious as to why a company new to the road-building programme in Jamaica should make such a grand gesture so soon. After Daisy's closing remarks, the interviewer was left with nothing to say but a lame thank you.

It was noted by those who understood the secondary education system in Jamaica that Mason Barratt had not offered the scholarship to those who had already passed their Higher Schools certificate and were therefore ready to enter university in the United Kingdom. Mason Barratt was instead viewed as being opportunistic, taking advantage of the publicity surrounding Daisy's achievement in the lower-level Senior Cambridge exams.

Since Hamilton did not have a sixth-form intake of its own, Daisy transferred to St. Marriott to complete her Higher Schools certificate in preparation for university. She remarked later that she had been well received and very well treated by the students of her new high school. She attributed it to their maturity.

FOURTEEN

(1958)

Daisy was experiencing her first summer in England, having started her university course the previous September. She was proud that she had conquered her fears about always being the eldest in her class at secondary school. She remembered how she'd wondered whether JJ and her auntie would see her decision as her being ungrateful if she decided not to go through with pursuing university studies. She now wanted to show them just how grateful she really was for the opportunity they had given her to attend not only a university,but a prestigious one as The London University, beyond her wildest dreams, and she asked for God's guidance in finding a way to make that happen.

She was pleased that she'd gotten through her first winter without the degree of discomfort she had expected. She, however, had spent more time in her accommodations than she'd wanted, unable to visit many sights she had promised JJ she would. He had listed the many things she should see as soon as possible so she would not be like so many before her, unable to talk much about London, and sometimes England, having spent most of their time in an unbalanced mix of sporting and studying, with sporting being too much. At the same time, he was at pains to point out that he was talking more about the young men. She promised she would not disappoint him.

London was a lot warmer than she had anticipated. Sure, she knew it would get warm in the summer, but she had never associated London with such summer heat. She was glad she did not expose her ignorance to anyone. There wasn't a cloud in the sky, and there was a gentle breeze, yet she chose to sit in the library instead of going outside like the vast majority of the students. She chose a seat that did not have anyone beside her so she could spread out her books as much as she wanted. She was going to enjoy the peace of the library instead of trying to concentrate over the din of the chatter that would have surrounded her outside. She thought those who were outside had great powers of concentration, or at least greater than hers.

After working diligently for some time, Daisy became aware of the young man some twenty yards or so away from her who seemed to be looking at her or at someone sitting close to her. As she was in the last row of tables with only the wall behind her, she thought he might just be looking at her. Daisy rubbed her neck as if it was a bit stiff and turned her head from side to side, stealing a glance to see who was the closest to her on either side that the young man might be looking at. On her right, she noticed two Indian girls sitting together, their heads buried in their books. On the left was a bespectacled blond girl who seemed angry with the world. Daisy resumed her work, pretending not to notice the young man, but she was becoming uneasy, as she could not concentrate anymore.

After deciding that the young man was looking at her, Daisy raised her head and stared right back at him with a frown on her face. Instead of turning away or lowering his glance as she had expected, the young man smiled. Daisy was surprised and found herself smiling, too. Just when she was contemplating what to do next, the young man picked up his books and headed straight in her direction.

He stooped in front of her, smiled, and said in a whisper, "Milton Swift." Daisy looked directly into his eyes, trying not to smile.

"So, what is it, Mr. Swift?"

"Milton Swift. I am a stranger here, too. From Sierra Leone. I guess you have seen me before. I have seen you before."

"Well, you guessed right. I am a stranger here, too, from Jamaica."

"And what about seeing me before?"

"I may have done."

"Well…you know, my grandparents came from Jamaica. Nearly all the coloured guys are from Ghana or Nigeria, and I just wanted you to know…you know…"

"You know, what?"

"Well…you know…why are you being so awkward? I am just trying to be friendly."

"Well, hello, Mr. Swift. I am Miss McIntosh. Daisy McIntosh." She started to laugh. Milton reminded her they were in the library and that she should be quiet. Daisy found herself relaxing more and more. She was secretly pleased that Milton had come over to her, but she was also surprised at her friendly reaction to him.

Milton was lean and bespectacled and had a short Afro. He seemed a couple of inches under six feet. Over the next few weeks, the two struck up a friendship that scared Daisy sometimes because of the ease with which she found herself being familiar with him. He told her he was from a wealthy family. It was just a matter-of-fact statement; he did not seem to be boasting, and Daisy let it rest. She thought it was the reason he had his own private rented accommodation in Earls Court, an area more expensive than most at the time. She was also impressed by some of the stories he told her about his family. For example, he had an uncle who at forty-two was the deputy head of the police force. He quickly added that he was well qualified for the job because of his law degree and the special training he'd undergone in the United Kingdom. He was more qualified than anyone else in the police force. The head of the force was soon to retire, so his uncle was expected to become his country's most senior police officer. The idea that having the right qualifications could get you so far so quickly impressed Daisy.

Milton's plan was to open his own pharmacy as soon as he returned to Sierra Leone. He wondered if she would consider joining him when she finished her studies. He explained that she would be at home in Sierra Leone because there were many people with Caribbean ancestry there. She would be guaranteed a good job. She would be in high society. He would also arrange for his mother to meet her when she was on her next shopping trip to London to restock her stores.

For the few months they dated, Milton asked few questions of her, and she volunteered little. He was content that she was tall and beautiful and that her father was a tax officer and her mother a businesswoman—a good background for a wife.

Daisy never really took him seriously in his talk about her going to Sierra Leone with him until he showed her a letter he'd received from his mother asking about her and at the same time reminding him about his responsibilities to ensure he got a good degree. She was both impressed and annoyed that he had written to his mother about her. To her, meeting parents was a serious thing, and in her mind she wasn't ready for that. Seeing the letter made her a bit wary. She recalled the stories she'd heard from some of her African colleagues, stories that implied that decisions regarding marriage partners were not as straightforward as Milton had said, as people from such classes went according to family decisions. So, Daisy reasoned, if Milton was from the type of family he described, there would have been somebody already set up in Sierra Leone for him.

Daisy enjoyed her time with Milton. He took her to restaurants and the cinema. He was not one for dancing much, and although he was invited to a few house parties by Caribbean friends, he rarely went. Whenever she found herself wishing he would go to some of the parties with her, she consoled herself with the thought that she was at least not disappointing Papa JJ.

She had no regrets about dating Milton that summer and up to just past the New Year. She found Milton to be kind and interesting. She managed to visit Kew Gardens and many of the other typical tourist attractions and was in a position to answer some of the questions JJ might ask her. She knew that although he himself had never been to Britain, he could talk about it as if he had. Such was his interest, backed up by reading.

If asked how the relationship ended, she would probably say that they'd both decided to concentrate on their studies, and their feelings for each other just died. But it was still a summer she looked back at with a degree of pleasure. It left her thinking about a possible life in Africa.

Daisy just missed getting a first-class degree. Though disappointed, she was more disappointed that JJ was not present with her Aunt Ruth at her graduation ceremony. She offered no excuses for not getting a first to maintain the standard she had set herself. As far as she was concerned, each phase of her life was different, with its own challenges, and all she had to do was her best.

Preston Hart was very proud of his achievements within Mason Barratt. He accepted that he got his break because of his army contacts, but the rest was due to his talent and the hard work he put in. When he told his wife, Jessica, that he was going to take up a post in Canada, she was not too keen on uprooting the children, nor did she want to contemplate the alternative—leaving them in a boarding school in England.

He had gambled on approaching Frank Bingham to make a case for not transferring him, relying on how sympathetic Bingham, overseas director and a major shareholder, was. That sense of understanding gave Hart false hope, and though his transfer was delayed for three months, he had to take up the post in Toronto.

Hart tried his best to persuade his wife that a Canadian education for their teenage son and daughter would be just as good as anything England had to offer. In the end, he was not sure what made her decide that Canada would be OK. He was just glad she'd agreed.

Hart could trace back to his great-grandfather, an artillery man, whenever he wanted to state his military pedigree. He often wished his line was the Guards. How he envied the words *the Guards* as they slipped off the tongues of the young men in conversation. It was not that he was ashamed of being in the Royal Artillery. Back then, he just knew it did not have the same sound. He recalled that as a young officer, it didn't catch the attention of the ladies as much as those who could say "the Guards."

He wondered how much help having been in the navy was to Bingham in his achievements. He also wondered whether his own military links had anything to do with his move to take up the post of human resources director in Toronto, being responsible for the Caribbean as well. He recalled the first meeting he'd attended on taking up his post. His deputy, Mark Lovell, was introduced as being a former Black Watch, *Canadian* Black Watch. Hart wanted to ask

Lovell if he'd ever played rugby for the Black Watch on a forces tour to England. That tour held bad memories for Hart because it was at an after-match drinks that his fiancé met and eventually went off with one of the Black Watch players. Although he had never told anyone, that was the real reason Hart did not want to go to Canada—the possibility that he might run into her. It did not matter that the vastness of Canada and the travel and work opportunities that existed worldwide meant that such a meeting would have been highly unlikely. Hart knew that. He was scared nonetheless. He had truly loved the woman, and she made him a laughingstock among his colleagues, who did not have an ounce of sympathy for him. His mother was no different, being more scathing in a letter to him: "I told you she was not your type. I told you, but you wouldn't listen. No good turning to Jessica now. She won't have you."

Years later, when he reminded his mother about the hurtful letter and the fact that he and Jessica had been married for many years, she replied that he was just lucky. He was content with that.

Hart spent eight years with Mason Barratt before leaving the company to join UM Technologies, a fast-developing drug company that needed a steady hand to run its human resources department. He remembered Bingham's words: "Hart, you are a good people's man. We will miss you. I wish you well."

On her return to Jamaica from university, Daisy did not get the call she was expecting from Mason Barratt as JJ said she would, and not being sure what she wanted to do, she started applying for jobs with the civil service, ending up in the education department. After three months in the civil service, the call from Mason Barratt came. She immediately thought they wanted her to work for them; an appointment was scheduled for her to meet with Bingham in a couple of days to discuss her future.

On relating the story to JJ and her aunt that evening, Daisy noticed that JJ did not seem excited for her, behaving as if he'd known about it all along. She had learned not to say the first thing that came to her mind, and so she kept quiet although she wanted to ask him about his involvement with the company in her behalf.

On arrival at the hotel, she was met by Bingham and the new Hamilton headmistress. They agreed on the details for Daisy's interview to join UM Technologies. On joining UMT, Daisy found that everybody seemed to know about her and the Mason Barratt prize. She hoped it would not distract from her performance or put too much pressure on her to deliver more than she was capable of. Soon it was clear that she was finding her feet and was someone to watch, someone who should be exposed to as many opportunities as possible.

Joining at the same time as Daisy were two Brazilian girls. They were all put in the same management-training programme. One of the tasks Daisy was assigned was preparing presentations about the company. She was very nervous about it at first but soon found that she was able to put into practice much of what she had been taught.

Disappointed at not finding her colleagues or those one level above her very accommodating, she decided to concentrate fully on her work. One day, the managing director, Abraham Carter, invited Daisy and the other management trainees to sit in, on the first part of a meeting he was having with his directors. Carter made it plain that he was after results. He implored the directors to identify a group of capable individuals and give them the tools to deliver the results. He was in a hurry. He emphasized that the competition was tough, but he felt they had the people and ideas to succeed.

After the management trainees left, Carter underlined the fact that to be successful and compete with the major drug companies, they had to aim at the third-world market and that having a few third-world executives rather than third-world folks hidden away in the laboratories would help. He saw it was a straightforward public relations exercise, which, if handled properly, could reap great benefits.

Following Carter's talk, one of the first steps was a recruitment drive at the universities. Not all the directors were keen on the idea. They felt that, being relatively unknown, the big drug companies would overshadow them. They had a go nevertheless. Daisy was a member of the information team, and that is how she met Gregory Hart, a chemistry lecturer.

Gregory was a long-haired, bearded, young white man of medium height. He had been thinking about quitting the teaching profession for something else, not knowing quite what. He had popped in to talk to all the visiting chemical companies that visited the university and had asked general questions about their products and markets, careful not to hint that he was thinking about a job with them.

When he visited the UMT stand, he found himself looking at the tall black woman talking with expressive hand movements that at times gave the impression she was handling a delicate flower. He was captivated by the passion she seemed to be displaying. He watched as the students seemed to be captivated by her, and he decided to move closer. It was then that he noticed her Jamaican accent, with each syllable being clearly defined. "That," he told himself, "is what has the students spellbound." He smiled and went his way. Unknown to Gregory, Daisy had noticed him, too.

Gregory phoned his father later that evening and asked him if he still thought it unwise for the two of them to be working in the same company. His father reiterated that in the normal scheme of things, that sort of thing happened from time to time; still, he agreed that his being head of human resources made things a little tricky.

Then he said, "Thought you had settled into being a university lecturer. What's brought this about?"

"Just getting a little bored, I suppose. It's just one of many ideas I have in my head."

"I see. What about the business idea, being your own boss?"

"Too stressful. Not cut out for that."

"Well, not too late to nip back home and join the army. Short-term commission would be just the thing to give you time to think. You're not too old, you know, and no longer having that young lady to worry about anymore. Think about it."

Thinking about it was the last thing Gregory was going to do. First, not having to think about his former fiancée, Charlotte, was not as easy as his father seemed to be suggesting. Second, being unshaven and growing his hair long was his way of driving the message home to his father that the line of artillery officers in the family had come to an end. He, at least, would not continue it.

Daisy's progress within UMT was steady rather than spectacular in comparison to that of the other management trainees. They were told they would still be doing a large amount of scientific work, but she was aware that her colleagues were getting much more lab work than she was. Whereas they were being invited to take part in projects by a variety of scientists, only Mr. Petrowski seemed to look out for her. She was grateful to him for that.

She was content with the variety of work she was exposed to and very glad to be working on the induction programme for new graduate employees.

Daisy was settling into her routine well, and enjoying knowing exactly what she would be doing each day she arrived at work. One morning, just as she was getting her usual coffee before settling down, Carter called out to her.

"Daisy, come meet Peter King."

Wondering who Peter King was, Daisy walked towards Carter, who was standing in the doorway of his office.

"Peter, Daisy McIntosh."

"Good morning," said Peter, who was seated at the coffee table. Carter motioned with a sharp movement of his head for Peter to stand. He did and offered a handshake. Daisy, not pleased with the discourtesy shown to her, nevertheless shook hands. They all remained standing.

Carter continued, "Now look here. We are going to have a few changes soon, and I think you two better get to know each other." Peter smiled. Daisy wondered what was going on. Carter interrupted her thoughts: "Peter is a consultant who will be helping us with the reorganization. He is going to need your help in understanding a few things. Anyway, that won't begin for another month or so, and there will be a meeting to brief everybody before then."

"Yes, sir," said Daisy, smiling and nodding as she left.

Within a couple of weeks of joining the company, Peter quickly took on the air of being in charge and so made a lot of enemies, interrupting managers and supervisors at will with no regard to what they might be doing at the time and the importance or urgency of it. The managers and supervisors complained among themselves until one decided to talk to Daisy about it. They told her that Peter had no time for their explanations as to why something he wanted explained or a conversation he wanted to have could not happen there and then. The managers and supervisors were obviously scared that Peter might report them to Carter as being uncooperative. They hoped Daisy might help Peter understand.

Daisy explained that she was not in a position to override anything Peter did, but she said she would see what she could do.

After a meeting with Peter, she was able to report that he had agreed to give the managers and supervisors more notice whenever possible, but he emphasized that he had deadlines to meet and that information like statistics should be readily available. He emphasized that part of his work involved looking at how quickly some data can be produced, and an immediate response to his requests was crucial to that aspect of the investigation. Daisy told him she understood and that she would explain such to the managers and supervisors.

Two weeks after the meeting, things were running smoothly, and Peter was content with his progress. Carter called Daisy into his office and told her that she would be working with Peter full-time on the reorganization project and that she would be getting a pay rise. The assignment was for six months. When Carter asked her if she had any questions, she couldn't think of any. Just as she was about to leave, he said, "Remember, you are *my* representative. Peter's report will have to be scrutinized. You will be part of that team. Good luck."

Daisy stepped out of the office walking tall. She had an opportunity to shine for the boss, direct. Then the reality of what she was about to do hit her. She had no clear instructions as to her exact role working alongside Peter. *Liaison* was not a good enough description for her role, especially with it being full-time.

Within a month, Peter had a team of three in addition to himself and Daisy. Daisy noticed that the team members were spending a lot of their time on telephone calls with other organizations, and from what she could hear, the conversations had nothing to do with the UMT project. She asked a few questions, and from both what they said and questions they refused to answer, she concluded that they were doing work for other projects they were handling and charging their time to UMT. She decided to investigate further. If she was correct, she would tell Carter and, she hoped, impress him even more. After all, he had told her she was his representative on the consultancy project. She had to act.

Just before leaving work the next day, Carter called her into his office.

"What's the matter, Miss McIntosh? You look somewhat nervous."

Daisy smiled. "Nothing is the matter, sir."

"Well, look here. I am flying off to Brazil in a couple of days, and I want you to know I am very satisfied with how you are handling things so far. All the directors have been told to give you any assistance you need. So don't be shy to ask for help."

"Thank you, sir."

"You are doing all right. You are asking the right questions. You are making sure the routine work and the consultancy proceed without too many hitches. You are not getting in the way. That's the main thing. If you need to talk to anyone, Adrian Sylvester is your man."

Daisy was quiet for a moment. She thought it was not the right time to tell Carter, especially as Mr. Sylvester was the finance director.

"Any questions?"

"No, sir. Thank you."

"I know this is new to you, but I want you to know that I have every confidence in you. You have come a long way, young lady. All will be well."

"Thank you, sir."

Daisy felt more confused than before. What did Carter mean by "You have come a long way?" Was he just talking about her work? Had he delved into the details of her background? The thought that he might know everything unnerved her to such an extent that she did not go to work the following day. She wished she had, however, because the number of telephone calls she received from colleagues seeking assurance that she was OK made her feel guilty for being at home. She scolded herself for being a bit silly.

Carter could hardly have been airborne when Adrian Sylvester, a balding little man with a permanent smile, called Daisy into his office. He beckoned for her to take a seat and immediately left the office, leaving her sitting there alone. Daisy kept shifting in her seat to make herself comfortable whilst she waited. On her arrival at the company, Sylvester was one of those she could not figure out. At first she thought he did not like her being there, but later she found that his attitude was the same with everybody. She wondered whether his staff alerted him to the fact that she had been asking questions about how the consultants spent their time. Sylvester returned some minutes later and apologized.

Then he said, "I know you don't quite understand how things work here. So I'll give you a few pointers." He explained that he was in charge of all things financial, that regardless of what Carter had said to her, the financing of the consultancy was *his* day-to-day responsibility. He added that he was appreciative of her concern about how the consultants spent their time, but any queries she had should be put through him and not through anyone lower down the line.

Daisy was expressionless. She was sure he had left her there alone deliberately, perhaps just abusing his power. She was not happy about it, but she knew she had to keep her peace. She wanted to ask a few questions but remembered something JJ had taught her: *"Gather your thoughts before you throw the words out there. You cannot drag them back."* She said nothing but "OK." She was struggling inside, however. She wanted to ask him how he saw her role, if he really wanted her to be bothering him every time she had a query instead of one of his managers, whether she was wrong in asking the questions she had asked, and what he thought of her asking those particular questions. Then, just as quickly, she realized that what he was really saying was that she should not ask questions about the funding of the consultancy.

In the weeks that followed, Daisy kept her head down and worked diligently with Peter, concerning herself only with work as it related to the reorganization. She endeared herself to the managers, whose day-to-day work suffered far fewer disruptions as the project got underway. In the end, she was commended by Carter for her work, including the briefing on progress she gave at a directors' meeting.

Life in Canada was a little different from what Daisy had hoped it would be. Her experience at university in England told her she could have fun among fellow Caribbean folks. "Meet a trusted one, and soon there will be a party or two to meet others," she had learned. But it wasn't quite that easy in Toronto. First, they didn't live in tight groups as they did in London, and second, most of the women in the families she came across, including those in the church community, did not warm to her as she had hoped. She was not sure of the reasons. She began to secretly hope the long-haired lecturer would phone and ask about her or find an excuse to bump into her somewhere. In the end, she decided to just buckle down to her work and take trips back to Jamaica as frequently as she could.

FIFTEEN

(1966)

On her more recent visits to Top Ground, Daisy had been able to look Mr. Mills in the eye and watch him look away. Geoffrey was different. He would always look at her with a half smile, a sense of satisfaction, a sense of achievement that unnerved her, irrespective of her outer appearance. She was also aware that he had turned into a so-called man of the people—a man who did not let having failed to become member of Parliament by a few votes dampen his spirit. He was a hero to his supporters. He had helped put Plummers on the map in a positive sense, replacing the negative image cast by Luvvy's murder.

Daisy thought how nice it would be to expose him for what he was. Then, just as suddenly, she realized she was in the same position as the night it had happened. She was in the dark. She did not see his face. She told herself the easiest way of dealing with him and the incident would be to avoid seeing him. She could achieve that by visiting Plummers less often. But then again, she felt she would be playing into his hands. She decided she would not let him torment her. She had done nothing wrong, so why should she be punished? In fact, why should she punish herself? No. That would not be her way. She would hold her head high. She admitted to herself that Geoffrey was the one person she hated. Despite her attempts to abandon the word *hate* from her mind, she secretly wished him dead. She wished he would burn in hell.

Mrs. Burrell-Salmon was chosen to give the address on Old Students' Day in keeping with the tradition of selecting individuals who had proven themselves in their professions or the community, people whose adult lives were shining examples for others to follow.

She was a businesswoman extraordinaire, moving into a field dominated by men and developing a successful company that hired out building machinery, including cement mixers and excavating equipment. She did this even though her husband, a pharmacist, was at first lukewarm to the idea. He did not know that she had been paying attention to her father, who ran a fleet of buses, and that she had failed in trying to get him to diversify into construction, which was to her a lucrative business.

When Mrs. Burrell-Salmon said she could not deliver the address because of overseas business commitments that had come up suddenly, the members of the school management board had a heated debate in their effort to come up with a suitable replacement. It was not that they did not have suitable candidates. It was just that they automatically wanted to give first consideration to those who'd been considered when Mrs. Burrell-Salmon was first approached.

Unfortunately, the unsuccessful candidates had been made aware that they had lost against Mrs. Burrell-Salmon, so when approached, every single one declined, making it known they had no intention of being second best. That breach of the management's privacy principle was a disappointment to the board. They speculated who the culprits were, weighing up the friendships that existed between different members of the all-female board and the individuals concerned, but they never did find out.

The process of getting a replacement so the event could go ahead as planned became more heated when they had to select someone who had not previously been under consideration. They also found that pressure to hurry things along was being put on them by a government minister with links to Mason Barratt. In the end, pressure was put on the head to contact Daisy McIntosh, who was credited with gaining the school more applicants and better-qualified applicants in the years immediately following her winning the prize.

Many felt they were being pressured to consider Daisy for the wrong reasons, and there were threats of resignation. One member stated that at age thirty, Daisy had too many youthful years ahead of her and so could still do all sorts of despicable things to bring shame on the school. She pointed out that the risk of a person bringing disgrace on the good name of the establishment after making an address was the very reason the policy of bestowing the privilege on a mature person with a sound track record had been established. Another member pointed to a court case that had occurred a couple of years earlier in the United States in which a former student of one of the more famous high schools went to prison for hiring a hit man to kill her mother-in-law so her husband could inherit a fortune. She said that though the woman was mentioned as an old girl of the school, it did not harm the school's recruitment the following year. She also made the point that people were mature enough to recognize that a school could not be held responsible for the acts of its former students, even though it quickly took credit for the good they did.

Despite the harshness of some of the discussion, Daisy, who was still working in Canada, was invited, and she immediately accepted. Daisy suspected that aspects of her background may have been known to some whilst she was at the school, Soldier's suicide included, as it had been reported in the press. At the time, the things that were of interest to readers were the presence of the soldiers by the river and the fact that a statement had been taken from them, plus speculation about why they were at Dalbeattie and questions about how they got to know Morag Sanderson and much else. She was fully aware that although, having been a child, she was not in any way involved, people tended to look down on the children of those who were involved in such things. She also knew that the folks in Plummers were thinking that her aunt had rescued her from a dull, dead-end life and that she should be grateful for the chance she'd been given to become famous by winning the island's Mason Barrett prize.

After entertaining such thoughts, Daisy wanted to shout from the hilltops, "No. No. No. I never had sex with my stepfather!" The fact that that seemed more important to her at that moment than being raped by Geoffrey confused her. She wished he could be present to see her on the dais, to hear her words and witness the adoration she would be getting. She wished she could see his face at such a moment.

She put her hands over her face and blew hard, as if exhaling daemons from her lungs. She then looked in the mirror and spoke to herself: "Tomorrow, you, the country girl who liked to 'play high,' as some of your Kingstonian classmates sometimes said of you, you are going to be the star. Tomorrow those who did not find a lame excuse to absent themselves because it is you, Daisy McIntosh, who will be giving the address, who will be looking down at them from the dais, they will be listening to your words of wisdom, words of appreciation, words of inspiration to the current crop of students. Tomorrow, you, Daisy McIntosh, you are going to be a star."

After a few seconds, because of her Christian beliefs and her fear of retribution, she immediately scolded herself and said aloud, as if some distant voice was commanding her to do so, "Be humble, my child. Be humble. Hatred requires more energy than love. There is only so much energy about. Be humble."

Anxiety, fear, excitement—all these emotions were keeping Daisy awake. She began to doubt that she had done the right thing by rejecting her aunt's offer to stay with her in her room, just offering company so she could relax and help her focus on the positive. She wished she had accepted. She wanted to be little Daisy again. She wanted her aunt's reassuring arms around her as they had been the morning after Geoffrey. She wondered how her aunt would react if she knew how grateful she was for the hugs that followed, in spite of having to endure the beating first. She had often told herself it was worth it, but she would of course never admit such a thing to anyone.

She reflected on what she had read and had been told about marriages and births related to her classmates and felt a mixture of happiness and jealousy. She remembered how, when she decided not to visit Richard anymore, it was because of a voice that came to her in the dead of night. She wished she was like those who could go up in front of a church audience and share their inner thoughts with strangers. She wanted to find an answer to the question, "When did you get to know Jesus?" It was something her friend Margaret had asked her when she professed that she was on the way to being a true believer. It was a question she did not understand and so could not answer. She considered herself intelligent, yet she struggled with what seemed such a simple, straightforward question. It was a question that stood in the way of her taking that extra step towards an understanding that would make her more like Margaret.

She thought of Margaret, now a doctor in the United States, and wondered how she was able to know from such a young age what she wanted to do, how she was able to be so focused. As if a voice commanded her to do so, Daisy turned her thoughts to the address she would be making. She picked up the copy of the 1838 proclamation that had ended slavery.

She wondered if she should defy her aunt and Papa JJ and refer to it as she had planned. She thought of Jamaica's independence four years earlier and the euphoria and pride that came with her island's being a recognized independent state. She wondered how things might have been had the idea of a West Indies Federation become a reality, as JJ had told her it should have been. She realized that all those thoughts of nationhood would have remained dormant in her mind had it not been for the imminent opportunity to share her thoughts with others.

It seemed to Daisy that it was appropriate to draw attention to the emancipation document in her address. JJ had explained to her that Hamilton was not like the big high schools that could pick and choose their students. The school had to accept almost any student it could get, and so the last thing it would want to do is alienate the white ones. In his view, making the emancipation a point of reference could put off a few and harm the intake, especially those from Canada, Venezuela, and the Cayman Islands. She understood the argument, but she was so fired up that she decided she would make her decision on the night of the address, whether to include the reference.

She also wanted to remove from her memory the short, wild period before her Senior Cambridge exams. She knew JJ was very proud of her. He'd restored her faith in the decency of a grown man around a young girl who was not his blood relative, but she restricted her new-found trust solely to him. Still, he had released her from the prison of mistrust that had engulfed her.

She knew her aunt Ruth was equally proud of her, even though she did not express her feelings as JJ did. She wondered if her aunt's lack of expression had anything to do with the loss of her own daughters, and she hoped her aunt would enjoy Old Students' Day and demonstrate her pride in her as she would have with a daughter of her own. She wanted her aunt to let go, to free herself—to be like her Papa JJ and just smile and laugh and show her emotions a bit more.

Daisy's plan included departing from custom and not restricting her speech to talking about the school, past and present teachers, and fellowship. She wouldn't just give a pep talk to the students, giving thanks to specific teachers and extolling the virtues of hard work and dedication and making sacrifices now for greater achievement in the future but still enjoying the wonders of childhood and fun growing up. She would instead find time to discuss treasured friendships of childhood, of those less fortunate. She would mention Martha, who had taught her to sew and who was like a mother to her in her youthful years. She would recall, silently, the times she'd rescued her after she'd been beaten up by Soldier.

It was not long before Daisy had a sudden strength and joyfulness about herself. She got up from the stool. She frowned and smiled and made mocking faces of joy and sadness at herself in the mirror before saying aloud, "Yes. Yes. Yes. I will show them!"

The prize that Daisy had craved the most at Hamilton was being head girl. She was bright. She was pleasant. She was caring. She was not good at sports, but she was good at sewing and embroidery, things she taught others to do, and she had the support of a few teachers. She believed the so-called money parents influenced the decision that went against her, the country girl. She became bitter and told JJ that she was certain at least three girls, one the niece of the headmistress, had prior knowledge of some of the examination questions. When he told her to look at the exam results and the scholarship as better rewards, she dismissed his way of seeing things. Studying abroad and seeing the security that existed with exam papers reinforced her view of what she'd called foul play back then.

Staring at herself in the mirror, Daisy thought she heard her little baby brother, Clinton, crying in the room next to her. She looked around, closed her eyes, massaged her face, and sighed loudly. She found herself thinking of the day she'd met him for the first time since they'd parted in Plummers.

Clinton grew up with his mother's relatives in Manchester. He had a decent, though not spectacular, childhood. He was with a family who had grown-up children. He was like one of the family. He did not know much about his sister until he was about seven years old, and though Daisy often thought of him, she rarely asked about him. It was whilst she was in secondary school that she felt the need for a brother to talk to, like some of her friends had. She had such thoughts in spite of the fact that Clinton would have been far too young for any meaningful conversation. She was happy to be in touch with him now. It was JJ who took the initiative, taking her to visit him one day when her aunt was away in New York. All Daisy knew was that she was going on a day trip to the country, and it was not Plummers.

When they arrived, JJ said, "This is where your brother lives. The lady is Aunt Doris."

Daisy did not react. He was about to speak but then changed his mind. His eyes were fixed on her face, but she kept looking straight ahead. They sat in that uneasy silence for about two minutes, though it seemed longer. The silence was broken when JJ left the car, cupped his hand, and washed his face from the standpipe.

Daisy began to look around. She noticed that the house was the first past the cane field and that the next was a little way from it. It looked isolated, with the cane field on one side and a bare, ploughed field on the other. She tried to imagine what her brother looked like. She wondered who Aunt Doris was, what she was like, and what she knew about her.

JJ's return to the car coincided with three little boys, barefooted, but otherwise very neat and tidy in matching blue shirts and kaki short trousers, being led by Doris down the path from the house to the gate where the car was parked. JJ leaned forward and whispered to the driver, and the driver got out and walked a little way from the car. Then he peed in full view of them. Aunt Doris appeared to be about seventy years old, dressed as if she was going to church with her wide brimmed hat and red shoes. She ushered one of the boys forward and JJ opened the door for Daisy to get out.

"Clinton, say good morning to your sister Daisy," said Aunt Doris. Daisy smiled at Clinton, but he just stared back at her. She cupped his chin in one hand and rubbed the top of his head with the other. She found the experience a bit strange. There was no emotional contact. Clinton did not look like her mother or Soldier. It was as if she was dealing with a total stranger. She suddenly remembered to greet her Aunt Doris, who, like Clinton, instead of speaking, just smiled.

After a few minutes, she learned that the other two boys had been taken in by Doris, her mother's sister. They looked like they were well cared for. Daisy noticed JJ fiddling in his shirt pocket, and she watched as he handed Aunt Doris an envelope. Something about the silent passing and receipt told her it was something they were accustomed to. She decided not to ask.

Years later, Clinton did well enough at school to get a job with the Port Authority in Kingston. He was now twenty-two, and they kept in touch occasionally. He told her he was a bit uncomfortable with her type of people, not in a bad sense, but rather in the social sense. They kept their distance but were quite friendly to each other on the few occasions they met in adulthood.

SIXTEEN

JJ was finding it difficult to come to terms with the retirement that was facing him. He managed to hide his fear and appear cool and calm for his beloved Daisy, but the strain of doing so was taking its toll. In addition, he no longer had the confidence he once had as he rapidly lost influence, as younger work colleagues gained modern specialist tax and business qualifications and became the sought after 'private' advisers. He soon found that only the much older business associates seemed to value his time-served experience. As his 'outside' income dwindled, he found he did not have as much spare cash for gambling on the horses as before, and his whole social world began to crumble. Worst of all, his friend Rogers had less time for him as well.

What really hurt JJ was not that Rogers was being unhelpful. After all, he always sent a car to drop him here or there if he could, and on occasions he would allow him to use the taxi firm the nursing home had an account with. The fact that Rogers seemed to be avoiding spending social time with him was what hurt him most. He thought Rogers should at least be grateful for his introduction to Daisy. He also knew Daisy was aware of the change in the relationship between them, but he was not going to sulk. He was not going to behave in any way to distract from the happiness of her big day.

Ruth's social life, on the other hand, had taken an upward turn. She had become involved in local politics and met some interesting people, which caused her to spend less social time with JJ. She was content with the new setup.

The Old Students' event was being held in a hotel by the waterfront. Many thought it was because it was not the peak tourist season and therefore not costly. What they did not know was that Mason Barratt was footing the bill in exchange for publicity. The company would feature the event in its annual report with pictures in order to show its philanthropic side. The company hoped it would help them curry favour with other Caribbean governments with whom they were negotiating contracts for airport and road-building projects.

Old Students' Day was like a government or movie event, with well-dressed people milling about and flash cameras going off all the time. There was a sense of excitement in the air. As folks began to arrive, young women with clipboards cornered those soon to be photographed or already photographed and asked for their names and a little background information. There was an emphasis on noting the names by which guests had been known at school, just in case a name had changed through marriage. Some of the guests wondered whether they had come to the right event, such was the professionalism that was evident.

Unlike previous Old Students' Days, during which folks had time to mingle before settling down to listen to the opening remarks from the head of school, this time, the emphasis was on getting everybody seated early. Many were not pleased with that. There was mumbling that the ceremony would begin with many people absent because some would be coming just for the speech, which they expected to start later. Unusually, however, nearly everyone was in the hall by the time stated on the programme.

"We will begin in two minutes," came a bellow through the loudspeaker, with a high squawk at the end of the sentence. Daisy looked at JJ and smiled. She was nervous, and it showed. JJ tapped her on her arm to assure her that all would be well.

About five minutes went by before another message went out over the loudspeaker: "Sorry for the delay, but we will be starting in a moment." There was frantic changing of seats behind the first two rows of reserved chairs as friends moved to sit together. Daisy was at the end of the front row, with JJ beside her. She returned the smiles and greetings of everyone who came up to greet and chat with her, though she did not recognize many of them. The hum of conversation was interrupted by a loud clearing of the throat over the loudspeaker by someone who was out of sight. Then the lights dimmed, and three women in long, flowing gowns walked onto the stage, singing the school song. Everyone stood, and those who knew the song joined in. Small though it was, Hamilton was putting on a show to rival those of the larger, better-known secondary schools.

At the end of the song, there was loud applause. Next came a short welcoming speech by the head girl instead of the headmistress. This was a change Daisy had pushed for. She looked at JJ and smiled. She had succeeded in having her own way to make the day a students' event, when even JJ and her aunt had said the school would not agree to it.

After mentioning the distinguished guests and paying tribute to Mason Barratt for funding the scholarship all those years ago, the girl introduced Daisy to polite applause. She went to the microphone with her notes and found that she was much more nervous than she had expected. As planned, she tried to make eye contact with JJ. However, peering into the dimly lit audience, she found it difficult to pick out individuals.

She laughed nervously and began, "You know, I spent a long time preparing these notes, but standing here tonight, seeing all you wonderful people—and forgive me for picking out the current crop of young ladies studying hard to achieve what many of us have already achieved and more—I do feel a need to deviate from my prepared remarks. It's not that I am abandoning the essence of what I had planned to say, it is just that—."

Before she could finish, Mrs Jones, the headmistress, a very tall, slim lady who seemed to demand attention by her very appearance, walked over to her with a piece of paper in hand. She whispered to Daisy, then took over the microphone: "We are pleased to announce that Mr. Geoffrey Marshall, adviser to the minister of agriculture, was able to get away from his meeting and join us. Some of you might not know this, but Mr. Marshall hails from the same place as Miss McIntosh." There was applause as Mr. and Mrs. Marshall were led to the seats in the front row, across the aisle from where Daisy had been seated. The headmistress smiled at Daisy, nodded for her to continue, and drifted away.

Daisy gave a nervous smile in return and started to cough. She took a sip of water, but the coughing did not stop. The coughing continued to such an extent that everybody seemed to be murmuring their concern. JJ dashed onto the stage to comfort her and whispered, "You can't stay on the podium like this. You must leave." She squeezed his hand in agreement as they were ushered behind the curtains at the rear of the stage, where she was immediately surrounded by members of the hotel staff. One person fanned her face whilst another held a glass from which she took sips of water. After a minute or two, Mrs. Jones appeared backstage. She whispered to Daisy, who nodded in agreement. Mrs. Jones then returned to the platform and assured everyone that Daisy would be OK, but, so as not to delay the programme, she had agreed that the head girl, Clarissa Gomez, would read her original speech. On hearing the announcement, JJ looked questioningly at Daisy, who nodded. JJ smiled and went back to his seat, leaving Daisy sitting on the chair in the care of one of the hotel workers.

At the microphone, Clarissa waited patiently for silence, but the murmuring in the audience continued. It was only when Mrs. Jones walked purposefully to the dais that there was a hush. For her part, Clarissa read the speech with gusto, and there was a tumultuous applause at the end when she implored the current crop of girls to stick to their dreams, come what may.

It was, by all accounts, a splendid Old Students' Day speech, marred only by the coughing fit that beset Daisy and prevented her from delivering her words herself. Everybody sympathized with her. The newspaper reporter made a point of telling her she would get good coverage the next day. Daisy herself posed for many photographs with various people, many of them strangers. At one point, she worried about what might happen should Geoffrey want to take a picture with her. She was relieved when she learned that, due to urgent business, he had left and would not be attending the closing reception.

At the reception, Daisy chatted with the managing director of Mason Barratt as well as with Mrs. Jones and several past students and well-wishers. She noted that only a few of her fifth-form classmates were in attendance, and, of those, few bothered to come over and chat with her.

Mrs. Jones was basking in the glory of the evening. She was told that there had never been an Old Students' Day like it. She was disappointed that she had not had time to talk with Mr. Marshall and Daisy together, but she was grateful, nevertheless, that he had taken the time out to attend.

When most of them had drifted away, JJ suggested to Daisy that they leave. He orchestrated their departure, making sure she said formal goodbyes to the Mason Barratt representatives, the press crew, and Mrs. Jones and Clarissa. As to how things went, JJ assured Daisy that, despite her coughing fit, the evening had been a success. He was happy that she had done her part and had left out the emancipation reference, and Mason Barratt and the school board were very happy as well. Daisy looked questioningly at him. She did not understand his linking of Mason Barratt and the school board in that way.

During the taxi ride home, JJ and Daisy were silent. She remained puzzled by JJ's comments, which suggested that the event had been a massive public relations exercise for Mason Barratt instead of the usual celebration of the school and its students. Her mind was full of questions. Had her aunt told JJ about what Geoffrey had done to her? Did JJ know that the coughing fit was faked to buy her time to decide how she was going to cope with Geoffrey's presence? Did her aunt know that Geoffrey would be there? If so, had she faked her own illness to avoid him? She looked across at JJ and smiled. He smiled back.

"You all right?" he asked.

"Yeah. I'm all right. I got my points across."

"Did a good job, that head girl."

"Yea, she read it with passion. It was as if she had read it before. It was kinda strange, listening to it."

"Well, you did at one time say that is how you wanted to do it. Must be careful what you wish for."

"Um…." The silence resumed as she remembered how she'd wished for Marshall's presence to hear and see her.

Whilst the Old Students' Day celebrations were going on, the five ladies were having a great time, chatting and laughing. The serious business was partly behind them, and so they let down their guards and became less formal, having a break, although still addressing each other as Mrs. This and Mrs. That. Miss Knight, the hairdresser, was the exception.

The women discussed a wide range of topics, from who had the most control over her husband and how it was achieved to tips on how to make the best rum-laced cake. It was an unusual conversation; people like Mrs. O'Neil and Mrs. Lopez would normally be reserved in such company. Also, they didn't have a clue about doing any of the things they were giving tips about. They each had maids (yes, plural), yet for some reason, they were keen to listen and even ask questions.

"Mrs. Hunter?" It was then that Ruth realized she was somewhat in a dreamworld. She had not heard what preceded her name being called. She raised her head.

"Sorry. My mind was on other things. What is it?"

"You sorry you not there?" asked Mrs Lopez.

"To tell you the truth, yes," she replied with a sigh.

"She will be all right. No point going to something like that and having to get up every minute, disturbing people in the process," replied Mrs Lopez.

"It would be like being in an outside seat in an aeroplane and being disturbed every minute as people want to pass you," added Mrs. Grant, the librarian.

"That's why it's first class or nothing for me," chipped in Mrs. O'Neil, scrutinizing her bone cigarette holder. You could hear a pin drop as she finished speaking.

"What? What? Why everybody looking at me like that? I am not the only one here who travel first class," she continued.

"Not all of us lucky enough to marry that well, you see," said Miss Knight, suddenly sitting up in the couch, as if doing so, would give her words more meaning.

"My dear, it is nothing to do with luck. It is a simple matter of who one meets in the circle in which one circulates," replied Mrs. O'Neil.

"No need for that," said Mrs. Lopez, who was a customer of Miss Knight's. The hairdresser herself did not feel a need to respond. Over the years, she had been privy to many of her clients' secrets, and she was proud of being in the circles in which she now moved. She saw herself as high-class, from a good family, and she knew most of them acknowledged that. She also credited herself as one who had elevated the art of hairdressing into a thriving business. Nobody could walk off the street into her salon. Her services were by appointment only, and only if she knew you or if you were well recommended.

Her clients were not quite the cream of society, but they were not far from the top. Yet some of them owed her money, and their husbands would be aghast at how much. When Mrs. Lopez once dared to suggest that she should come and style her hair at her home, Miss Knight flatly refused and invited her to find another hairdresser. The matter was never raised again, and Mrs. Lopez did not find another hairdresser.

Sensing that things might get out of control, Mrs. Lewis, the hostess, cut in: "Ladies. Ladies." Her interjection had the desired effect. With everyone quiet, she went into a speech, reminding the group of the purpose of the gathering: to identify and support a female candidate to run for election to the House of Representatives.

"Doris, you have to learn to talk to people like grown-ups, you know. You always behave as if you talking to your pupils. Come on, man," chided Mrs. Grant. They laughed, knowing that the two had known each other since childhood. Mrs. Grant continued, "And you know something, I still think Miss Levy fit the bill. Yes. She would be the ideal candidate."

"*Ideal* is a bit strong, don't you think?" said Mrs. O'Neil, to no one in particular.

Mrs. Lopez added, "Good...yes. She has done a great job behind the scenes at the party head office, and she is on enough committees to have influence. But I still think she is too young, and I don't think the men would vote for her. And without the support of the men, she wouldn't stand a chance. Also, it would be better if she was married. She doesn't look too well, either. We need a sturdy, mature, no-nonsense woman."

Realizing that all eyes were on her, Mrs. Grant laughed and said, "Yes, I am sturdy. I am mature. I am no-nonsense. That's as far as it goes."

"I will test the idea of Miss Levy with the party chairman. After all, Rose Leon showed it could be done," said Mrs. Lopez, whose husband owned a series of ice cream parlours, and was attending only because she wanted to keep up with the group who all worshipped at the same church.

"Mrs. Hunter, what you think?" asked Mrs. Lewis.

"Well, I really don't know. I am just...Look, please excuse me. I have to go. I am not feeling too well. I also want to be home when Daisy gets back."

"But...but..." Mrs. Lewis did not continue.

"I am sorry. I really have to go," Ruth insisted. Mrs. Lewis gave in.

"OK. I'll call your taxi." After the two women left the room, the others exchanged glances, no one wanting to voice the obvious question: what was going on with Mrs. Hunter? There was a lull in the conversation until Mrs. Lewis returned.

Walking back into the room, she asked, "So, where were we?"

Instead of an answer, there was a chorus: "Come on. Tell us, then. What's up with her?"

"She is just not feeling well. Tell you what, let's have some ice cream."

Mrs. O'Neil was not to be deterred. "Come on, Beatrice. What's up with her?" she demanded. "She was not well enough to go to the Old Students' thing, but she look well enough to me—and to the rest of us. So tell us—what's going on?"

"I can only tell you what she told me." And with that, she left the room to get the ice cream.

On arriving home, Ruth noticed that lights she had left off were now on. The purse she had started to open remained closed as she wondered what to do. She had not expected JJ and Daisy to be home as yet.

"Ma'am…I reach you gate," said the taxi driver.

"Come to the door with me. I don't remember leaving so many lights on."

"What? You might have t'ief in you house, and you want me to come wid you? I am not a policeman. I will drive you up the road to the police station."

Before she could respond, the front door opened, and JJ peered out. As the driver put the car in gear to drive away, Ruth said, "Stop. Stop. It's all right. It's my husband. He is home earlier than I expected."

"Just pay me, ma'am, and let me go. I don't want to be a witness to any t'ing between husband and wife."

"It's nothing like that," she replied. She paid him and headed up the short pathway to the door. The driver did not drive away immediately. Instead, he watched as JJ held the door open for his wife and they disappeared inside. In the living room, Ruth walked over to Daisy, who reclined on the couch with one leg stretched out on the seat and the other resting lightly on the floor. Her eyes were closed, and she seemed at peace. JJ went to sit on a chair nearby.

Ruth glanced from one to the other. "What's the matter with you two?"

"What you mean?" replied Daisy, surprising Ruth, who had been expecting an answer from JJ.

"Well, you could cut the atmosphere with a knife."

"How did your meeting go?" asked JJ.

Daisy broke in before Ruth could answer. "Auntie, tell me something, did you know Mr. Marshall was going to be there?"

"What you talking about?"

"It's a simple question, Auntie. Did you know Mr. Marshall was going to be there?"

Instead of answering, Ruth turned to her husband. "JJ, how come I am the only one without a drink?" JJ walked over to the cabinet and poured a small glass of ginger wine. Daisy sat up and stared at her aunt who made no attempt to answer the question. She watched as Ruth took her drink from JJ whilst avoiding her gaze.

"So, Papa," Daisy persisted, "no questions? That means you know Mr. Marshall was going to be there as well, right?"

"No, I didn't," JJ said unusually sharply. Then he added, "Anyway, what difference would it make if I knew? They can invite anybody they want."

It dawned on Daisy that her papa JJ might not know the full story of what had transpired between her and Mr. Marshall. "Well, he is a politician, and they like to get themselves into everything. Me and him being from the same district is not enough reason for him to get pride of place, though. That's all."

"So what's the big deal?" asked JJ angrily.

"You confuse me sometimes, you know, Papa. Sometimes I…never mind. I am relieved it's all over. Thank you very much for everything." With that she jumped up and hugged JJ tightly and gently let him go. Ruth, who was at first open-mouthed and seemed disapproving of the long embrace, broke into a smile as Daisy stepped back.

JJ continued to hold her hands, then smiled and said, "The speech was very good. No—excellent. Excellent. Extremely well received. No—delivered *and* received. You were great. I am proud of you."

Later Ruth went to Daisy's room and explained that she had never told JJ about the rape. She had kept her word and had not mentioned it to anyone. It was important to her that Daisy believed her. She volunteered, however, that she did mention that Soldier had beaten her up and that was the reason for deciding to have her live with them. Daisy was quiet throughout her aunt's little chat. At the end she said, "Thanks for that. I was wondering."

"I hope Mr. Marshall didn't spoil it for you. I really hope so. I just didn't know what to do. God knows I asked for guidance when I found out he was invited. Not going was the best I could come up with."

"No, he didn't spoil it for me," Daisy lied.

"Well, I think I'll have some rest. Goodnight." With that, she left the room.

The following day, the *Daily News* featured the school event, mentioning many of the people who had been present, particularly those who were past students or prominent in society. Miss Prentice, though having taken no part in the event, was also featured for her part in helping Daisy in her younger years. Daisy was a little put out by that, as she felt it would have been more appropriate to include Miss Prentice for helping her to win the prize years earlier. She knew JJ had had a part in briefing the headmistress and wanted to ask him about what seemed to be nothing but blatant publicity for Miss Prentice, who was now well established as a private tutor as well as serving as a board member of the school. She decided against it. As for Hamilton High, it was riding high on the publicity.

Daisy was pleased that the article simply reported that she'd had a cough and had been assisted by the head girl, who read her prepared speech. The price she paid, however, was that she had to share the limelight with Clarissa, the daughter of a banker from the Bahamas. The story was accompanied by two photographs. The larger was of Clarissa, and the other of Daisy. Ruth was angry that Daisy's photograph was the smaller, but Daisy was just pleased that it showed off her lovely dress and her curves. It was as if she'd known how things would go. She was content.

The reporting of the event on the radio and in the press upset many because it took a lot of the shine away from an event that was held at the American embassy that same night. On the society page, the report and sketches of the ladies' outfits were from the Old Students' Day event. It attained a level of interest that no one had envisaged.

Mason Barratt was pleased with the work done by its PR machine. The company had increased its scholarships in Jamaica to two per year, adding one for sports at a college in the United States. It was a notable thing for a British company.

The firm was disappointed that it had not been able to expand its contract work in Jamaica as much as had been hoped, but it was confident that the provision of the first scholarship and the associated publicity had helped it to win contracts in other Caribbean islands. The firm also made it known that it was committed to featuring the event in its corporate annual report. JJ did not think the likely expenditure would have justified the benefits, but he admitted to viewing the situation through a different lens than that of the company's public relations machinery.

SEVENTEEN

The clandestine meetings between Daisy and Rogers began whilst she was still in secondary school and continued on her return from university and on her holiday visits from Canada. In time it became a routine affair, as if they were simply safe with each other without a hint of commitment. Ruth and JJ acknowledged the relationship, but neither attempted a parent-like lecture or comment. Ruth wanted to say something but was afraid of upsetting Daisy, and despite her pleading, JJ refused to say anything to his young friend. He hoped that things would simply sort themselves out, and he was ready for any outcome.

Three months after the Old Students' Day celebration and during the many telephone conversations, Daisy told her aunt that she needed time to decide on the path her life should take. She said she was not sure that what UMT was offering was what she wanted. Ruth was sure that this was not the real reason and that Daisy was thinking about a return to Jamaica. She was convinced Rogers had something to do with it.

"Whatever you decide, my dear, you will have my full support," Ruth told her.

JJ, on the other hand, told her that although he was tempted to tell her to follow her heart, he couldn't help thinking she was being a bit reckless and suggested she take a little more time to consider her options before making such an important decision. Daisy surprised him by saying she had given it sufficient thought and that she would follow her heart. She added that she did not feel obliged to give a detailed explanation to anyone. After moments of silence, JJ told her he felt her reason was more than she was saying. She laughed and hung up the telephone without saying goodbye. JJ looked at the phone and shook his head. "Wow!" he said before hanging up.

In the six months Daisy was away, Ruth had sold the craft business, and JJ was a bit depressed due to his upcoming retirement. He had no idea what he was going to do with himself. It was as if he had just woken up and was told he was due to retire.

The ladies had failed to get a female candidate for their constituency, and Ruth was using her spare time a bit differently, mostly on learning a bit about commercial catering and volunteering with a group of ladies who were lobbying the government for work programmes for young girls who had little to do.

There was tension in the home as JJ wrestled with his depression. This was not helped by Ruth constantly reminding JJ that she'd told him years earlier to put some thought into his plans for retirement. She recalled how he did not want to talk about it, emphasizing that he would have no problem with money because of his very long service. Ruth was surprised that he could not think beyond the financial aspect of retirement.

Daisy was not too sure Rogers had any confidence she would keep her promise. After all, several years had passed since their first regular nights and weekends together, and when she suggested it was better that he did not attend the Old Students' event, his simple OK had her wondering whether he was still interested in her. She decided to be brave and come back from Canada to be with him. Together they would create a family. Together they would develop Pelican Nursing Home into a business that retiring North American and well-to-do local folks would clamour to use.

She was convinced she and Rogers could be a great team. Rogers had the money and local connections. He had curbed his wild ways, or at least that's what she believed. He mentioned that he did not want to be penniless and be a laughingstock to those who thought his mother was crazy to leave the business in his hands. He felt they were waiting to see him fail. He no longer valued his mother's opinion about anything. She'd left with a lot of the cash from the business, and in all the telephone conversations they'd had since then, she had not once asked him how the business was getting on. He had convinced Daisy that he was not doing it for the good of the family name. No—he had grown up. He had seen so-called friends come and go. He realized that he had to make something of himself, and at the age of forty-four, it was time.

Travelling in her business suit to South America, staying in top-class hotels, and being treated with the utmost respect as a representative of UMT is the picture that was laid out for Daisy by the executives. It was an attractive one. She thought about it and the alternative of a life with Rogers—developing the nursing home, moving on to bigger things like what Mrs. Burrell-Salmon had managed to achieve, and gaining respect from her own folks as a successful businesswoman. The latter seemed to be the bigger calling. She was confident she could put into place the marketing skills and strategies she had developed with UMT and from JJ and that she had the determination to rise above all she had been through to succeed. She knew she was ready.

"Roy," said Daisy, smiling as she spoke on the phone.

"Cowboy here," came the reply as he recognized the voice immediately.

"Guess what?"

"Yes, Precious?"

"Well…"

"Yes? Yes?"

"Well…"

"You mean to say?"

"Yes. Come and pick me up right now."

"You mean right this minute?"

"Yes. Right this minute." She laughed.

"Nice one. Nice one. Coming right now."

Daisy looked at the phone and smiled before hanging up. She was glad she had kept her word a few days earlier and telephoned him within a day of being home as she said she would. She had already decided how to break the news to her aunt and JJ.

Ruth was the first to return home that evening, and she looked quizzically at the pink envelope sitting on the centre table as she entered the living room. She also noticed that it was unsealed and not addressed to anyone. She walked instinctively to Daisy's room and noticed that it was bare of all her belongings. She walked back out and headed to the drinks cabinet, pouring herself a rum and coke. She opened the fridge for ice but closed it immediately and downed the drink, clenching her teeth and shaking her head from the burning sensation she got in her stomach. Then she opened her mouth wide and breathed out before sitting on the couch.

"Well, well, well. Guess it was destined to happen," she said before looking around the room, at the floor and at the ceiling, as if she was looking for a missing item.

The phone rang, and she let it ring out. It rang again. She picked it up and listened. The person at the other end was also silent. She hung up. The phone rang again.

"Yes, Daisy dear," Ruth answered.

"I knew you knew it was me."

"You are a big woman now. You didn't have to do it that way, you know. Rogers there with you?"

"Yes."

"So I take it you not going back to Canada."

"That's right."

"You let them know?"

"Yes."

"You are wasting a golden opportunity, you know. A lot of people will be disappointed with you, perhaps even JJ and the school. Boy, they will be disappointed."

"You going to wish me well?"

"Of course. Of course. I hope you will make it, you know, official between the both of you."

"So you haven't read my note."

"Oh God...no."

"All right, we will stop by later."

She was caught off guard to hear Daisy say "we," speaking for both herself and Rogers, but Ruth replied, "Of course. See you both later."

Had she read the note, Ruth would have known that Daisy and Rogers were planning to marry soon and that she had already advised her Canadian employers of her decision not to return to Toronto, citing the marriage as the main reason. She would also have been surprised that the wedding plans were as advanced as to the date and the place and that it was going to be a very private, quiet affair.

Soon after that first evening chat and with the wedding day fast approaching, Daisy decided they would meet with her aunt and JJ to have a chat about the plans. Ruth decided it would be at her home.

Arriving early and alone, Daisy said Rogers had to see someone and so couldn't make it. She added that JJ would not be there either. Ruth did not ask how come Daisy knew that when she, the hostess, did not. What she did not know was that Daisy wanted to give her a hand and restrain her from drinking too much to calm her nerves.

The early arrival upset Ruth's plans, as she wanted time to think. She wanted time to do just what she wanted and how. She was aware of Daisy's influence over her, and she was becoming uncomfortable with it. She felt that if she tried to hold her ground, the day would end in a quarrel, and she did not want that. At least, not on such an occasion. In addition to that, she didn't want Daisy to see her working from the notes and recipes for making sorrel drink, something someone like herself, brought up in the country should have been able to do.

To Daisy's surprise, when she arrived, her aunt did not have a drink handy and was busy in the kitchen.

"Shall I get you a drink, Auntie?"

"Good idea. Lots of ice." Without asking, Daisy poured ginger wine for both of them. Daisy realized her aunt was expecting something stronger, and they both laughed when Ruth screwed up her face on taking the glass from her. They toasted each other. Ruth emphasized marriage, children, and long life. Daisy concentrated on the word *friendship*, telling her aunt that they were embarking on a new relationship of friendship—good, lasting friendship. This surprised Ruth, who hesitated for a moment, looked at her niece, smiled, and nodded before drinking to the toast.

Over lunch of red snapper, sweet potato, rice and peas, fried plantain, avocado and vegetables, Ruth told Daisy how disappointed she was that the wedding was going to be such a private affair and how un-Jamaican it was. Daisy responded that she was in full agreement with Rogers since he found out that so many of his so-called friends were not friends at all. He simply wanted to start as he meant to carry on. Ruth pointed out that she was disappointed that with her business training she did not recognize that the last thing business people should do was alienate potential customers, and that was what Rogers was doing, even if he did not realize it. Daisy's response was that to them, their business was the nursing home, and their wedding was their private concern. Ruth told her that she probably spent too much time with non-Jamaicans, hence her attitude.

Ruth was unhappy that the wedding was going to be at a north coast hotel and that Rogers and Daisy would catch a flight later that afternoon for a honeymoon in the Cayman Islands. As far as she was concerned, that sort of wedding was not for Jamaicans. Daisy reminded her that apart from the honeymoon, her marriage with JJ had also been a very private affair. Ruth's explanation was that it had been that way because they were both married before.

Ruth was about to continue when she hesitated, laughed, and asked, "What was that word again?"

"What word?"

"Forget already?"

"What?"

She laughed. "Let's drink again to *friendship*," said Ruth.

Ruth wanted to ask if Daisy had contacted her father about the wedding and whether he would be there. Unsure as to how Daisy might react, she shelved the idea and asked instead if Mrs. Rogers would be coming. She was very surprised when Daisy said no. Daisy did not tell her that when she suggested going to meet Mrs. Rogers in Toronto, Rogers told her it wasn't a good idea. In fact, his exact words were,

"People poison her mind against you already, and it would be like hard work to win her over. One day we'll do it together."

The reason put forward to others for Mrs. Rogers not coming was that she was not well and flying would make her condition worse and that Rogers had no intention of delaying the wedding just so his mother could attend.

Instead of commenting on Mrs. Rogers further, Ruth asked, "Told your father?"

"You know I'm having lunch with him tomorrow."

"You know full well I mean *your* father, my brother."

"How many fathers do you want me to have at my wedding?"

Ruth did not answer. She decided not to even ask if her brother was aware of the wedding. When asked what she would do concerning her friend Thelma and anyone else in Plummers, Daisy replied that once back from the honeymoon, she would be writing to Miss Martha and Thelma and that she would also visit them with her husband one day.

"And just in case you are wondering, my brother will be there," said Daisy. Ruth smiled and said she was glad to hear it.

"What about Margaret? Will she be there?"

"I am afraid not." She did not say she had not invited her, and Ruth did not ask why she would not be there.

Part of Ruth's plan had been to mention her plans for a catering business, but she decided to shelve the idea. She would let the discussion be about Daisy and the wedding.

Daisy made the arrangements to have lunch with JJ at the hotel restaurant. This time, he would be her guest.

"I remember the first time you took me here," she told him. I was so nervous. All those people looking at us. So many of them knowing you." JJ smiled. He remembered it well.

"I guess you noticed that only a couple acknowledged me now. How quickly things change," he responded.

"Even I know that the staff has changed. It's been a few years, you know. People move on."

"I guess so," replied JJ.

"Tell me, what you think about the wedding plans?"

"Wait. You invite me here to talk about wedding plans? Me?"

Daisy laughed before saying, "Well, you have had two, so you should know a thing or two."

"You teasing me, right?" Daisy laughed so loud that JJ had to remind her where they were.

"Just so you know, Roy was going to have the wedding in the Caymans until he found out you were scared of flying."

"How did he find that out? We have never discussed it."

"You, a man who knows all about contacts, ask a question like that? Anyway, isn't that thoughtful of him?"

"I guess so." After a little silence, he asked, "Your father coming?"

"My father?"

"Yes. Your father."

"Auntie didn't tell you?"

"Tell me what?"

"She asked me the same thing yesterday."

"Well, there are certain things we do not share. People tell different people different things, and we like to respect that."

"I see."

"Well, you might as well know that I have been instrumental in getting your father to drive up to the Canadian border see you. I thought it was important. I am happy you met. Now, is he coming?"

"You should know he can't come."

"Yes he can."

"What?"

"Lots of people slip contract and travel back as someone else. Anyway, from what you are saying, you haven't invited him, right?"

"You have been my father for seventeen years, and you will be my father on my wedding day. I won't have two fathers present. Too complicated," she said. Daisy and JJ looked at each other in silent admiration as they smiled, touched glasses, and sipped their wine.

As for her choice of Rogers as a husband, JJ volunteered to her that Rogers had once told him he would marry her one day, and that though he did not say it then, he thought Rogers was a dreamer and had no chance. They both laughed at the story.

It wasn't long before the intended wedding became known to a few, and JJ found himself being accused of "letting the side down" by allowing his daughter to marry for money. The story was that the only reason an intelligent girl like Daisy would marry someone like Rogers was his money. JJ was also seen as having encouraged the relationship since Daisy was a young girl, and that, too, brought a measure of criticism from colleagues and friends. Some went as far as suggesting that Rogers must have some secret for JJ not only to have encouraged the relationship but also to have formed such a close friendship with his daughter's suitor, something they found unusual. They did not know that JJ and Rogers's friendship preceded the couple's meeting.

When Daisy explained that she would be joining Rogers in running the Pelican, both Ruth and JJ tried to convince her that the business was not substantial enough to give them a good living, nor was it challenging enough for her. They felt she should seek other challenges and lend a hand in the business when necessary. They also feared the marriage would suffer from such a close daily working relationship. Daisy was adamant that that was what they wanted, and although she recognized the risks that would be how her life back in Jamaica would start.

Things were going well for the Rogers family. They moved further into the Saint Andrews hills as the Pelican developed into a thriving business. They bought No. 25, had a driveway in an arc from the far boundaries of both properties, and constructed a reception area in the gap between the two, giving the appearance of an American ranch-type building. They provided trips to the theatre, Hope Gardens, and the mineral baths for those able to manage the journey and redesigned the backyard to encourage those able to take gentle walks around the yard. They removed the number twenty-five so the address remained No. 23 Alpha Gardens. The staff wore uniforms, and a uniformed guard was obvious twenty-four hours a day.

Ruth managed to persuade Rogers and Daisy to give up the hassle of doing the catering on-site and instead buy in the service from her. The only complaint from Rogers was that he felt he was running an "old people hotel." It didn't stop him thinking of planning to open another on the north coast.

JJ noticed that he was being excluded from family discussions. He was now the outsider when it came to talking about the expansion of the nursing home. Things had radically changed. Daisy and her aunt were having detailed business discussions, and their relationship took on the flavour of that of best friends or sisters. Sometimes JJ had to listen to his wife and Rogers talking and laughing like old friends late into the night, using business terminologies he knew Rogers had only recently learned. He felt insulted. He was an outcast in his own home and was getting to dislike the late visits of his friend. He remembered the discussions he used to have with Daisy and how Ruth used to be jealous. Now he knew how she'd felt. He was at times tempted to remind Daisy of what he had done for her, just as her aunt had done, but he couldn't bring himself to do it. He thought of ending his life in as dignified a way as possible. Such was his depth of feeling. Such was his shame. It had to be dignified, if not for himself, at least for Daisy and his son, who had been in touch with him in recent years and who was doing well in a government job in Toronto. He was not worried about himself. It was the fear about how his suicide might affect them that stopped him from going ahead with it. Yet the idea would not leave his head. He realized it was time he got himself together.

JJ noticed that his many friendships were waning. The ladies no longer gave him a second glance, and he was not being invited to parties and seaside outings as before. Ruth's friends hardly acknowledged him. His no-drinks policy had failed, and once he had a drink too many, he had a tendency to talk a lot. Sometimes it was about his glory days with the women. At other times it was about individuals and what he had done to help them develop their businesses and how ungrateful they were, pretending to not even know him these days. His drinking partners were now folks he would not have associated with in years gone by. Things had gone badly wrong, so wrong that even Oliver severed links with him.

When Rogers answered JJ's call to meet for a chat, it was very painful for JJ, especially as he had to beg Rogers to promise not to let the ladies know about his call, even if he declined to meet. As far as JJ was concerned, he was dealing with a new Rogers. It was a Rogers who had a mean wife who didn't want to pay for anything if she could get it for free. It was a Rogers that used to pretend he was strong but was now being manipulated by his wife and her aunt. JJ wanted an opportunity to show them all that he still had it in him to counsel wisely. He wanted to show them that he understood why they had sidelined him. He wanted to be back on track, and he needed help to do it.

Rogers also had things he wanted to say, and he was glad for the opportunity to meet with JJ. From past experience, he decided he would get in first and say what he had to say whilst driving. It didn't matter that it was JJ who had asked for the meeting. There would be ample time for JJ to say his piece. He knew that JJ was a more willing listener in the car. He didn't know why, but it just happened to be that way, and that's how he'd play it. He was, however, taken aback when JJ insisted on saying his piece first as they drove along. He said he had things to say, and since he'd called the meeting, it was his prerogative to speak first. Rogers was amused by this and let JJ speak.

JJ told him how disappointed he was and how insulted he was by the way Rogers had lined up with the ladies against him despite everything he had done for him. He reminded him of their long friendship, of contacts he'd linked him up with, of how he'd gotten him into places that even with his money he could not get into. Rogers waited for him to mention Daisy, but he didn't. JJ had made a conscious decision not to mention her.

Rogers listened in stony silence. When it was clear that JJ had finished, he said, "So how you plan to fix all of that?"

"Fix what?"

"You telling me about what you see is wrong. What is in your—how you say it? Your power to fix? Yes, that's it. So what you plan to do about it?"

This was new to JJ, Rogers talking to him like that, talking to him the way a father talks to a son. He was uncomfortable with the role reversal. "It looks like being married to Daisy is like being back to school," he said.

"What you talking about?"

"Before you married, you couldn't put a sentence like that together." Immediately realizing what he'd said, he continued very quickly, "Don't take offence, my friend. Sorry. I am a mess. I know. I know. I am sorry."

"Well, you telling me you can't or you don't want to fix it?"

There was silence for a while before Rogers continued. "Look, don't think for one moment I liked keeping you out of things. I have been batting for you all the time, but I have to agree with the ladies that you have to sort things out yourself, and I didn't want to take any blame if anything happen to you."

"Happen to me? What you mean?"

"Look. The ladies figured that if we left you alone, sooner or later you would, well, see a bit of sense and be youself again. I had to go with them."

"What you mean by *anything happen to me?*" JJ insisted, thinking of his suicidal thoughts. There was no response from Rogers, and they drove in silence until they arrived at the Barrel.

The Barrel was the bar Rogers and JJ usually stopped at on their way home from Caymanas Park races, a small circular building with a canopy to protect customers from the sun or rain that was frequented by people from all walks of life. It had been years since JJ had been there.

The bald-headed, bearded Casanova spoke in a whisper. One almost had to lean towards him to hear what he was saying. Built like a barrel himself, he had eyes that stared right through you. It was as if he was saying, "I not only see you, but I know what you are thinking."

"Casanova. Long time, man," shouted Rogers from his open-top car.

"You sporting a lot of gold, man," whispered Casanova, staring at Rogers' gold watch and bracelet. "Hear married life tie you down but it don't look bad for you at all," he continued. Rogers laughed as both he and JJ approached the bar.

"Red Stripes as usual," said Rogers. JJ gave an acknowledging smile to Casanova. Not one for smiling, he nodded his acknowledgment instead. Rogers was the first to walk away from the window.

As JJ was about to turn and follow, Casanova said, "The look on you face tell me you have another assignment for me, boss. Right?" JJ choked on the sip of beer. He stared at Casanova in disbelief, his eyes popping out of his head.

"Assignment? What assignment?"

"Left, right, left, right, halt," he said, followed by a nod and a wink.

"Look. I don't know what you talking about." Taking a couple of steps towards Casanova at the window, he continued in a slow, forceful voice. "You don't know me. Understand? You don't know me. And don't you ever talk to me like that again." He turned and walked the few paces to the car, all the while looking back at Casanova as if he was checking to see if Casanova was following him.

Rogers's shout to look out came just as JJ walked into the side of the open car door, the bottle flying out of his hand and into the car, spilling most of the beer over the seats and over Rogers. JJ flicked his wrist, which had been hurt by the impact, as Rogers began cleaning up the car.

"What's up, man?" enquired Rogers.

"Let's go! Let's go!"

"But—"

"Let's go!" he screamed.

"All right, all right. Calm down. Calm down, man," said Rogers, accompanying his words with hand signals. After a few minutes of driving, during which Rogers kept stealing glances at JJ, he stopped the car.

Before Rogers could speak, JJ said, "How the hell did he know that it was me the job was for?"

"What you talking about?"

"He wanted to know if I have another assignment for him."

"No, no. It's you who tell him now. He's been trying to find out for years. I don't conduct business like that. I deal with a man who deal with a man who deal with a man, and so on. Nobody can get back to me. Anyway, that done with years ago, and as you know, things worked out differently. So is that what make you vex up so and smell up me car with beer?"

"Look, man, you know I never like that man from long time. The man frighten me. Don't like how he looks at me. Next thing you find my body in a gully or some such place."

"Stop being dramatic."

"Wait, you know words now—sorry…sorry."

"You are a joker. Let's go get you another beer."

"No. I don't want a beer. In fact, I think will not have another beer from today."

"What? Another whiskey I can understand, but a beer?"

"Just take me home."

"OK. OK," said Rogers as he pulled away.

EIGHTEEN

(1968)

It was unusual for a policeman to return to take charge of a station in which he had previously served at a lower rank. So it was a surprise to those in the know when Sergeant Furlong, a good-looking man with a Clark Gable moustache, was announced as the new officer in charge. It was also a surprise when he had a little gathering in the garden of his home for a few special guests.

It was a small gathering that included the headmaster of the elementary school, the JPs, the postmistress, a doctor, the head nurse at the clinic, Mr. Chin Yee, who owned the bakery and the biggest shop, and Morag. Geoffrey was invited, but he could not attend.

There was a handy helping of curried goat and rice, fruit punch, beers, rum, and whiskey. The evening went well, with everybody mingling and chatting freely. What the guests didn't know was that Furlong was putting into practice some aspects of the training he'd received in the management courses he'd attended and so wanted to know what concerns, if any, the folks had about law and order. He was particularly interested in what changes there might have been in the years since he'd left Bramley. They were proud to tell him that things were relatively quiet, with no serious crimes having taken place since the Luvvy murder nineteen years earlier, contrary to the national trend. When he asked about the less serious crimes, they said he would be in a better position to answer that as, from their perspective, such involved the regular traffic stops by the police and people being booked for minor infringements. "That's something I am sure you can do something about," said Nurse Williams.

"Nurse, you sure that's the reason they stop you?" asked the sergeant, evoking laughter from the others. Nurse Williams joined in the laughter because she knew the sergeant knew she was speaking on behalf of others.

Geoffrey stopped by the following day. He and Furlong chatted over drinks on the veranda. He was catching up on what had gone on the previous evening. Furlong commiserated with him for his election loss.

Manny, who had been away for many years, much of the time incarcerated for theft and wounding, was cutting the grass around Furlong's house. He had poor eyesight, was getting frail, and looked and moved like a man many years older than his years. He had, however, continued his old ways since returning to Plummers, supplementing the food given to him in return for little chores or out of pity, with his habit of stealing people's foodstuffs from their farms. In general, people seemed resigned to the fact that he would steal, but since he never took much and did not steal from just one person, most let him be. One or two felt his persistence should be curbed, and so it was that he ended up in jail and was given a token sentence of three days. Manny's time around the yard was a relief compared to the alternative—being incarcerated in the hot jailhouse.

On hearing Geoffrey's voice, Manny stopped chopping and cocked his head to listen more intently. He thought the voice sounded like that of the man who'd stuck the gun in his ribs those years ago. The only thing was, the man had a slight American accent then. Manny continued chopping, but the voice haunted him. He stopped and moved into a position where he could see the person's face. On seeing it was Geoffrey, he shook his head, telling himself he had made a mistake, as he would have recognized his voice years ago.

It was mid-afternoon a few days later, and Geoffrey was visiting over at Dalbeattie, something he had been doing during the last years before Kenny passed away a year earlier, at age seventy-six. His visits had become even more frequent in the previous years, especially when he became an election candidate. As far as he knew, his former boss appreciated and looked forward to his company as they sat silently on the veranda, looking out to sea. Now the scene was being repeated with Morag, except with chatter and drink.

Morag, dressed in an old evening dress that had become a bit tight for her, was unusually quiet, as she sat on the veranda under a home-made canopy, where she had stayed earlier as a rain shower passed. It was something she often did despite being told she would die from pneumonia from such a practice.

"So, why are you so formal these days?" she said with a smile.

"Am I? Didn't notice."

"You don't notice a lot of things."

"Like what, for example?"

"Like I don't have many visitors anymore."

"Well, you didn't have to put all your eggs in one basket with the soldiers."

"Officers! Officers! Soldiers make them sound common. They were officers."

"Well, officers then," he said with a smile.

"Anyway, they were not coming here for me. It was the mixed Indian-Negro-Chinese girls, all very pretty girls from Outa-Bridge they liked. Tell me something—how come there are so many pretty girls in the Red River area?"

"Long story of sailors who used to come in there years ago when they still had a wharf. Long before my time."

"I never understand men. Still, the officers were good company. They provided good conversation and news. I got to know what was happening back home, better than anything that was in the press. Gosh, it can be so lonely up here sometimes. One can be so out of touch with what's going on around them." She looked at him, silently inviting him to continue the conversation.

He said, "Anyway, what's so urgent?"

"Urgent?"

"Well, the message gave the impression of urgency."

"Yes. It's Manny. He's working over at Sergeant Furlong's."

"Not quite working. He's doing a little bit of yard clean-up instead of being locked up in the hothouse. Short sentence for some farm theft. His usual thing. The sergeant just using the jailhouse as a place for him to sleep."

"Oh. So that's the arrangement. Anyway, I have found out that it is not only the white man whose tongue is loosened by white rum, you know."

"What you mean by that?"

"Hear that when Manny has a drop of white rum in him, he too has a loose tongue."

"What is he saying?"

"That he hanged Soldier and choked Luvvy to death and that he was paid to do Soldier, and Luvvy just got in the way."

"No. Manny doesn't talk like that. That's a film script."

"Well, I might not be quoting him exactly. Anyway, he couldn't say who paid him to do it. Said it was dark."

"I see."

"Said he saw me and the army officers walking by the river and so on—the type of thing that is common knowledge."

"He's crazy. Doesn't make sense for him to be admitting to something that he could hang for. Anyway, how come you know all this and I haven't heard any of it?"

"I lied about not having a friend. I have a new one—Sergeant Furlong. He and I had a very long chat. You see, when Manny was in prison, they found out he had some sort of terminal illness. Also, Sergeant Furlong—let's say Malcolm—he said the Luvvy case was used in his sergeant training programme for officers to come up with possible alternatives to known outcomes of a case. Something like that. Anyway, he said that one bright spark came up with the exact alternative of hanging and murder. You'll be happy to know that the bright spark was not seen as being very bright."

"Well, nobody can pinpoint me. Manny didn't see my face, and he didn't hear my real voice. I have nothing to worry about."

"Don't have to think that far. He believes Manny somehow heard some officers talking about the course and just link the whole thing with the details everybody knows about anyway."

"So what do you have to worry about?"

"Me? Where do I come into it?"

"Well, you paid for it."

"Who can prove that?"

Geoffrey thought for a moment before saying, "So we have nothing to worry about, then."

"There you go again with *we*, this time." Geoffrey and Morag sat silently for a while, each wondering what the other was thinking. Then she said, "Why isn't Mrs. Furlong here as well? They don't usually put single sergeants in charge, do they?"

"Why didn't you ask him?"

"Talking about ask, when you going to visit your English relatives?"

"How come you switching things so?"

"Oh, never mind. Tell me—whose idea was it to go for such an elaborate way of doing it, and on a day when I had visitors as well?" She paused. "No. No. No. I don't want to know any of the details. Just be aware that, out of curiosity, Malcolm might just decide to start asking a few questions. You never know."

"He wouldn't ask a question like that."

"I know that. But…"

"You're really scared, right? You just jumping from one thing to another. Look, just remember this. There is no way I would go down alone if it comes to it."

"You are worried. Pretending to be brave. So much to lose."

"All I know is that it wouldn't stop with me."

"How come?"

"What reason would I have? Everybody know you wanted to kill him those years ago when he rub up himself against you and only Mr. Sanderson put some sense into you."

"You trying to tell me you didn't have a reason to hate him? To see him put away?"

"Yes. That's what I am saying. After all, I wouldn't have the money to pay for something like that."

Morag took a sip and looked straight into Geoffrey's eyes. She was smiling. Geoffrey was puzzled. The smile turned to a smirk. Geoffrey was even more puzzled. "So according to you, it's all about money, right?" she asked.

"No. No. Not all about money but it's a big part."

"What about getting rid of a love rival? No…no…no…*love* is not the word. Sex—yes, a sex rival. The lure of sex with a defenceless little girl."

Geoffrey opened his mouth to speak, but no words were uttered.

Morag looked at him whilst her smirk changed gradually to a smile. "What you have to say about that, then? See, with money you can find out anything."

"You are drunk. You don't know what you saying. Hot sun and whiskey got you confused. That's one thing that is a legacy of the soldiers."

"Officers! Officers! Damn you! Officers!"

"OK, OK, OK—officers. They leave you with a real taste for whiskey. No wonder you can't forget them."

"Just think back to that night. Where were you supposed to be? And do you remember the reason you gave me? Remember? Said you fell asleep. Mind you, that might have been true. The youngster exhausted you, eh? You are pitiful."

Morag excused herself and went down the stairs that were the exit to the veranda. Geoffrey poured himself two more whiskeys whilst she was away. He also used the time to think of the stories he had heard about her, how she might have been responsible for the death of Jean Sanderson, to whom she'd been a nurse. He thought they were just wicked rumours, as from his observations during the period he worked for them, Morag didn't seem the type of person who would do something like that. He also thought of her patience and devotion to her late ailing husband, despite her actions with the officers on some weekends. He heard her coming up the stairs and instinctively picked up his glass. He then pushed the glass a little farther from his reach. He found that he was having second thoughts about her.

Morag moved from the table to the rocking chair and began to rock it gently. Geoffrey watched her close her eyes, and he noticed she was smiling to herself from time to time.

"Geoffrey," she said, her eyes still closed. "You forget you were our bookkeeper? You forget you knew how much cash we kept in the safe?" He did not respond, and she continued. "His silence lasted six years, you know. Often wondered what was going on in his head, in his silent world. I am sure he could hear. Sure of that, even though he would never answer a single question. That is how I would want to go. Just go to sleep and never wake up. That's kind to everybody around you. Kinda neat."

Geoffrey did not hear the last few words. He was wondering why she had encouraged him—almost forced him—to attend the Old Students' Day event. He remembered the detailed questions she'd asked him on return. He remembered her disappointment on learning that Daisy had taken ill and could not read her speech. He thought she must have sent him as a form of punishment. He was getting uncomfortable.

"Geoffrey, remember who you dealing with, you know." Her pronunciation became more Scottish. "Remember that though you think you are a big shot now, you still have us to thank for everything. You have me to thank for quite a lot, even though you may not know it. I want you to know also that I have been hearing about what you said in defence of your friendly chats and drinks with me. You know—old fowl and chicken? I have my sources."

Geoffrey looked at her, wide-eyed, but said nothing.

Morag opened her eyes, took another sip, slammed the glass on the table, and jumped to her feet. Her face was cherry red. She began speaking in what seemed like a lisp, with spit flying everywhere. "How much of the money did you pocket? Tell me. Tell me. You only paid him—God, you are pathetic."

For the first time, Geoffrey became concerned that someone might just be within hearing distance of them, and he aborted his attempt to say anything as he walked to each end of the veranda before resuming his seat.

Then he heard, "Do you know I could have had you arrested?"

"Me? Arrested? What for?" He was thinking of her comment about the money.

"That little girl. Why did you do it, Geoffrey? Why did you have to do it? She could so easily have been my family. You knew how I felt about Soldier and her."

Geoffrey thought, "If only you knew. I was the first." He thought about her reference to family, and it did not make sense to him. He also noticed Morag was sobbing. He reflected on the fact that she was now talking freely with Sergeant Furlong. He needed to think. He decided it was time to leave, as it was beginning to get dark. He headed towards the stairs.

Through her sobbing, Morag said, "Goodbye, Geoffrey." He did not answer.

Troy, the Dalmatian, got up as if to say his own goodbye. Troy and Geoffrey knew each other well. Nevertheless, Geoffrey kept an eye on Troy as he descended the stairs. He hoped nobody else had heard the exchange between himself and Morag. He looked back towards her. He descended a few stairs and looked back again. He did not see the rope tied at ankle height across the step where the staircase curved.

NINETEEN

Daisy was not happy that her first visit to Plummers with her husband was to be for Geoffrey's funeral. She had agonized about it for a couple of days and surprised her aunt by seeking her opinion as to whether it was a good idea to go. She was disappointed when Ruth said the decision was for her to make, without giving her a steer. She thought about having a chat with JJ but decided against it, fearing she might end up talking to him about the rape. In the end, she decided she would go. She hoped that witnessing his leaving might bring closure to the years of heartache the traumatic incident had brought her. JJ and Ruth decided not to attend.

Some of the local people made fun of Geoffrey's death, saying, "Soldier's duppy kill him." First, they said, Geoffrey took Daisy away from Soldier, and then he started to fraternize with Morag, where Soldier could see him from his grave. It was at times difficult to distinguish between those who were making fun of the situation and those who truly believed it.

Another story was that Morag was a clever murderer. They said that first she killed Jean Sanderson, then she suffocated her husband when she got tired of looking after him, and she killed Geoffrey because he refused to play the part of the soldiers who no longer came by. Also, when Morag made it known that she would not be attending the funeral, just as she had not attended Soldier's, many saw her decision as being linked to her having some guilt. None of these stories were taken seriously, as there was never an investigation by the authorities. They were nevertheless popular among some of the people.

JJ's view was that the stairs were a bit steep, and a man with a little too much drink could easily trip and fall as they said Geoffrey had done. Also, the injuries he received, putting him in a coma for two weeks, were consistent with the way the winding staircase was designed.

Nobody knew how much Morag prayed during the period between the fall and Geoffrey's death. She wanted him to survive and be forever conscious that she knew about his rape of Daisy. It would have been a means of punishment.

As it turned out, nobody had heard of any disagreement between the two. Geoffrey always visited during the daytime, returning home to his family by nightfall. The evening of the fall was no different. The whiskey in his stomach was said to have been a contributing factor.

Daisy and Rogers arrived early so that her husband could meet Martha, Gladys, and a few of the others she was keen for him to meet. The people warmed to Daisy. The little girls, too young to have known her before, ran behind her as she went from house to house. The younger ones who knew her chatted excitedly and passed the word around: "Miss Daisy come back." Every few yards, it was "Miss Daisy."

Some folks talked about her in the third person yet loud enough for her to hear, things like, "What a nice young lady she turn out to be!" and "What a pretty lady. Plummers should be proud." Daisy smiled through it all. She was being treated like royalty at the funeral of the man who'd tried to ruin her life. Rogers smiled, too, obviously proud of his wife.

Geoffrey's funeral was the biggest ever held in Plummers. It was like a political rally with parish counsellors, party officials, and the church congregation of Plummers. Many individuals and families drove into the district that morning, and the number of goats killed and liquor drunk was more than anyone had ever seen for any event in Plummers. Mrs. Marshall surprised everyone by deciding she would have nothing to do with the funeral arrangements. Geoffrey had a wife, she reasoned, so all she had to do was to attend like any grieving mother would do for a child. Even when her daughter-in-law asked for her help in organizing the catering, she refused without giving a reason.

Instead of ensuring that the travellers from far away had a meal after the funeral service, the ladies in charge of the catering put their effort into giving the children of the district a feast to remember, remembering what happened after Soldier's burial. Consequently, there was very little food left for the adults when they returned from the church and the graveyard.

Whilst many mumbled their disappointment and disgust, Geoffrey's mother invited a select group, including the politicians, to her house for food and drink, including jerk pork, and an array of neatly cut sandwiches, with ginger beer and tea for the ladies and whiskey, rather than cheap rum, for the men. The amount she had prepared suggested she had expected the situation to arise. Daisy was not among those invited.

By the time Daisy and Rogers were ready to leave, Daisy was surrounded by a variety of people who showered her with gifts of foodstuff that she would otherwise have had to buy in Kingston. She had come prepared with lots of small change, and she counted out the money carefully to each person before putting the foodstuff in the car. It was what she had expected.

The people gathered to wave the couple goodbye. It seemed royalty had visited. As they pulled away, Rogers turned to his wife and said, "Precious, you were like a princess up there. Bwoy, the people love you bad! That was nice. That was nice. For a while it was not like a funeral at all." Daisy said nothing. She was in deep thought.

"Precious, you are on a new path of life now, you know. All the bad things are behind you. Trust me." He squeezed her arm gently.

She turned and smiled at him before saying, "Just keep your eyes on the road."

"You safe with me. You know that."

"I still wish I was the one to tell you about it. I suppose Papa was doing what he thought was right."

"Of course. He just didn't want me to overhear anything and think the worst, as he put it."

"It's like a big load off my shoulders."

"But you can't keep punishing youself for the wrong other people do. That not right. Remember, your stepfather beat you up. You didn't do anything wrong." Daisy looked at her husband and smiled.

Things at home between JJ and Ruth were improving. He was eating more and putting on a little weight. He had not managed to cut out the beer, but he was drinking far less than before. He was also in a position to reject invitations if he didn't feel like going. He was on better terms with everyone. What mattered to him most was that he was now a part of the team working on the expansion of the Pelican and close to his dear Daisy. The ladies were happy that their deliberate alienation of him had worked.

Rogers was in a good mood. The Pelican was getting good reports in the press, and the bank wanted to use the front of the building to make an advertisement for TV and the cinema. To his surprise, the nursing home was also in a position of having to turn away applicants.

Daisy was pleased with herself. She was happily married and had persuaded her husband to think big, at least bigger than he had been thinking before. They were proving to be a good team. They were running a good business establishment, though not a big one, and their bank manager was happy with them.

Ruth was grateful for the opportunity to play a part in the development of the Pelican, and she had extended her catering operation to include providing meals for conferences and weddings.

JJ had new friends. He played dominoes some evenings and table tennis others. He was following a new lifestyle and was once again sought after for advice and assistance by individuals and some small businesses. He was regaining the respect he'd enjoyed when he was working.

When his lawyer called him, Rogers could tell from the tone that all was not well. This was confirmed when he learned that the promised loan from his bank manager friend to open a second branch of the nursing home on the north coast was no longer available.

Having spent a lot on the plans and bought an old school building, Rogers was unhappy at the news. He was also a bit concerned because despite pressure from his wife, who was unhappy with the lawyer, he had refused to change lawyers. She wanted him to take more control of the business affairs because she didn't like the way the lawyer, who was his parents' lawyer, seemed to be dictating matters rather than giving advice. She also thought he was disrespectful to her, not wanting to talk to her about any business matter, however minor, even though the business was in both their names.

"Precious, we have a problem. We not getting the loan."

"What? How come?"

"That's all he said. Said the bank manager said he couldn't manage it at the moment."

"That doesn't make any sense. What exactly did he say?"

"I tell you before, you shoulda been a lawyer. You should be in court. Always questions, questions, questions. Sometimes I 'fraid to tell you anything."

"We should have done it ourselves. Used our own bank. Some friend his banker turned out to be."

"Precious, what can I say?"

"I think we should go direct to the bank ourselves, after all the time, work, and money we put into it. The business plan is good. It's sound. How could we not get the loan?"

"That's it, Precious."

"His friend at the bank must be planning to do the business himself. That sort of thing happens a lot, you know. I don't have a good feeling about this at all."

Daisy was upset. She had given her soul to the development of the business. She had suggested that he discuss the matter with his mother before talking to his lawyer, but Rogers did not want to do that. He did not want to involve his mother, as he felt she had treated him badly by walking away with a lot of the cash his father had left. He could not come to terms with the fact that the cash legally belonged to his mother.

Rogers was the one who was displaying patience. He was the one who wanted time to work out an alternative plan. He was confident that all would be well. His coolness about not getting the loan worried Daisy.

A few days later, the Pelican was mentioned in the press in a story about the development of small businesses. The article mentioned the former Daisy McIntosh as director and the brain behind the expansion and highlighted it as an example of how a small business, properly managed, could grow. Rogers was aware that the article was due and that JJ was behind it. Daisy was not overjoyed by what seemed to be yet another secret kept by her husband. She did not see the business as being big or important enough to warrant the article, and she was suspicious that it had come at the time the development loan was refused. She was also annoyed that she was not mentioned as Mrs. Rogers. She thought it was time she had a heart-to-heart business chat with her husband.

Over the next few days, Rogers had discussions with his bank, alone. Daisy was again upset, this time because her husband excluded her from the meeting. He had discussions with Ruth, also alone. Daisy didn't like that either. From time to time, Rogers simply said, "Precious, everything will be all right. Trust me. Everything will be all right."

Such comforting words did not pacify Daisy because she knew that Rogers associated with one or two people involved in the business of marijuana, and he had once mentioned it as one way of dealing with financial problems. She wanted to talk to him about it, to beg him not to take a chance, to think of his family, the good name of his parents, of how far they had come together as a couple, of what she had given up to be with him in Jamaica. Yet, despite all these thoughts, she did not utter a single word. Then she remembered what JJ had said about the dangers of married couples working closely in business. She decided to wait and see what happened.

Later, when Rogers saw her worried looks, he said, "Everything will be all right, Precious. Trust me. I know what you thinking. I won't do anything illegal. I won't shame you. I won't disappoint JJ. Just trust me." Daisy smiled but said nothing.

It was near the end of the month and just after four on a Monday morning, and Rogers was driving his Land Rover along the winding road. He had made the trip before and was confident he would be OK. Just as he passed the white-washed cart wheel that was nailed into the coconut tree, he turned off the road. The vehicle rocked and rolled along the dirt track for about four hundred yards. He stopped and switched off his lights. He was a little early. He could not be just on time or be late. Others were watching, and had to feel sure things were all right. He listened for the humming noise that would mean the plane was approaching. He waited for what seemed an eternity. He looked at his watch every few seconds, at no time acknowledging the time. He began to sweat. He wondered if something had gone wrong. It was not supposed to be that late.

"Keep calm, mister. He has to come. He has to take this load. It's a must," said his bodyguard, seated beside him. Rogers did not reply. Then he heard a click that sounded as if a pistol was being prepared to fire. He froze. Instead of hearing a gunshot, he saw the oil lamps being lit in parallel lines. Then he heard the sound he was waiting for. The noise got louder, and the landing lights of the little plane flicked on for a short while before the plane touched down, turned, and came to a stop about fifty yards from where he was waiting. The oil lamps went out immediately, as if controlled by a switch.

Rogers was sweating more than usual, and his fingers gripped the steering wheel in nervous anticipation. He watched and listened to the hustle and bustle of the plane being loaded, engine still running. The bodyguard ran out towards the plane and returned with a satchel just before the plane roared its engines. He chucked the satchel through the open door of the Land Rover and dashed back to the plane as it began to taxi in the direction it had come from. Rogers became afraid. He was now alone. That was not the plan. He had to get out and away quickly.

He had a quick look at the cash and noted the wad of dollar bills. He smiled, put the satchel on the floor, took his revolver from his waist and laid it on the seat beside him, put the vehicle in gear, and pulled away. He would wait till he got some way along the tarmacked road before having a quick count of the cash, even though there was nothing he could do if the amount was incorrect.

As he approached the road, a large tree branch crashed in front of him. He screeched to a stop and watched as dust overtook the Land Rover. Before he could put his hand on his revolver, a gunman opened the driver's side door with an outstretched hand.

"The money," was all he said, grimacing.

Rogers hesitated. He looked ahead and saw another gunman between the Land Rover and the tree branch, pointing a rifle directly at his windscreen. The nearby gunman didn't see Roger's revolver. He knew if he hesitated a moment longer, the other gunman might approach and open the other door. Rogers calmly handed the satchel to the gunman beside him. He was disappointed, as he had always told himself that he would prefer to go out like a Wild West gunfighter than be gunned down in cold blood.

Almost immediately, he felt the warmth as he wet himself. The man in the glare of the headlights, with his rifle pointed to the windscreen, motioned a safe route around the fallen branch. Rogers drove away, sobbing like a child. He noticed a pickup parked facing the opposite direction and assumed the gunmen would be heading that way. His mind was in turmoil. He wanted to stop and run back with his gun at the ready to retrieve his money before the men got away. Then he thought of his wife's words and decided to head home.

Rogers stopped in the driveway, trembling. He seemed to have run out of tears. Daisy heard the vehicle pull up and waited for her husband to appear. After a while, she went to the vehicle, tapped on the window, and ushered Rogers inside.

"How you know I was out 'ere? And what craziness you going on wid, coming out a de 'ouse in you nightie at this time o' morning?"

"Heard you pull up."

"But…but you wouldn't normally come out here like that at this time of the morning. I don't understand. What's going on?"

"You tell me. What's going on?"

"Keep you voice down, Precious. Keep you voice down. What happening? What going on? I don't understand."

As Rogers walked behind her towards the house, Daisy said, "You smell like a ram goat."

"Wait a minute. Is it you behind it?"

"Behind what?"

"How come you don't even ask me where me coming from or anything like that? Even when you know I coming from the Pelican you full of questions."

"We're going into the house, aren't we?"

"Precious, you? You? Lord, I don't believe it." Daisy turned and smiled at her husband but said nothing. He continued, "Bwoy. I don't care what time it is. I need a drink right now."

"Just go have a shower."

"I hope this is a dream. It have to be a dream."

"I'm going back to bed. Oh, before I forget, we better make an appointment with the bank for next week."

"What?" asked Rogers.

It was too late for the *Daily News*, but it made the morning radio and television news, and the evening newspaper carried a picture of the crashed plane with a short story:

A small plane loaded with ganja crash-landed on a beach on the island's south coast, killing the two occupants, so far unidentified.

Local fishermen said the engine was spluttering and the pilot attempted a landing on the beach. The plane was partly submerged with its cargo of marijuana. The police believe that two burned-out vehicles found about fifteen miles away are linked to the crashed plane and are continuing their investigation.

A few months later, after being invited to dinner at Dalbeattie, JJ found himself pinned against the veranda wall by Troy, who was on his hind legs, his paws on JJ's chest. Standing like that, Troy was almost as tall as JJ. He panted and dribbled; the dog was in a playful mood. JJ continued his fake smile and chuckle even though he was scared. Morag was enjoying the spectacle and continued to sip her drink.

Bored or disappointed that JJ would not play, Troy came down on all fours and walked slowly away towards the stairs.

"I really don't like dogs, you know. Well, not like that. Dog is dog, and I am sure you notice that we in Jamaica don't treat them like people."

"Um," said Morag, taking another sip.

"So, when you going to tell Oliver, then?" JJ noticed she was talking more like a Jamaican of late.

"Tell him what?"

"Are you another one who takes me for a fool?"

"What you talking about, Mrs. Sanderson?" He still found it uncomfortable addressing her as Morag, though she had often told him to.

"So you want me to spell it out, do you?"

"Yes. I haven't got a clue about what you talking about."

"Let's put it this way: did your Mr. DeMar—I bet you that is not his real name—did he tell Oliver that the job was done by somebody else…by another paymaster?"

JJ shifted in his seat. He took a sip of his drink. He rubbed his hands over his balding head. He looked towards the stairs and saw Troy lying a few feet behind him. "Is that what the important thing is you want to talk to me about?"

"No. It is not. But we have to clear up a few things before we get to it. So, what is your answer?"

"I don't know where you get your information from, but I don't know what you are talking about. I don't know any DeMar. Of course, you know I know about Oliver. But he's abroad, and I am here in Jamaica. I don't travel. He skip contract. I don't know where he is."

"So back to the question. When you going to tell Oliver? No—let's start again. That fellow DeMar, the Pan Am worker—did you have a direct link to him?"

"I told you already that I don't know him."

"You sure about that?"

"What you on about, Mrs. Sanderson?"

"I can contact him, you know. I can get to him. I can let him know."

"Let him know what?"

"That you took his money under false pretences. You did. You did. Whoever you paid, or said you paid, didn't do the job. It was already done, by someone else."

Instead of thinking about what Morag was saying, JJ was thinking about his rehabilitation and wondered if she was aware of what he had been going through. He looked for signs in her face of any glint of pity. He saw none.

To break the silence, Morag asked about Rogers and his family, and she added that JJ was lucky to get such a lovely lady like Ruth. JJ's expression did not change. He listened as Morag told him how, by coincidence, they both seemed to come up with the idea that Soldier had to go. His reaction came when she told him he had made a mistake by going after the wrong man and that he should have gone after Geoffrey.

"Why Marshall?" he heard himself ask.

"Ah," she laughed. "See—I could be a good detective. Anyway, I know it was not your idea." JJ remained silent. Morag continued, "You want me to believe she didn't tell you?"

"Which *she* you referring to now? And tell me what?"

"Your wife…or even Daisy herself, for that matter."

"Now I'm really confused. I really don't know what you are talking about. What did Marshall do?"

"Damn you!" she said, pouring herself another drink. JJ looked towards Troy. The dog seemed to be asleep.

"So, you didn't know you were going after the wrong man. You didn't know that Marshall raped Daisy. You didn't know that Soldier never did anything sexual with Daisy. You didn't know that *nobody*, for that matter, had ever done anything sexual, proper sexual, with the little girl before Marshall raped her. Is that what you telling me?"

JJ wanted to tell her that he'd only found out about the rape when Marshall died. Just then, Agnes cleared her throat to announce her presence. As she entered the veranda from one of the rooms, Troy ran towards her. She put out an outstretched hand, and the dog stopped in its tracks and slowly returned to where it had been lying.

"Anything before I leave, Miss Morag?"

"Don't think so. Have a nice weekend."

"Thank you, ma'am." JJ smiled at Agnes. He had given her a few dollars earlier when she'd presented him a tin of potato pudding for him to take back with him.

As Agnes went back inside, Morag said, "How times have changed. I now have a different person for weekends. Still, it works well. This place is like a weapon in itself. It's really a secret weapon."

JJ was silent. He didn't understand the statement. He looked towards Morag, who had her eyes closed but appeared to be in deep thought. He looked at the stairs, at Troy, at Morag again. He looked over the side of the veranda and the distance to the ground.

"You like the way things have changed in Jamaica in recent years?" asked Morag. JJ was not expecting a question like that. He needed to think before answering. Morag continued, "If I were a Jamaican, I would be happy with a lot of it." As he struggled to come up with a comment, she added, "It can't continue like this, though. There will have to be a change. In fact, there will be a change." Morag was disappointed that JJ was not joining her with the drinking as he had done before whenever she popped in to Kingston, but she did not let that stop her from enjoying drinking. Dusk was fast approaching, and JJ thought it was time to get started back to Kingston.

"So, what was the real reason you wanted to see me?" he asked.

"Oh, yes. I need your help with some paperwork. Things I need to submit to my lawyer. Can't allow him to dictate what I should do. Kenny used to say that the lawyer is there to do what you want him to do. Don't ever put him into the position beyond giving you good legal advice. Don't know if he was right, mind you. But that was his position. So I want to make sure that when things go before him, there is little room for him to try and tell me what to do, in the general sense. Do you understand?"

"Yes. I understand."

"OK. I'll get the papers to you in a couple of weeks or so."

"Is that it?"

"Yes. That's it. I will get the papers to you."

"But you could have said that by phone."

"Why go to Port Antonio to telephone? I am paying you for your time here right now. Correct?" JJ did not reply to that before calling the driver from the cellar, where he was having a little nap.

A week later, Ruth was on her way from the hairdresser when she decided to pop into the pharmacy. She caught a glimpse of someone she thought she recognized as Agnes. The person was talking to someone who was hidden by a row of shelves. Ruth turned swiftly and went back to her taxi.

"Just wait a minute," she said to the driver. He did not reply but instead watched her through his rearview mirror. He noticed she looked a bit anxious, as if she was hiding from someone. Then he noticed that she wrinkled her brow and half closed her eyes in concentration as a lady left the pharmacy. Ruth was just about to get out of the cab when she saw JJ step out of the pharmacy as well and into the cab parked a little way behind the one she was in. She sat back in her seat and exhaled loudly as the car pulled away.

"You OK, ma'am?" asked the driver. "Want me to go get what you want?" he enquired.

"No. No. That's all right. I have change my mind. Let's go."

On the way home, Ruth was trying to figure out why Agnes and JJ just happened to be in the same pharmacy in Kingston at the same time. She had not seen them talking; she was sure, however, that Agnes had been talking to JJ.

"Driver, sorry, but turn back. I have to go back to the pharmacy."

"But one is just up the road, ma'am."

"No—no. I have to go back to that one." The driver did a U-turn and headed back to the pharmacy. The woman at the counter, looking very business-like, immediately recognized Ruth as a previous customer and gave her a welcoming smile. Ruth cleared her throat nervously.

"I hope you don't mind, but a few minutes ago, a lady in a white hat and, and an umbrella—she was standing over there talking to somebody."

"Yes?"

"Don't think bad of me, but, but…"

"Yes?"

"I don't want a name, even if you know it."

"Yes?"

"I just want to know if she was talking to a tall, slim man in a blue shirt. That's all."

"Yes." Ruth smiled and thanked her. The woman looked around the store with both palms open and asked, "Yes?"

Ruth smiled and said, "You know, I need some new curlers and a new hot comb." On the way home, Ruth couldn't help laughing to herself for buying a hot comb she did not need.

It proved very difficult for Ruth to raise the subject of JJ and Agnes meeting in secret. After agonising for longer than she had intended, she asked:

"You still doing stuff for Dalbeattie?" JJ lowered his newspaper and peered over the top of it, only his eyes showing.

"Why you ask me a question like that?"

"Just answer me. Yes or no." She decided to take an aggressive tone, which she would try to maintain.

"I just want to know what could have brought on a question like that after all these years."

"You have something to hide, then. OK." She sat there looking at him, making him realize that although the lowering of her tone suggested she was finished, she wasn't.

Feeling obliged to continue, JJ said, "I do a little paperwork for Mrs. Sanderson. The plantation lawyers deal with the other stuff."

"So why a secret meeting with Miss Agnes—and in a pharmacy at that?"

JJ lowered the newspaper to his lap. "Since you asked, I am going to tell you a story. Once I start, you will have to hear it all. I will even wake you up in the middle of the night to finish it if you walk away. You must hear it all. That's the only way it would make any sense. The choice is yours. Want to hear the story?"

Ruth was silent for a little while before getting up and walking away. JJ took this to mean she did not want to hear anything. In fact, Ruth felt that whatever it was, it was not going to be pleasant, and she was trying to put unpleasant things behind her. She thought it must have something to do with Soldier or Geoffrey or both, and she did not want to risk hearing anything about either.

"No. I do not want to hear anything about it," she said, her voice fading as she headed to the bedroom.

TWENTY

(1971)

Just before the third anniversary of Geoffrey's death, JJ and Daisy received identical letters of invitation from Morag. They were to meet her at Hotel Wentworth, Montego Bay, the following week for a discussion. There was no mention of the matter to be discussed. Daisy was intrigued when Ruth pointed out that the meeting date was the third anniversary of Geoffrey's death. When JJ did not seem surprised to receive the invitation, Daisy had a chat with Ruth. Ruth advised her not to ask him about it but to go to the meeting, since he was going. Daisy kept her eyes on her aunt, waiting to see if her countenance betrayed her prior knowledge. Ruth kept her eyes firmly in her book. Although she remained suspicious, Daisy said nothing. It was three days before she told her husband about it, hoping he would share his thoughts with her. Instead, he too said to just go. He added that he would drive them there on the day.

"Mr. Hunter and Mrs. Rogers to see Mrs. Sanderson," said JJ to the hotel receptionist.

"Just a minute, sir." After a moment she added, "The elevator to floor number six. Room 607 is on your right when you exit the elevator."

"Thank you," said JJ. He turned to Rogers.

Before JJ could speak, Rogers said, "I'll be in the bar. Not too early for a beer. See you later."

JJ turned and led the way to the elevator as Daisy followed, gliding across the floor in her long, flowing, colourful dress. Rogers kept his eyes on his wife, but Daisy did not look back.

JJ was about to knock when the door opened and a smiling Morag, dressed in an ankle-length light-blue dress that looked a bit too big for her, said hello and waved them inside. Her face had become more round of late, even though she had lost weight since their last meeting. Her breath smelled strongly of whiskey, a change from the gin and tonic she usually drank, and JJ thought the weight loss and the drinking were linked. JJ looked around, hoping to see the drink and a glass. He would gladly break his vow on this occasion, but Morag had hidden both glass and drink. She could do nothing about her breath.

Daisy and JJ sat together on a couch whilst Morag, gathering up the bundle of material that surrounded her ankles, sat in a single-seater opposite them, with her back to the window. It was a grand suite with a sea view, which Daisy was enjoying, thinking of Plummers. Suddenly her thoughts were interrupted.

"I guess you are wondering why we are meeting in Mo'bay and not Kingston, which would have been nearer and more convenient for all of us."

Neither Daisy nor JJ replied.

"You seem very nervous, Mrs. Rogers. Am I that bad? Do I have that bad a reputation?" Daisy smiled but said nothing. "Mr. Hunter, you knew this day was not far away. As you know, Mrs. Rogers, Mr. Hunter helps me with a lot of my paperwork. As I was saying, I told you, I cannot stay at Dalbeattie any longer. I have no links here. In fact, I have no links with anyone back home, either. It's pitiful, really."

Morag and JJ exchanged looks that signalled agreement with some of what was said. Daisy's knitted brow signalled she had questions. She, however, said nothing.

Morag continued, "It's no longer fun at Dalbeattie, and I just exist. I am grateful nonetheless that I had the opportunity to experience life here in Jamaica. There's good and bad everywhere in the world, and your Jamaica is no different. Now, to business."

She handed Daisy a two-page document. When it was obvious Daisy had finished reading it, Morag asked if she had any questions. Daisy looked towards JJ, since she understood he was aware of the contents, but he was avoiding her gaze.

Morag, looking directly at Daisy, said, "It carries a proper seal. It is genuine, in case you are wondering."

Daisy smiled nervously.

"Well?" asked Morag.

"Why are you doing this, Mrs. Sanderson?" asked Daisy.

"I am a messenger in all of this. It is from the estate, which is a family thing. It never belonged to Kenny alone. Look—it's a long story, Mrs. Rogers, but I think your mother would have had it had she been alive."

"My mother?"

"Yes. Your mother. The Sanderson men are very strange, I tell you."

"Don't understand that."

"I am happy for you. In a way, it is like a payback. No…no…wrong choice of words. Look, I now feel your mother is owed nothing. I feel better. So you see, it is not really for you that it is being done."

"Being done by whom?"

"Don't worry yourself about that. Just listen to me. I am the messenger in all of this. It's complicated, but it's well deserved."

"I am totally confused."

"If it makes you happy, you might like to know that I have, in a way—in a very small way—done enough for you already. Wouldn't you agree, Mr. Hunter?"

"I…I…I don't quite know what you mean," JJ stammered. Then he thought about Soldier and Marshall. The look on his face told Daisy he was hiding something.

"Doesn't matter," said Morag. Then, looking straight at Daisy again, she said, "I want you to know that no matter what you have heard in the past or what you will hear or read in the future, you and your mother were loved by people who loved you for who you are." The mention of the future, concerned Daisy. But before she could speak, Morag continued: "Life has its ups and downs, my dear. Some people have more ups than downs."

Daisy began to think of her own life's passage. She said, "Mrs. Sanderson, I am not coping too well with all of this. You are speaking in riddles. You are confusing me. You say—I mean…according to the document, I have been given seventy acres of the Dalbeattie property, including the flat area by the sea bordering Red River. I can't quite imagine what seventy acres is, but it sounds like quite a lot to me, and I am not even sure who is giving it to me—or why. You talk about my mother. You mention the Sanderson men. I do not understand all of this. It's like a name game. I am confused. And my mother—I still don't understand how she fits into this."

"Your mother was a loyal employee and a friend to me. She kept my secrets. I did not—I could not—repay her properly. That is all you need to know, young lady. That's all you need to know." Then, getting to her feet, she continued, "Now, let's go down and eat."

"No. No. I am not going anywhere until you explain a few things."

"What? You making demands now, are you?"

"Yes. I am. I think you owe it to me, since you brought my mother into it."

Morag rubbed her forehead whilst she bought some time. Then she said, "OK. May I sit down?"

Daisy smiled at Morag's mockery. JJ laughed.

Morag continued, "We are going to be talking about women business now, Mr. Hunter, so how about waiting for us downstairs? Order your drink, and have them charge it to me. If they dare make a fuss, just tell them to call me. They know you are my guest, so let them dare call me. Oh—take this envelope as well, an outline of the area. As you know, you will hear formally from my lawyer about your fee."

Addressing JJ directly, Daisy said, "Papa, can you tell me?" JJ took the envelope and, without even looking at Daisy, headed for the door.

Morag said, "Mr. Hunter is well acquainted with these things, my dear. You should know that. But this is not his story to tell." Morag took

JJ's place beside Daisy. She then opened her heart to her and told her just about everything about her life, beginning with being a little girl in Fife, Scotland. She told of her nursing career and how her parents had died within weeks of each other, her mother going first and her father following, presumably from a broken heart. She told Daisy that her tough exterior was a protective mask she'd developed because she was alone in the world—she'd been alone from the day she decided to leave Fife until she married Kenny. She mentioned taking care of Jean Sanderson and the unkind rumours that she had something to do with her death so she could marry Kenny. She told her about the parties at Dalbeattie with her husband's blessing. She said she thought at the time that her husband was very thoughtful, and it was for that reason she personally cared for him so much.

"What do you mean *at the time?*"

"Still questions…questions…questions."

"What's all this about the soldier and the land?"

"Let sleeping dogs lie, my dear."

"No. You must tell me. Please, Mrs. Sanderson." Daisy attempted to pat Morag's hand but held back. Her hand shook as it hovered.

Morag leaned forward, raised her left hand, and trapped Daisy's hand between both of hers as she spoke. "All you need to know, my dear, is that your mother at one time thought your father might have been one of the Sanderson family members who came here on a visit. Took a little while for your mother to be sure, but as you can see, you are the image of your aunt."

"Did the soldier know?"

"Not then."

"What you mean, *not then?* When did he know?"

"It's a bit complicated. No need to bother your head. Put it this way: he knew after it was clear that he was *not* your father." At that point, Morag let go of Daisy's hand and sat back.

"Now, why would he be told something like that afterwards? Doesn't make sense to me. I think you are keeping something from me. Be honest with me, Mrs. Sanderson—please. It's not fair."

"Fair? Fair? Want to talk about fairness?"

Sensing Morag's growing anger, Daisy said. "Sorry. I didn't mean to...." Then, changing the subject, she decided to seek an answer to something she'd never believed. "How do you feel about the rumour that you suffocated Mr. Sanderson?" Morag was taken by surprise by the question, and she glared at Daisy as if to say, *"How dare you?"* Daisy retained her composure even though inside she was chastising herself for angering Morag. Morag seemed to be disarmed by Daisy's calmness.

"What if I did? Not saying I did it. My question to you is, what if I did?"

"I suppose I would feel a bit uneasy."

"Would you, now? And would you want to hand me back the gift?"

"There you go again. So it's from you."

"You still don't understand, do you?"

"Did you do it?"

"You are not as smart as I thought you were. Mind you, you are smart, book-wise. I think we better end it now. We are late for lunch."

"But did you do it, Mrs. Sanderson?"

Morag stood, arms akimbo, taking up a common Jamaican female stance when anger abounds. She stared at Daisy as her face changed into different shades of red. Daisy did not change her expression.

After a moment, Morag eased her arms to her side before calmly saying, "Whether or not I did it is none of your business."

"You are a remarkably straightforward person. Were you like that with my mother? Did she like that about you?"

"So you want to know some details about your mother now, do you? Thought it strange you didn't ask before."

"She isn't here to speak for herself, so I have no way of knowing if what you would say would be true."

"Calling me—I mean, suggesting—I am a liar, are you?"

"No. Just being practical."

Morag, who was heading for the door, stopped. "Practical? Practical? What blooming nonsense." Daisy thought about her father not paying any attention to her in her early years and began to suspect why. Morag continued, "Tell me something, did you regret Marshall's death?"

Daisy was surprised by the question and did not know how to respond.

"What he did to you was despicable. Horrid. Should have been castrated."

"And to think Auntie promised not to tell anybody, and it's all her fault," responded Daisy, covering her face with her hands and making sobbing sounds.

"Cut out the drama. You are as tough as old boots. Think I don't know what you've been up to over the years? I know everything about you. Everything! You hear me? Every damn thing!" She waited a few moments, but Daisy did not respond.

She continued, "You are daring. I give you that. Bloody daring and a bit stupid. Still, you get enough from it. And as for that vulgar husband of yours…"

Daisy still had her hands over her face. She was wondering what Morag was talking about. What exactly did she know when she said *everything*?

Morag continued. "Don't fret. That Marshall thing is still a secret. The people in the district don't know, if that is what you are worried about. What's more, they still believe Soldier committed suicide."

"What you mean, *believe*?"

"Don't worry your little head about that, either. He deserved to die for the way he beat you up. But you know something?"

Daisy interrupted, "Mrs Sanderson, wasn't Papa's death suicide as the police said?"

"No. It was not." And before Daisy could speak again, Morag became visibly red in the face and continued, spit flying as the alcohol began to take hold of her body: "You could have spoken up. You could have saved his life. Could have said he did not, did not touch you. I mean, the sex thing. But you kept quiet. I believed he was guilty, and so did countless others. And as for that auntie of yours…"

When there was no response from Daisy, whose face was still buried in her hands, Morag added softly, "No. It was not suicide. It was murder."

She waited again for a response, but Daisy was still quiet.

Annoyed that Daisy was not responding, Morag shouted,

"Murder! You hear me? Bloody murder! You played a dangerous game, flirting with Marshall. You led him on. Made him think it was all right. You knew very well what you were doing. But that episode with you that night ruined things for me. We were supposed to…"

Daisy's heart was pounding, ready to burst through the walls of her chest. She removed her hands from her face. Her lips began to quiver, her chin dropped slowly, and her teeth bared themselves as she flew out of the chair, her steps restricted by her long dress and her fingers were set like claws about to strike.

Morag, as if expecting the reaction, pulled a revolver from her handbag, cocked it, and said, "One more step, young lady, and you are no more."

Daisy stumbled as she came to a halt, her hands in the air as if it was a holdup. She was trembling. Tears ran down her face. She feared Morag would fire if she took another step.

"Sit down! Sit down! And get yourself together," screamed Morag. "Think you are smarter than me because you have travelled and have letters behind your name? Don't forget that I know all about you, lassie."

Daisy walked backwards to the couch, fearing that if she took her eyes off Morag, she would be shot.

"As I was saying, Geoffrey Marshall should have been with me that night instead of with you. Don't look so surprised. I was a good looker back then. He was also one of us—well, partly. Oh, yes. It makes a difference. But never mind. I have had enough of your questions. Not answering any more. You just get on with your life. Just be glad you are not like me."

"What you mean by that?" Daisy asked haltingly. The women stood in silence for a little while, eyes locked, as if seeing who would blink first. Daisy slowly regained her composure and began to relax. As if it was a sign to calm down, Morag put the gun back into her handbag and leaned backwards on the door. Daisy made several attempts to speak but gave up each time before finally saying, "Are you telling me that you know they murdered Papa?"

"Yes. And take comfort from the fact that he did not touch that girl Luvvy. He had no part in her death. Now, go to the bathroom and freshen up. We are late for lunch."

Daisy ignored Morag and asked, "You know all of this all these years? And I suppose you know who killed him as well, right?"

Morag hesitated before responding. "As far as I know, your aunt and your father—your real father, that is—know as well. I mean, know that it wasn't suicide. They might not know exactly who the killer is. We had to do something. None of us knew at the time that Soldier was innocent of messing with you. We knew about the beatings. Sure."

"What? You had something to do with killing Papa as well? Wait a minute. Mrs. Jean Sanderson…your husband, Papa, Mr. Marshall—you mean to say you are a real killer, Mrs. Sanderson?"

Daisy watched as Morag took the handgun out of her bag again.

"No. Please, Mrs. Sanderson, please. I don't deserve this. It's not fair," she pleaded, tears running down her face again.

"Shut up, you silly girl. I kept Kenny going, helping to reduce the debt the hotel in Singapore was running up, educating the younger Sandersons, maintaining their crazy, expensive lifestyle in England. And what do I have to show for it? Nothing! Nothing! I tell you. Want to know something about fairness? Well, I am not even a Sanderson. How do you like that? That is a surprise, right? Tell you something else. It was a bogus official who officiated at my wedding. Yes. Didn't know at the time, mind you. A family-only wedding. The Sandersons—well, the older ones—they knew all along it was bogus. But it didn't matter to them. You see, they got a nurse for their man. That's it. They got what they wanted. All I was to them was a goddamn nurse. How do you like that? The only decent one among them is that young officer, Alex, who could so easily have been your father. Well, you know what I mean. He wants to have nothing to do with this place. That's where you come in, when he asked about your mother."

"What did you tell him about me?"

"You are not listening to me. You are no different from the rest of them. Just thinking about yourself. You haven't even asked me, not even out of curiosity, what I am going to do now that I am leaving that godforsaken place. I am trying to tell you, girl, that I am a laughingstock to the lot of them and their friends. You hear me? A bloody laughing stock. But you know what, they won't forget me. The Sanderson name will be all over the British newspapers. Ha!"

She was still laughing when she put the handgun to her temple and pulled the trigger.

Morag would have been disappointed with the meagre press coverage her death received in Jamaica and Britain. It was put down to depression of a drunken lady who could not cope with getting old. She was referred to as Morag McDonald, housekeeper to the late Kenneth Alexander Sanderson of the Dalbeattie estate, Plummers, Jamaica.